# GREEN GROW THE VICTIMS

# GREEN GROW THE VICTIMS

A HILDA JOHANSSON MYSTERY

## Jeanne M. Dams

Walker & Company New York

*To the memory of my dearly beloved father*

Copyright © 2001 by Jeanne M. Dams

First published in the United States of America in 2001 by
Walker Publishing Company, Inc.

Published simultaneously in Canada by Fitzhenry and Whiteside,
Markham, Ontario L3R 4T8

Library of Congress Cataloging-in-Publication Data

Dams, Jeanne M.
Green grow the victims : a Hilda Johansson mystery / Jeanne M. Dams.
p. cm.
ISBN 0-8027-3355-7
1. Johansson, Hilda (Fictitious character)—Fiction. 2. South Bend
(Ind.)—Fiction. 3. Women domestics—Fiction. I. Title.

PS3554.A498 G74 2001
813'.54—dc21

00-054549

Series design by M. J. DiMassi

Printed in the United States of America

2   4   6   8   10   9   7   5   3   1

# Preface

IN writing this work of fiction I've taken a few liberties with South Bend history. The county fair in 1902 was, in real life, a sorry affair, poorly attended. The public's expectations had been raised by the Columbian Exposition of 1893; county fairs paled by comparison. In 1903 the St. Joseph County Agricultural Society, sponsor of the fairs, called it quits and surrendered the fairgrounds to the board of commissioners, which eventually turned it into the city park and zoo now called Potawatomie Park. It wasn't until 1915 that a fair was again held in the county. This time it was named the Interstate Fair and was held in the fine new Springbrook Park, which later evolved into the amusement park called Playland.

So the fair I've described is more like those held somewhat earlier, or somewhat later, than the period of the book. Further, the election is totally unlike the real November election of 1902. Though the Democrats had indeed taken over city government in the spring election, and the new mayor was indeed an Irishman named Fogarty, in the fall election for county, state, and national offices, the Republicans swept the field. A sole Democrat, one Patrick O'Brien—and you can't get much more Irish than that—was elected to the county council, running unopposed. Clement Studebaker, Jr., also running unopposed, was elected to one of the other seats on the county council. That much is true. The rest is a fairy tale.

There really was a tunnel leading out of one of the cellars at Tippecanoe Place. No one now seems to know where it led, or why, nor has anyone I've been able to locate known what it looked like. I've never seen it myself, as the doorway is now—shades of Edgar Allan Poe—solidly bricked up.

The Kentucky mine explosion is fictitious, but the 1902 coal strike is not. Nor have I exaggerated the conditions that prompted the strike.

The immigrant situation I have described is true in essence, though probably not in detail. Immigrants were preyed upon by opportunists, both before they left their native lands and after they arrived in America. Many were made to work off their passage, often serving as indentured servants for years after the passage price had been repaid to their "sponsors." The more unfortunate among them, particularly those who spoke no English, were victims of liars, thieves (many times at Ellis Island itself), and crooks of all kinds. They were despised as inferiors, deprived of their rights, and blamed for the ills of their adopted country. Movements to close off the United States to "undesirable" immigration arose periodically.

And are matters all that different a century later?

# 1

So far the year 1902 has broken the record of the past decade for immigrants landing [in New York].
—*The New York Times* (editorial), May 4, 1902

So." Sven Johansson dropped his large, square hands to the table with an air of quiet satisfaction. "The end of September, you say?"

"No later. Probably sooner, depending on when there's space available on a boat."

Sven's sister Hilda shivered suddenly, though the parlor of the tiny house was stiflingly hot. "A month, or a little more! For such a long time we have not seen Mama and the others, and now, in a month . . ." She had to stop talking. There seemed to be a large lump of something hard in her throat.

Hilda's younger sister, Freya, sniffed and applied a handkerchief to her eyes, but Gudrun, the eldest sister, was made of sterner stuff. "There is much to do in only a little time. We must find a home for them—"

"Oh, Gudrun!" Freya was impatient. "They can live here for a little while—"

"Seven of us, here? There are only two bedrooms, and we do not have enough beds."

"Our house in Björka is not much bigger, and there were eight of us there, with Hilda. Nine, when Papa—"

"Yes, well," said Mr. Andrews, standing up. "I'll leave you to work out the details. But—ahem—haven't you forgotten something?"

Sven stood. He topped the other man by several inches. "It is here, Mr. Andrews," he said with dignity. He unlocked the beautifully painted box that rested in the center of the table, opened the lid, and removed a large black bag tied with a drawstring. He handed the bag to Mr. Andrews.

"You have it all?" Andrews hefted the bag.

"It is all there. You will count it, please."

"No, no, if you say—"

"Please count it, Mr. Andrews. We would not want to think we had made a mistake."

With a shrug, Mr. Andrews untied the bag and shook the money out on the table. It was in neat bundles tied with twine, bundles mostly of dollar bills. It took Mr. Andrews quite some time to count out four hundred dollars. To the Johansson family, it was an immense sum of money, every penny they had been able to save for the five long years they had been in America. The three women had worked as domestics and Sven in the Studebaker wagon factory, and they had set aside everything they could, made every possible sacrifice, for this moment.

"And that will pay for everything?"

"Everything. Mr. Vanderhoof arranges every detail. Their passage, the train to Göteborg, rooms there while they wait for the boat and also in New York while they wait for the train to South Bend, their food—everything."

Sven held out his hand. "Thank you, Mr. Andrews. It was good of you to come here on a Sunday. I am sorry to break your Sabbath, but it is the only day we four can be together, you see. We are very thankful for your help."

"Ah, it's Mr. Vanderhoof who does it, really. I only carry out his orders." He shook the proffered hand. "You'll be hearing from me as soon as I know exactly when you can expect them."

After he had left, the family sat down again around the table. Gudrun was pensive.

"I had forgotten," she said quietly in the Swedish they used among themselves, "how hard it was, the journey from home. How long and uncomfortable, how frightening. And we had Sven to protect us. Erick is only eleven."

"But Mama will be with them," said Hilda. "Mama is strong, and she is brave. And they will know what to expect, because we have told them. They will be fine. And soon, soon, we will see them all. I can hardly wait!"

"Be patient, my sister," said Sven. "As Gudrun has said, there is much to do before they arrive."

They all finally agreed that the family would live temporarily in the little house until jobs and housing could be found for them. There would be seven of them: Sven, Gudrun, Freya, Mama, and their three younger siblings, Elsa, Birgit, and little Erick. It would be crowded, but at least they didn't have to squeeze in Hilda; she was head housemaid for the Studebakers at the biggest mansion in town, Tippecanoe Place, and lived there.

So the three of them, and Hilda in her time off, scrubbed and painted and improvised. Sven, talented with his hands, built trundle beds to go under the big beds; the two youngest girls would sleep on those. Mama could have his bed; he and Erick could sleep comfortably enough in the shed until winter set in hard, and surely by that time more permanent arrangements would have been made.

But August turned to September, and golden summer began to flirt with autumn, and there was still no word from Mr. Andrews. One bright, warm Sunday close to the middle of September, Hilda rebelled.

"New curtains, I think, for the parlor," Gudrun was saying. "I will make them, and you, Hilda, can hang them on Wednesday—"

"No."

Gudrun blinked. "You will not have your afternoon off this week?"

"I will have my afternoon off. I will not use it to hang curtains."

"But—"

"Gudrun, I have had no time to myself for weeks now. I did not mind, but everything is now done that must be done. You can make more work for yourself if you wish. Me, I wish to have some fun. Patrick has asked me to go to the fair with him on Wednesday, and I intend to go."

Gudrun set her lips together tightly. She approved neither of Hilda's independent spirit nor of her friendship with Patrick Cavanaugh. An Irish Catholic was not an appropriate friend for a Swedish Lutheran, and though she wouldn't admit it, even to herself, Gudrun was horribly afraid that Patrick was more than a friend to Hilda. But Gudrun had delivered endless lectures on the subject, lectures to which her strong-willed young sister had paid not the slightest heed, so now she conveyed her disapproval silently.

It made no impression, and Hilda did not change her mind. Wednesday afternoon found her flying up the three flights of stairs from the basement to her room after her lunchtime duties were completed, grumbling in Swedish with every step. She was supposed to have the whole afternoon off, but she was running late, thanks to the Studebakers' fussy and tyrannical butler, Mr. Williams. He had thought of several extra things for her to do, not caring in the least that she was in a hurry today. Changing out of her maid's uniform into nice clothes would require considerable time.

Hilda had never been to a fair before. Björka, the village of her birth, had been much too small and much too poor for such gaieties, and for most of her years in America she had been able to snatch neither the time nor the money for amusements. Her energies, like those of her siblings in South Bend and of so many other immigrants, had been focused on making and saving money for the family immigration fund.

Her friend Patrick, however, had been here longer, and his many family members were all here with him. He didn't earn a great deal as a fireman, but he had a little money to spend as he wished. So he had asked Hilda to go with him to the fair, and she had been delighted to accept.

There would be, Patrick had told her, wonderful things to eat, popcorn and ice cream and candy and Vienna sausages in rolls. "Wieners," they were called, or else "hot dogs," for reasons Hilda did not understand. There would be displays of sewing and needlework and preserves and cakes and cookies and pies, and prizes for the best entries. There would be prizes for the best animals, too, and all the animals would be on display. Hilda's very soul yearned for cows and goats and pigs after so many years away from the farm. There would be commercial displays featuring such locally manufactured products as Singer sewing machines and Oliver plows and, of course, Studebaker wagons and carriages and maybe even a new Studebaker automobile—rumors had been rife all summer that Studebaker's planned to begin manufacturing automobiles. There would be horse races, and a merry-go-round, and games where one could win things, Patrick said, and best of all, oh, most wonderful of all, there would be a balloon! A genuine, beautiful, miraculous balloon, and she, Hilda, was to have a ride in it!

She donned her corset for the occasion, not without a struggle. One needed help to get one's corset properly hooked, but her good friend Norah Murphy, whose room was next door and who was also going to the fair, had finished her work and left the house at least half an hour before. So Hilda sucked her stomach in to suffocation point and managed somehow. Then came her nicest corset cover and petticoat, and then the important outer layer.

Her sisters, for her birthday in June, had given her a length of pink-and-white-striped muslin. Hilda had made it up into a very fetching skirt in the new gored style and had trimmed an old, plain white waist with lace removed from a nightgown Mrs. George Studebaker had discarded. Together they made an ensemble that flattered Hilda's slim figure and Swedish fairness. The mid-September day was sultry, and she would roast in all those tight layers, but the effect was what mattered.

Her old straw hat with its drooping blue feathers did

nothing for her, however. With an impatient gesture Hilda
snatched off the feathers. The hat would look better plain,
or—yes! She rummaged in a drawer, found a length of pink satin
ribbon (also salvaged from the nightgown), wound it artistically
around the hat, and pinned the creation firmly over her thick
coronet braids. There. Her gloves were only lisle, not kid, and
they were somewhat rubbed, but they were clean. They would
have to do.

She looked at herself in the small mirror above her washstand. What little she could see pleased her. If no one was
around to catch her at it, she'd take a better look later in the big
hall mirror on the second floor. That one was intended for the
use of lady guests, who would come up to primp before making
their entrance down the grand staircase to a party. Hilda had no
business using the mirror, but she sneaked a glance anyway on
her way downstairs and was satisfied. She wished she had a
parasol, but they cost too much. Never mind. She looked nice,
and she knew it, and Patrick would be impressed.

Patrick was waiting impatiently when she came up the outside stairs from the kitchen entrance in the semi-basement of
the great house.

"Ye've been long enough about it!"

"Patrick! Do you have nothing else to say to me? Do I not
look pretty?" She revolved before him.

Patrick thought she looked pretty enough to kiss, but he
knew better than to say so, or to act on the thought. Hilda was
happy enough to walk out with him, but she steadfastly refused
even the mildest display of affection. And she was, Patrick
thought glumly, probably right. If they should ever cease to discipline their feelings, who knew what might happen? And their
families would— Well, Patrick didn't even like to think about
that.

So he said nothing but, "Sure an' you do, though it's not you
should be sayin' it. An' you're *late*, me girl! We'll miss the streetcar to the fairgrounds if you don't hurry!"

The electric railway had added extra runs to accommodate
fairgoers; Hilda wasn't especially worried. Nor did she intend to

put herself out to please Patrick. "It is too hot to hurry," she said firmly. "If we miss one car, there will be another soon." Patrick muttering, they set off down the back drive.

Luck was with them. When they reached the center of South Bend, the corner of Washington and Michigan Streets, the trolley was still there. It was crowded. They would have to wait for the next car or else stand, and it was a long ride.

"Do not grumble," Hilda said to Patrick, who was beginning to do that very thing. "We will feel the breeze more if we stand on the outside."

"Huh! What breeze?"

"There will be a breeze when the car starts, and it will be cooler."

"Not much."

Hilda frowned. "You are very cross today, Patrick. If you will not change your temper, I will wish I had not come. What is the matter?"

He made a face. "Sorry. I don't mean to be a bear. It's me uncle."

She laughed, and then grabbed Patrick's coat as the car started off with a lurch. "You have many uncles, Patrick! And many aunts and cousins and I do not know what else. Which one worries you now?"

"Uncle Dan. Daniel Malloy, me mother's brother."

"Oh." The single syllable spoke volumes. "The one who is—"

"The one who's goin' to send us all to an early grave with his shenanigans!"

# 2

Every political good carried to the extreme must be productive of evil.
—Mary Wollstonecraft, *The French Revolution,* 1794

HILDA smiled at the sound of the word. It was new to her, but she could guess what it meant. Patrick's uncle Dan was a flamboyant man, an important dry-goods merchant who had decided to get into politics. His campaign for the one disputed at-large seat on the county council had been making local news for the past few weeks. First there had been the speeches designed to secure his nomination. Dan Malloy had a glib tongue and an Irish wit, a winning combination. He'd been able to make monkeys out of his possible Republican opponents without ever being truly offensive.

Furthermore, the political climate of South Bend and St. Joseph County was changing. In the May elections the Democrats had swept the mayoral and the city councilmanic elections, breaking the Republican stranglehold on local politics. Not only that, the new mayor was Irish, one Edward Fogarty. The Democrats astutely decided that an Irishman stood a good chance of helping to bring county government into the Democratic fold. Malloy was nominated without much fuss.

That was when the real fun had begun. Malloy made more

speeches, drawing larger and larger crowds with his humor. He wrote letters to the newspapers. A gifted caricaturist, he drew sly little cartoons, had them printed up, and distributed them as flyers all over the community. Hilda had especially liked the one with the donkey in the checked coat and porkpie hat, shillelagh in hand, chasing the elephant out of town. The elephant bore a distinct resemblance to John Bishop, the Republican candidate, whose nose was rather long.

The South Bend *Tribune*, as Republican a newspaper as ever published an editorial, made huffy remarks about turning politics into a circus and referred repeatedly to Clement Studebaker Jr. and his dignified campaign. (Hilda's feeling was that, since Mr. Studebaker was running unopposed, he could afford to be dignified.) The rival, and rabidly Democratic, South Bend *Times* retaliated by printing Malloy's next cartoon on the front page. This time the elephant was a circus elephant, blundering about the tent and pulling it down while the donkey stood fearless in the midst of the crowd. His head held high, he kept the tent off the frightened children.

Bishop lost his temper. He challenged Malloy to a debate, which was duly scheduled at the Odd Fellows Hall. Malloy, wearing his usual black-and-white-checked coat and green porkpie hat, arrived on a donkey and rode it right into the hall, nearly causing a riot. When a furious Bishop threatened to cancel, Malloy murmured something about an elephant's capacity for creating a bigger stink. Bishop and all the Republicans stormed out of the hall, but the Democrats stayed to drink the beer that Malloy had thoughtfully provided.

Hilda was not officially allowed to read the newspapers, which contained news that Mr. Williams thought unsuitable for a young woman's consumption. She read them anyway, snatching opportunities when his back was turned, and she had followed the whole Malloy campaign. "I think he is funny," she said, clinging to her handhold as the trolley car stopped abruptly to pick up yet more passengers. "He is interesting. If I could vote, I would vote for him."

"Hmph! Just shows why you women never will get the vote. No sense of what's important."

"Patrick! Do you mean that you will not vote for him? Your own uncle? You are a citizen now; you can vote."

"Oh, well—I'll *vote* for him, I suppose. But he's makin' a laughin'stock of the family, and I don't like it! The Malloys have been here for a lot longer than the Cavanaughs. They're Americans now, and they should act like it."

"You are too—too stuffy." It was her latest piece of American slang. She repeated it. "Yes, stuffy. If he is funny, it is only so that he will be elected, and then I think he will be a good councilman."

"Ye haven't heard the latest," said Patrick gloomily.

"What? What has he done now?"

"He's challenged Bishop to a greased-pig contest at the fair."

A well-mannered young woman could not, in a public conveyance, burst into loud guffaws. Hilda nearly strangled in her efforts to keep her laughter within seemly bounds. The corset didn't help. Her face grew red; she shook.

"But Mr. Bishop will not do it, will he?" she asked when she could speak.

"I doubt he wants to, but he's agreed. A lot of the farmers are Republicans, and they'd likely take offense if he refused. They think he looks down his nose at 'em anyway."

"His nose would be good for that," said Hilda, beginning to giggle again. "Patrick, do not worry. Mr. Bishop will not like what he must do, so he will look more foolish than your uncle. Everyone else will have a good time. And Mr. Malloy will be elected in November, and your family will be proud—the first man in your family to hold office!"

Patrick grunted again. "Just wish he could do it without bein' so rambunctious. He makes people think the Irish are clowns. Why can't he be dignified about it, like Judge Hagerty was? Now there was a *fine* example of an Irish politician."

"Judge Hagerty was old. And a judge must be dignified. It is not so necessary for a councilman."

They had reached the eastern edge of South Bend. The car

picked up speed for the rest of the journey to the fairgrounds, located between South Bend and Mishawaka. The ride grew so rough that Hilda was forced to cling for support to Patrick. He happily forgot his uncle.

Despite Hilda's predictions, there was little breeze even on the trolley car. She was hot and tired by the time they got to the fair and more than ready for some iced lemonade. While Patrick went to find some, she sat on a bench in the shade and stared and stared.

Huge tents were everywhere. Many of the closest ones, her nose and ears told her, held animals. She could hear the irritated cackling of chickens, the bleats of silly, nervous sheep, the occasional lows of cattle. Farther away there were the tents that must hold the home-arts exhibits, and farther still, the midway with the merry-go-round, the commercial displays, and the games of skill and chance. The racetrack with its grandstand was in the middle of everything. That was where the political speeches would be made and where, Hilda guessed, Daniel Malloy and the reluctant John Bishop would attempt to catch and hold on to a greasy, squealing pig. She giggled again at the thought.

And there, tethered near the grandstand, a gorgeous silk-and-rubber balloon swayed at its moorings, ready to take excited passengers up in its basket for a bird's-eye view of the fair. She could hardly wait for Patrick to return. Over the noise of the crowd, she could hear the joyous sound of the merry-go-round's organ. She could hear the raucous cries of barkers and the shrill laughter of children. She could smell popcorn and other exciting food. Where, oh where, was Patrick?

He was at her side, lemonade in hand. She sipped it delicately, as befitted her ladylike clothes, and then said, "Let us go, Patrick, and get something to eat, then go up in the balloon!"

Patrick demurred. "Look at the waitin' line, me girl! If we look around till the three-thirty race starts and most of the crowd goes in to watch it, there won't be as many people wanting to go up. We'll have a hot dog, if you want, but then let's go see what's to be seen."

So they strolled through the exhibits, eating their sausages. Hilda hobnobbed with farm animals to her heart's content, fine specimens that gracefully tolerated conversations with strangers, especially strangers with food in hand. All but the bulls. She had the sense to stay well away from them.

The home-arts buildings were next. Hilda oohed and aahed over the beautiful needlework, the perfectly preserved fruits, the jars of jelly glowing like jewels. Patrick's mild interest in the display of baked goods evaporated when he realized they were not for sampling. He wooed Hilda away. "Come on. Let's get some ice cream and go to the midway."

They chose fresh peach; it was cool and creamy and delicious. They ate it out of a rolled-up cone of paper which allowed the ice cream to drip. Nobody minded. They watched the people, all kinds of people—fat, thin, rich, poor. Patrick pointed one of them out, a heavyset man in a natty, brown tweed knickerbocker suit and sporting a beard. "Know who that is?"

"You should not point at people, Patrick. Who?"

"That's old Vanderhoof."

"Really? The one who— But, Patrick! You are not polite today. *Mr.* Vanderhoof. He is an important man."

"Sorry. He's important to you, I guess."

"Yes, to me and my family, and many other people he has brought here to America. You should speak with more respect."

"Yeah, well, you'd think he'd hurry up with gettin' your family here. If you've finished, let's try the midway."

The midway was a riot of color and noise where games offered their gaudy temptations.

"Coconut shy! Knock down the coconuts, win a prize for the lovely lady! Three balls for a nickel!"

"Shooting gallery! Try your skill! Step right up!"

"Test your strength! Ring the bell and win a prize!"

Patrick, who fancied himself good at such things and wanted to show off for Hilda, was minded to try. Hilda, always conscious of the need for thrift, wasn't so sure. At last she allowed him a trial at the shooting gallery. He missed the target all three times and went away grumbling that the rifle was improperly sighted. Hilda was wise enough to agree.

A little before three-thirty they got in line for the next balloon ascension. Patrick's prediction had been accurate; there were only two people ahead of them, a middle-aged couple standing arm in arm.

Hilda grew more and more excited.

"It is so big, Patrick," she whispered. "And so beautiful."

The balloon was painted in gorgeous colors, a scene of farms and rivers and castles on one side, the city of Paris, France, on the other. It bobbed and swayed at its tether in the gentle breeze, occasionally bouncing the passenger basket on the ground. The breeze grew a little stiffer; Hilda was glad her hat was securely pinned on.

The line grew behind them. At last the man in charge of the balloon stepped up to take their money. "Sorry, folks." He addressed those in the back of the line. "I can only take up the first five, and this'll have to be the last ascension of the day. Wind's coming up; won't be safe later."

There were mutterings from those who would be excluded, and Hilda turned to Patrick. "Ooh! We nearly missed—"

A man came up and touched Patrick's arm. "You're wanted. Come along." He was about Patrick's age and height, maybe a little taller, definitely fatter.

"What do you mean, come along? Hilda and me're goin' up in the balloon, an' it's our last chance, too."

"Your uncle needs you." The man, his bushy black eyebrows set in a frown, didn't even look at Hilda.

"You're holding up the line," said the balloon man. "Are you coming, or not?"

"Yes. Here's the money." Patrick handed over an amount that made Hilda blink, and helped her into the balloon's basket. As he made to follow, the man who had accosted him grabbed his elbow.

"I told you, you're wanted. This is a family matter. You'll come along *now*, young feller-me-lad."

He dragged Patrick away unceremoniously.

"Hilda—I'm sorry—you go—"

The rest was lost in the noise of the crowd. Hilda gazed helplessly after Patrick. She could not get out of the balloon by herself.

"Now that's a downright shame," said the woman who had gotten in ahead of her. "But it'll be all right. You just stay with me and my husband. We'll look after you."

Hilda wasn't so sure it was all right, but she was given no time to think. The pilot loaded two more people in, firmly turned away the rest, and arranged his passengers so that the basket would be properly balanced. Then he loosed all but the longest of the ropes holding the balloon to the ground. Silently, swiftly, they rose into the air. Hilda looked hard, but she could no longer see the hurrying figures of Patrick and the fat man. As the balloon rose higher and higher, all Hilda's cares were lost in the wonder of it.

The fairgrounds grew small. People became tiny, insignificant creatures crawling about the grounds. The merry-go-round was a pretty toy. The noise of the fair, oddly, seemed nearly as loud as ever, if not so clear.

The wind was stronger up here. The basket tossed and swayed. The balloon was still tethered to the ground, so there was no danger of their being blown away, but they were carried far from their point of ascension to a spot directly over the racetrack.

Hilda, alone on her side of the basket, could see the activity in the grandstand very well. Horses—they must be horses, though they looked more like small dogs—ran 'round and 'round, trailing flimsy-looking sulkies behind them. Other horses were being exercised outside the arena. One, hitched to what looked like a small green delivery wagon, was behaving badly, tossing its head, backing, curvetting, trying to rear. Hilda was amused at the groom's attempt to control it.

She could see the river from up here, and lots of trees, and church spires, and (if she looked across to the other side of the basket) the great golden dome that topped the main building at Notre Dame, far to the north. She could even, if she stared hard, see what she imagined might be Tippecanoe Place, nearly hidden by the big, lovely trees around it. She sighed. It looked from here like a dream castle, not the place of her unremitting toil.

Never mind, she thought. You are here now, and it is lovely. If only Patrick were here, too, to enjoy it.

The ride was over far too soon, curtailed by the pilot's concern about the wind. He reeled in the balloon, with the help of his ground crew, and helped them out.

"Here you are, miss," he said to Hilda, the last one to disembark. "Your young man gave me the money for his ride, too. You'd best give it back to him."

"He is not my young man, only a friend," said Hilda firmly. "But thank you. I will give the money to him."

She stood irresolute, however, as the balloon crew busied themselves tying it down securely against the rising wind. Where was Patrick?

She held up a hand to shade her eyes, peered around, and saw him running toward her. As he neared, she could see that he looked worried.

No, not just worried. Frightened. Very frightened.

"Hilda!" He stopped in front of her, panting. "Hilda, I'll have to send you home on the cars. Somethin' terrible's happened!"

Her blue eyes opened wide. "What, Patrick? What is it?"

"John Bishop's gone and got himself killed! And Uncle Dan's disappeared!"

# 3

Heaven has no rage like love to hatred turned.
　　　—William Congreve, *The Mourning Bride,* 1697

W HAT do you mean, disappeared? A man cannot vanish!"
"He has, though. We can't find him anywhere. And I'm sorry, but I've got to go back and keep lookin'. Here's some money. Can you get to the cars by yourself?" He gave her a handful of coins.

She dropped them in her pocket, at the same time handing back the money for the balloon ride. "Here. The balloon man gave it back. But do not be foolish, Patrick. I will go home in a little while, but for now I come with you. He will be here. I will help you look."

She set off at a brisk pace toward the grandstand and Patrick had no choice but to follow.

"Where do you think you're goin'? You can't—"

"Patrick! Do not argue! Tell me where Mr. Malloy was when you last saw him."

Patrick gritted his teeth. Arguing with Hilda was as productive as arguing with a fence post, he knew, but he was determined that she would not become involved in this situation. "Stop an' listen! I never saw him at all. We was lookin' for him, me an' me cousin Clancy. He was the one that come and hauled me away, you know?"

Hilda nodded.

"So we was lookin', and what we found was—was Bishop." He stopped and swallowed hard. "An' now the police are lookin' for Uncle Dan, too, an' I don't want—"

Hilda stopped and stared at him, horror dawning in her eyes. "The police? Why do the police look for Mr. Malloy?"

Too late, Patrick tried to backpedal. "Well, they— When a man is lost, the police—"

Hilda interrupted. "How was Mr. Bishop killed?" she demanded.

There was no help for it. If he didn't tell her, someone else would.

"He was beaten to death."

"With what?"

"They don't know, not for certain!"

"Then why are you so frightened?" She was relentless.

Furious and miserable, he shouted at her. "Because they found me uncle Dan's shillelagh lyin' next to the man's body! Are you happy now?"

Hilda put a hand on his arm. Her voice softened. "No, Patrick, I am not happy. But I do not believe that your uncle Dan has killed Mr. Bishop. And I think that we must find your uncle, and quickly, so that he can explain."

"Hilda, you don't understand! I don't want you mixed up in this. It's too dangerous, and besides, me cousin said—" He broke off, unable to find the words to continue.

Something in Hilda turned cold. If her corset had not held her upright, she would have slumped. Her eyes, all the happy animation gone from them, met Patrick's. "It is your family, *ja?*" she said at last. "They do not want me to concern myself?"

His silence answered her.

They stood looking at each other, oblivious to the noise and bustle about them. It had come, the moment they had both known would arrive sooner or later, the moment when the differences in their backgrounds would become a barrier between them. They had tried to ignore the problem, tried to pretend that they were only friends, that the differences didn't matter. Now they could no longer pretend.

"Patrick! Patrick Cavanaugh!"

It was Clancy's voice, raised to a bellow.

"Hilda, I—"

"You must go. I know. Do not worry. I will not come with you."

She turned her back to him and walked away without another word.

Patrick stood and watched her go. Twice he nearly went after her. Twice the set of her back, the rigid carriage of her head, made him think again.

"Patrick, yé great gomerel! Stop moonin' about an' come here *now!*" The bellow was even louder, the Irish brogue strong from stress.

Patrick turned on his heel and strode toward Clancy, his face a thundercloud. "An' I'll not," he said when he reached his cousin, "be ordered about by the likes of you, do you understand that? Now where haven't you looked?"

Clancy was bigger than Patrick, and a year older, but even when they were boys, Patrick had been able to best him. He was the best fighter in the family. Clancy looked at Patrick's clenched fists and high color and bit back whatever he had been about to say. "I'm tryin' the animal tents next, if you'd want to go down the midway."

They separated to continue their hunt.

Hilda had kept her shoulders rigid, had carried her head high, in case Patrick was watching. Now she slowed down and wandered aimlessly, blinking back tears and trying to think. It was stupid to cry. She was not crying. It was the dust, or the heat, or the discomfort of her corset, or—something.

She sank down on a bench in the shade and pulled her handkerchief out of her pocket. A cascade of coins fell to the ground; she bent to pick them up.

Patrick had given her a lot of money, nearly a dollar. She could stay at the fair. She could buy a souvenir, ride the merry-go-round, try her hand at the coconut shy.

And how much fun would she have doing any of those things by herself?

Why had Patrick run off with Clancy that first time? What had Clancy wanted? He'd said something about Uncle Dan needing Patrick, or wanting him. Hilda couldn't remember. But then, Patrick had said, they couldn't find Dan.

Clancy must have known where Dan Malloy was, must have been dispatched by him to find Patrick. If only she had asked!

She squared her shoulders. It was none of her affair. The family didn't want her help. Patrick didn't want her help.

She touched the handkerchief to her cheeks again. Surely there was dust in her eyes.

Which direction had Clancy come from, when he'd come to find Patrick? She had no idea. She and Patrick had been looking at the balloon when his cousin had come up behind them.

Well, then, where had they gone? Hilda thought hard. They had started off into the crowd, away from the balloon, along the side of the grandstand. Then Hilda had lost them, and a minute or two later, when the balloon began to rise and she was high enough to see over the crowds, she had caught no glimpse of them.

Could they, then, have entered the grandstand? They could have been under the seats, where she would not have been able to see them from above. If so, then Clancy must have expected to find Daniel Malloy there.

If she were to explore the grandstand, she might find—

She reined in her thoughts. She might find a number of Patrick's family members, all upset and ready to take offense. She knew the Irish temper. She might even meet Patrick again, and . . .

Resolutely, she found the archway that led out of the park and made her way to the trolley stop.

She arrived back at Tippecanoe Place at least an hour before sunset, the time she was due back on her afternoons out. The great house was silent, the family and servants all out except for the butler, who was probably snoring in his own particular chair in the servants' room. Hilda didn't care. Wearily she climbed the stairs to her room, got out of the clothes she had put on with such happy anticipation, and lay down on the bed.

Now that she was alone, she let herself cry. She told herself her distress was due to hurt pride. She, Hilda Johansson, who had solved two important murder cases when the South Bend police could not—she had been spurned by a family of ignorant Irishmen! She who was smart, she who could talk to people and learn things that others could not, had been treated with contempt.

Her thoughts turned in a new, equally unpleasant direction. She, who could have walked around the fair and learned a great deal, had walked away like a sulky child. And why? Turning over on her narrow bed and propping her chin on her hands, she faced the truth. She had walked away because she feared an encounter with Patrick. She feared the embarrassment, the hurt, the loneliness of seeing him turn away from her.

In a moment of inner honesty, she acknowledged bitterly how much she cared for Patrick. And now things would never be the same between them.

And that is a good thing, she told herself fiercely, flouncing again to lie on her back. It is not good to be friends with Patrick. Better to find a nice Swedish boy to marry. You could never have married Patrick.

Perhaps she did not want to marry anyone. She could not continue as a live-in maid if she were married, and she was proud of her status, proud that she lived in the finest house in town. The work was hard, though. Perhaps, after all, it would be better to have a house of her own, with a good, industrious Swedish husband and a lot of pretty blond children.

She pictured the children. Why, oh why did the boys all seem to have turned-up noses and unruly black hair?

There was a noise of hooves on the carriageway below: John Bolton, bringing the horses back from their exercise. Soon the great house would come alive again. The family members were all dining with friends, as they usually did on the servants' afternoon out, but the rest of the servants would be returning. Mrs. Sullivan, the cook, would start preparing the servants' supper.

Norah would come upstairs and change her clothes. Mr. Williams would wake from his afternoon nap and pretend he had spent the time reading the book that lay open on his lap. The sketchy supper of leftovers would be served, and all would be expected at the table.

Hilda quickly got up and wrung out a towel in the tepid water still in the washstand pitcher. She pulled the window curtains closed and lay back on her bed, the damp cloth over her eyes. If Norah looked in she would think Hilda had another of her terrible headaches and would leave her alone. Norah was her best friend, but Hilda couldn't bear the thought of talking to her, or to anyone, just now.

She lay and tried to think of nothing, but the sights and sounds and smells of the fair kept chasing through her mind. The smell of horses and hay and popcorn. The sound of the merry-go-round's organ, the cries of the hucksters.

Had there been other cries? The cries of a man being beaten to death?

Hilda shuddered. Mr. Bishop could have screamed as loudly as he liked, and if he had been even a few feet from possible rescuers, no one would have paid any attention. Animals squealed. Children shouted. The noises of the fair would have covered any cries of alarm.

Probably, she told herself firmly, the attacker had administered one hard blow to the head that had rendered Mr. Bishop unconscious, and he'd never felt anything that followed. At least she preferred to believe that.

But why had he been killed at all? And why so savagely? There were many ways to kill. Poison, a knife, a gun. One could drown an enemy, or push him down a flight of stairs, or, as had nearly happened to her on one occasion, set a building on fire around him. Beating implied hatred or vindictiveness, not mere expediency.

Or, of course, the killer could have been taken by surprise. Suppose—oh, suppose he, the murderer, had been doing something he should not. Stealing a racehorse, perhaps. Horse theft had, she knew, been punishable by death in some parts of

America, and though she wasn't sure, she thought it might be still. If Mr. Malloy had caught the man stealing, and the man had had a weapon in his hand—

Once more she brought herself up short. The weapon, apparently, was a shillelagh belonging to Patrick's uncle. She wasn't certain exactly what a shillelagh was; some sort of heavy stick, she thought. Why it was at the fair, and was found apart from its owner, were interesting matters for speculation.

They were, however, of no interest to her, she reminded herself for the tenth time. None of it had anything to do with Hilda Johansson. She had been told to keep out, and she was not one to be insulted twice. She would keep out.

Footsteps climbing the stairs. A knock at her door. She lay still and tried to breathe evenly.

The door opened. There was silence for a moment, and then determined footsteps crossed to the bed. The towel was snatched from Hilda's head.

"You're no more asleep than I am, Hilda Johansson!" Norah said briskly. "An' I don't care if you *have* got a headache. Get up this minute and tell me why you're doin' nothin' to find Dan Malloy!"

# 4

[With regard to the anthracite strike] it is freely predicted that the most serious labor struggle in the history of the country is about to begin.
　　　　—*The New York Times* (editorial), May 16, 1902

ORAH'S belligerence fanned Hilda's smoldering emotions into flame. She sprang from the bed, her eyes blazing.

"Do not tell me what to do! I will lie in my bed if I wish. And you—you will not come into my room again! My family is right. I ought to have nothing to do with you *Irish!*" She spat the word out like an obscenity.

Norah, astonished, backed to the doorway. Hilda stood facing her, hands on hips, her whole body trembling with rage. "Get out! Leave me alone!"

Norah opened her mouth, but Hilda had had enough. "*Go!*" she screamed, and slammed the door and locked it.

Then she threw herself down on her bed and wept until her head began to ache in earnest. Eventually she slept.

The room was dark when she was awakened by a tap at the door. "Hilda! Hilda, let me in. I've brought you a tray. I told Mr. Williams you had one o' your headaches. Hilda, I'm sorry."

Hilda lay rigid and said nothing. After a minute or two of more soft taps and whispers, she heard the chink of china as the tray was put on the floor. Norah's door opened and closed. There were sounds of movement in the next room for a few minutes and then the creak of the bed. A tap sounded on the wall between the rooms. Hilda made no response, did not even breathe until she heard Norah turn over.

Then there was only silence. Hilda lay awake for a long time, finally falling into a troubled sleep an hour or so before her alarm rang and she had to rise and begin the day's duties.

Her head still ached. She was exhausted by emotional excess. Nevertheless, she rose and dressed quickly and quietly. Leaving the spurned supper tray on the floor outside the door, she tiptoed downstairs, the better to avoid talking to Norah.

Their early-morning duties took the two women to different parts of the great house. Norah, the waitress, would be busy setting the family breakfast table in the semi-basement and then cleaning and tidying the state dining room before going to the kitchen to help with the servants' breakfast. Hilda's morning jobs were on the main floor, cleaning the library and drawing room and tidying the other rooms to be ready for the under-housemaids, the dailies who would arrive after the live-in servants had had their breakfast.

Hilda usually took a few minutes in the library to pretend that it all belonged to her. With its richly carved woodwork, its glass-fronted bookcases, its carved plaster ceiling and fine chandelier, its elaborate fireplace, it was her favorite room in the house. Today, barely glancing at the luxury around her, she went dully about her chores, taking care with the delicate ornaments only from force of habit.

The windowsills in the drawing room were covered with a fine layer of soot. They always were. In warm weather, when the windows were open, the soot came from the roaring chimneys of the bustling factories all over town. In winter the central heating in the house, along with the twenty fireplaces, generated soot along with heat. It had to be washed off every single day, and carefully, too. Dusting or careless washing left black streaks. They didn't show so much against dark wood. Hilda sometimes rushed the job in other rooms, but the woodwork in the drawing room was ivory colored.

There was less soot than usual today, though. It had been diminishing for some weeks, and it was not cause for rejoicing, for the reason was grim. A coal strike, now beginning its fifth month, had taken a terrible toll on small industry, and many of those soot-producing factories had been working on half shifts, or not at all, for some time now.

Hilda had a good deal of sympathy for the miners, who were little more than slaves. Some men worked twelve hours a day, seven days a week, for a little over ten dollars a week. Children, sent into the mines to earn what they could to keep the family alive, might make forty cents a day. And even that pittance was often owed to the company store, which held a monopoly on retail business in the mine field and charged exorbitant prices.

So the anthracite miners of Pennsylvania, under the leadership of a man named John Mitchell, had struck in May. The strike had grown and was now nationwide, including many bituminous mines as well. Coal had gone up and up in price; now little was to be had at any price. Oh, the big industrialists held huge reserves, and the railroads. They'd hold out for a while longer . . . But autumn was nearly here. If the strike continued into winter, suffering would be extreme on all levels of society. Even the Studebakers, with their almost limitless wealth, could not buy coal for their factories and their furnaces and their fireplaces if there was no coal.

Hilda had grown up being cold. Swedish winters were brutal and the family had never been warm enough. She feared the cold. She feared the effect on her family if Studebaker's were forced to shut down and her brother Sven were thrown out of work. Most of all, she feared the violence that threatened the mines.

For the owners had not allowed their mines to sit idle for long. They had hired strikebreakers, "scabs," men who knew little or nothing about mining but who preferred even that oppressive work to none at all. There were confrontations, of course, between the striking miners and the scabs. And most recently, and most horribly, the nation had been stunned and appalled by an explosion in a Kentucky mine that had killed seventy-three men and fifteen boys, the youngest only nine years old.

No one knew what had caused the explosion. Spokesmen for the strikers (some of whom were among the dead and wounded; the explosion had destroyed homes on the surface as well) claimed the inexperienced miners had touched off coal gas. Owners (none of whom had been scratched) claimed the strikers had deliberately touched off the blast to punish the scabs. Tempers were at flash point, and troops had been called out to control the situation, but they were of dubious help, since both sides assumed the troops were there to protect the other side's interests. It was a situation ripe for violence and yet more tragedy.

Yesterday Hilda had been vitally interested in the matter. Today she had forgotten it until the light coating of soot brought it back to her mind, only to be instantly dismissed.

She was scrubbing listlessly when she saw yesterday's South Bend *Tribune* lying on a chair where someone had left it last evening. It might have some news of the murder and disappearance, if the events had happened before the newspaper's deadline. There might be details that Hilda didn't yet know.

She went on scrubbing, concentrating on leaving no streaks.

By breakfast time her stomach was growling. She could go without food no longer. She crept down the back stairs and listened, and then, head held high, walked into the servants' room.

Norah was already seated at the table. Hilda slipped into her usual place next to Norah, saying nothing.

"I trust you are feeling better this morning, Hilda," said Mr. Williams in his usual pompous manner.

"A little, sir," she murmured.

"I could have told you the fair would make you ill. Too much heat and noise and excitement and unwholesome food. You'd have done better to take a quiet walk."

He had not heard the news, then. That meant the evening

newspapers had not carried the story, and the morning delivery boys had not yet arrived with their burdens of meat, groceries, and gossip. Good. Mr. Williams did not yet know just how bad the fair had been. And he need never know how bad it had been for her personally.

"Yes, sir," she said with such unaccustomed meekness that he stared at her suspiciously. But she had her coffee cup to her mouth; he let the subject drop and began to find fault with the consistency of the porridge.

Hilda spoke no word to Norah during the meal, nor did Norah attempt any conversation. Neither the butler nor the cook noticed, being occupied with their own quarrel. Anton, the footman, who shared meals with the live-in servants, concerned himself solely with his breakfast, and Michelle, the French ladies' maid, ignored them all. She never spoke much to the other servants, whom she considered beneath her. Only John Bolton gave them a curious look, but his policy was never to intervene in arguments, especially arguments between females. It didn't do to let them think they were important. Besides, a man could get hurt in a catfight.

The two women were able to avoid each other for the rest of the morning. After she had finished her own meal Norah had to serve the family theirs, while Hilda and her underlings hurried through the family bedrooms and bathrooms. Then there were the public rooms on the main floor to finish cleaning, while Norah made sure the family dining room was ready for the noonday meal.

Tippecanoe Place had been a house of mourning for nearly a year. Clement Studebaker, the fabulously wealthy industrialist who had built the house in 1889, had died peacefully in his own bed in November of 1901—the day before Thanksgiving. His widow still lived in the house, but the real master and mistress now were Clement's younger son, Colonel George Studebaker, and his wife. Hilda missed Mr. Clem sorely. He had been a great man and a good one as well. She didn't care as much for Colonel George, nor was Mrs. George as pleasant a mistress as Mrs. Clem. True, some things had been easier for the servants since Mr. Clem's death. There was no entertaining, which meant no evenings of working until midnight and beyond. But the routine daily work had to be done to Mrs. George's exacting specifications, so all the rooms had to be as clean as if guests were expected any minute.

Hilda was harsh with the underhousemaids that morning. She allowed no slacking, no chatting, but moved through her own work with breathless speed and demanded the same from them, reducing the youngest of them, a child of fifteen, to tears.

"If you must weep," said Hilda coldly, "do not do it where the family can hear you. And wash your face with cold water when you have finished so that they will not see your red eyes. Servants are not expected to have feelings."

When luncheon for both servants and family had been eaten and cleared away, the live-in servants were allowed an hour or so of rest before continuing with their work. As Hilda approached the back stairs, Norah caught up with her.

"Hilda, wait. I don't know what I did to make you so mad, and I don't like what you said about the Irish, but I'd as soon have it out as go about with chips on our shoulders this way. Won't you talk to me?"

"What do you want me to say?" Hilda was as brusque as she had been with the young housemaid.

"I want to know what's wrong. Don't you even want to hear the news about Dan Malloy?"

"No." Hilda began to climb the steep, narrow stairs.

"*No!* Why not? What's the *matter* with you?"

"I am tired. My head aches. I have no wish to hear about matters that do not concern me." She rounded a corner of the staircase.

"Ye don't care that he's still missin', and the police are sayin' he killed Mr. Bishop? Hilda, they've got a warrant out for his arrest!"

Hilda's footsteps faltered for a moment, nearly long enough for Norah to catch up. Then Hilda continued climbing the stairs.

"What the Irish choose to do is nothing to do with me."

And to Norah's further angry remarks she would make no reply.

She was too tired not to nap, but her mind even in sleep refused to relinquish the problem. She thrashed about on her bed, and when she woke to the pounding on her door, her cheeks were wet with tears.

She would not answer the knock. She had nothing to say to Norah, and it was not—she glanced at the alarm clock—not yet time to go back to work.

"*Hilda!*" The voice belonged to Mr. Williams and it sounded angry. "Are you deaf, girl?"

"Yoost a minute, sir!" In her agitation her accent reverted. She donned her wrapper, unlocked her door, and peered out.

"There are callers for you," he said, his manner at its most disapproving. "They are respectable gentlemen and gave me to understand that it was a matter of importance or I would not have come up to fetch you. I trust you realize this is most irregular. You had best hurry and not keep them waiting. They are in the small reception room."

"Yes, sir," she said anxiously, her mind casting about for explanations of this unheard-of thing. The *reception* room! That was where guests of the family waited. "Are they—is it my brother? Has something happened?" But no, they were gentlemen, he had said. Her family would have had to cool their heels in the servants' room.

There was no reply. Mr. Williams had already gone down the stairs, eager to forget that he, the butler, had been forced to deliver a message to a housemaid.

She dressed quickly and ran down the back stairs, but when she reached the great hall she slowed her steps to the gait expected of servants while in a part of the house where the family might catch a glimpse of them.

Her callers were waiting for her, two men she had never seen before. With them—she nearly tripped on the Persian rug when she saw—was Colonel George.

"Ah, there you are, Hilda," he said as she approached. She

curtsied and waited, dumb, for someone to say something that made sense.

"Let me introduce to you Mr. Murphy and Mr. Leahy, business associates of mine. I saw them waiting here and came in to speak to them, thinking they had called on me and Mr. Williams had forgotten to tell me. However, they have come on a somewhat different errand, which I will allow them to tell you for themselves."

The man named Murphy cleared his throat. "I have come, Miss Johansson, to ask for your help. It is my understanding that you have been—er—instrumental, of late, in discovering the truth about several matters that puzzled the police."

"Yes, sir." It was barely a whisper.

"Don't be frightened, girl!" Mr. Leahy spoke impatiently. "We won't eat you!"

"No, sir." She looked from one man to the other, bewildered.

"Perhaps you'd better let me explain," said Colonel George with a sigh, and turned to the maid. "These men are leaders in the community, Hilda. They are also, as you will guess from their names, Irish. They are troubled by the events of yesterday and convinced that Mr. Malloy is innocent of the charges being brought against him."

"And we've come—that is, his family have asked us—actually, we want to ask you . . ." Mr. Murphy seemed unable to finish a sentence. He fingered his tie.

"Malloy's family," said Leahy bluntly, "want you to find him, and they didn't want to come and ask you themselves. It's Mrs. Malloy, you see. She thinks you can do something. Young Clancy doesn't seem to agree, and I must admit I don't see the use of it, myself. It'd be better just to let Mayor Fogarty handle it, in my opinion. He's on the side of the Irish, or you'd think so. But Mrs. Malloy seems to feel he's too new to have much influence with a police superintendent hired by the old regime, and she's heard reports about you. Exaggerated, I dare say, but there you are."

"Oh, but, sir, I do not think I—you see, I have my duties, and I cannot—"

"I don't think we need trouble about that, Hilda," said Colonel George. "With no entertaining these days, there's not as much work to do, and the weather's warm—no coals to carry or that sort of thing."

Hilda would have rolled her eyes to the ceiling if she had dared. Coals to carry, indeed! That was the footman's job. And there was enough work to keep her busy, more than enough.

"At any rate, it won't hurt to give it a try, eh? I'll tell my wife you'll be taking some time off for a few days."

"It's very good of you, George," said Mr. Murphy, shaking the colonel's hand, relieved now that his awkward errand had been accomplished. "You'll let us know if you need anything, will you, Miss Johansson? Good day, then."

Colonel George saw them out the front door. Hilda was left holding her breath.

She expelled it slowly. She had been given no choice, no chance to speak her mind. She was being lent to Colonel George's friends exactly as though she were a horse—or a slave. She was not a slave! She was a free woman. Soon, she hoped, she would be an American citizen. She would not be ordered around!

Colonel George returned. "Well, now, Hilda, this is a lucky thing for you, eh? Get to run around poking your nose into the sort of thing you enjoy, and see that young man of yours at the same time!" He chuckled. "I just hope you come back to us. Don't let him woo you away, now! I'll speak to Williams about this; don't worry about your chores here for the time being."

Before Hilda could think of a reply that was both deferential and clearly negative, he had gone into the library and rung for the butler.

Hilda sat down on the nearest chair. She had never done such a thing before. Servants did not sit on the family's furniture. She did it now without so much as a thought.

She struggled to make her mind function in its usual cool, logical fashion, but too much had happened in too short a time. She was being pulled in too many directions.

Think, she commanded herself. You must think what to do.

Yesterday Patrick had not wanted her help. Today he, or at

any rate his family, did want her help. Mrs. Malloy had sent men to find her. But she, Mrs. Malloy, had not wanted to ask her directly.

That meant, she reasoned, that a Malloy was still unwilling to talk to a Swede. She was still an outcast, a Protestant. She could be hired to do a job of work, like any other minor subordinate, but an Irishwoman did not wish to have personal dealings with her.

And what of Clancy, who yesterday had been very rude? She realized he must be Daniel Malloy's son, but apparently he still didn't want her involved, still thought her beneath his contempt.

The idea made her simmer.

However, Mrs. Malloy had sent important men to ask her, men who were known to Colonel George. That meant that she was uncertain of Hilda's response and wanted to make sure she would agree. And that in turn implied a certain level of desperation.

Why?

Her anger began to diminish. The Cavanaugh-Malloy family might not like her, but they needed her, and badly. They knew the police were unlikely to do anything useful; she was their best hope. To that extent they were in her power. Her chin came up.

Moreover, she was being given the chance to abandon her routine, leave behind her mops and dust rags and brushes, the drudgery that was her life day in and day out. She was being freed from her prison with its rigid schedule of times when she must be in a given place occupied with a given task. She was being invited to come and go when she pleased and where she pleased, asking no one's permission, and to do the kind of thing she enjoyed most, investigate crime.

She frowned again. No, she was not being invited to do these things. She had been told to do them.

Was she stubborn enough to refuse to do the things she wanted to do simply because she had been ordered to do them?

Yes, she answered herself honestly, she was that stubborn. Was she also that stupid?

A sudden thought occurred to her. She rose and went to the library. Mr. Williams had apparently come and gone; Colonel George sat smoking his pipe and reading a book. He was more a man of leisure than his father had been. His business interests were not solely in Studebaker Brothers, nor were they of the sort that kept him at an office all day. Hilda privately thought that he was not half the man his father had been, but she had the sense to keep the thought to herself.

She cleared her throat and curtsied when Colonel George looked up.

"Oh, Hilda. I thought you had gone off to—do whatever it is you're going to do."

"No, sir. I think, sir. No, I—I been thinking." She was working hard to improve her English.

" 'Have been thinking,' " Colonel George corrected absently. "About what?"

"If I do what Mr. Murphy and Mr. Leahy want me to do, how will I be paid? I have not much money, sir. I cannot work for no pay."

"No, no, of course not. Nobody expects you to, girl!" Colonel George puffed rapidly at his pipe, looking annoyed. Hilda realized that he had not considered this aspect of the matter. And why would he? He had never in his life had to wonder where his money was coming from, or if there would be enough to buy both food *and* a warm coat for the winter. So long as Hilda held this job, she didn't have to worry, either, but if she lost it . . .

She waited. Colonel George sighed. "Suppose we say that I will continue to pay your wages as usual for a week. You'll be able to find the man in that time, surely."

If it was a question, it was phrased in such a way that Hilda did not have to answer. She was grateful. She had no idea how much time this task would require.

"Yes, well. At the end of a week, we'll see, eh? And I shouldn't wonder if you didn't get a nice bonus out of it from the Malloy family, as well. That'll be all, Hilda."

He nodded in dismissal. Hilda curtsied and turned away. The subject was closed for now, but she was far from satisfied. A week! She didn't know where to look, who to talk to. She didn't know what opposition she would meet, or what danger awaited her. And she seriously doubted that the Malloy family would pay her anything at all for her trouble. They didn't like her. They didn't want anything to do with her.

And if she was unsuccessful? If she had learned nothing by the end of a week? Would she still have employment—anywhere?

If she had dared, she would have returned to the library and told Colonel George in no uncertain terms that she would not become involved in the disappearance of Dan Malloy.

But she did not dare. Her family had almost no reserves, now that all their savings had been paid over to Mr. Vanderhoof. Until more could be saved, they could afford no disasters like the loss of anyone's job. And with Sven's in jeopardy, perhaps, if the coal strike continued, Hilda could take no risks.

Wearily she climbed the stairs to her room. There was no help for it. She must try hard to turn herself into a real detective.

# 5

... I did not even trust my own impressions, but it rests partly on what I saw myself, partly on what others saw for me, the accuracy of the report being always tried by the most severe and detailed tests possible.

—Thucydides, *The History of the Peloponnesian War*, c. 420 B.C.

S HE encountered Norah on the stairs.

"It's time to get back to work, Your Majesty," said Norah, her voice dripping with sarcasm.

"I do not go to work."

"Oh, so you've got the sack, have you? Thought you would, one o' these days."

"No, Norah, I— Do you have time to talk? Only for a minute?"

"Oh, now you're not too high an' mighty to talk to me! Well, it'll have to wait. *I* got work to do, if you don't, so I'd be obliged if I could pass."

Hilda didn't move. "Your uncle came to see me. In the reception room."

That captured Norah's attention, as Hilda had known it would.

"Me uncle? To see you? Which one? Whatever for? And

what was Mr. Williams thinkin' of, puttin' him in the reception room!"

"I do not know which one. His name is Mr. Murphy, so he must be one of your uncles."

Norah sniffed. "Oh, him. He's me father's only brother. Not that he acts like a relation, not him. He's gone up in the world and thinks himself too fine for the likes of us."

She seemed ready to expand on the theme, but Hilda didn't want to listen to Norah's family problems just then. She interrupted. "Yes, he is a rich gentleman, and he wishes me to find Mr. Malloy. Or Mrs. Malloy wants it, and sent Mr. Murphy to ask me. Norah, Colonel George has told me to do it, and I think I will need your help."

"Hmph! Seems to me you said you wanted nothin' to do with us Irish, and that's fine with me, thanks all the same."

"I did say that, and I am sorry, but I did not mean it. I was very angry with Patrick, and with his family. I am angry still, but I should not have shouted at you."

She waited anxiously while Norah's temper did battle with her curiosity.

At last Norah shrugged. "Ye'd do better to think before you have your tantrums, girl. One day you'll make somebody mad enough they'll not forgive you. I've me work to do now, but if you want to work with me, we can talk."

Hilda hesitated. "I do not think Mr. Williams will let me do that. Colonel George has told me that I may spend all my time at this other yob—job—and Mr. Williams will not like that. He will want to find fault with me. If I talk to you, he will say I keep you from your work, and he will scold both of us. I think it will be better if I leave the house now, but I will try to help you after dinner. Mr. Williams will be busy in his pantry then, and we can talk in private."

"If you like." Norah had almost forgiven Hilda, mostly because she was eager to be involved if something interesting was happening. All the same, she had no intention of making things too easy. "I'll be here, not like *some* as can come and go as they please."

She slipped past Hilda and went on down the stairs. Hilda stood, hands on hips, and looked after her. Really, the Irish *could* be . . . Then she shook her head. She'd better rid herself of that attitude, and in a hurry. She was guiltily aware that she'd been unfair to Norah simply because she was Irish. And she, Hilda, was going to be working very closely with the Irish for at least the next week.

She sighed. She was very tired. She would like nothing better than to continue her interrupted nap, but if Mr. Williams caught her, he would be incensed. To take time off from one's regular work to do a job sanctioned—very nearly ordered—by Colonel George was one thing. The butler might not like it, but he had no choice but to allow it. To take time off for rest was quite another thing. For that, she would probably be discharged. Sighing again, she plodded on up the stairs.

She thought for some few minutes about her clothes. If she went about her inquiries—and she still had no ideas about how to pursue them—in housemaid's dress, would she be more, or less, likely to be admitted to the places she needed to go?

In the end she decided to wear her uniform. Wherever she went, her first encounters would be with those of her own class, servants and laborers, mostly immigrants like herself. They would be more likely to talk to a woman who looked like themselves than to someone who looked like a lady, and Hilda flattered herself that she could look very much like a lady when she put her mind to it.

Besides, it would be a waste of her good clothes, of which she had only a small selection, to wear them where Patrick would not see her.

The thought of Patrick stung. Fiercely she dismissed him from her mind, only to be reminded again when she thought about money. She might need money, for carfare if nothing else, and she had none of her own; she had, as usual, turned all of her last week's wages over to her brother Sven. There was, however, money still in the pocket of her best skirt, Patrick's money. Ought she to use it, in the interests, after all, of his family?

No! She transferred it to the pocket of her black skirt with a fine gesture of disdain. She would find him and give it back to him. She did not want his money. She would ask Colonel George for money to meet her necessary expenses, and if he would not give it to her, she would go to Mr. Murphy.

Colonel George gave her the money, though with a bad grace. He was clearly becoming annoyed. "Never should have gotten mixed up in this thing," he muttered as he fished in his pocket. "More trouble than it's worth. Will a couple of dollars do?"

Two dollars! It would take her a month to spend that much. "Yes, sir, thank you, sir. I will keep an account of what I spend."

"Don't bother. Just get the job done, there's a good girl." He turned back to his book.

"I will keep the account, sir," she said firmly. "And there is one more thing."

"Well?" He drummed his fingers on the arm of the chair.

"I must know the Christian names of Mr. Murphy and Mr. Leahy, and their addresses. I may need to ask them some questions."

"John Murphy. Andrew Leahy. Don't know where they live, and they wouldn't want you bothering them at home anyway, but they're bankers. First National, both of them. See that you don't turn into a nuisance."

He changed his position in the chair so that his back was to her and pointedly picked up his book. Hilda curtsied, unseen.

Quite deliberately, she left the house by the front door. Such a thing was never allowed. Servants and tradesmen came and went by the door at the back of the semi-basement and the steep outside stairs leading up to the back drive. Hilda's action now was a defiance of Mr. Williams's authority and a small assertion of her independence. She might be doing Colonel George's bidding, but she would do it in her own way.

And the first thing she would do, she decided when she reached Washington Street, at the bottom of the front drive, was to go and see Patrick at the fire station. There were questions to be asked, and she wanted to give him his money back.

If she had other motives, she kept them sternly out of her mind.

It was a lovely, lazy day, the sort of day for dreaming. The sky was piled with masses of fluffy clouds, almost a summer sky, except that the purplish undersides of the clouds showed that fall was coming. Washington Street, the finest street in town, where the very wealthiest families lived and the very best lawyers had their offices, was looking its best, the lawns lush and green, the flower beds bright and well tended. Hilda was oblivious to the beauty around her. She was too busy considering a plan of action.

First she must learn what Patrick knew of yesterday's events. Patrick would not want to talk to her, perhaps. He would tell her to stay away from the whole matter. She tossed her head. She would have a thing or two to say to Patrick about that, and she would make him tell her everything.

Then she would go to the police station down the street. If she was lucky and Patrolman Lefkowicz was on duty, she could probably learn from him what the police knew of the murder and the disappearance. Patrolman Lefkowicz was her friend, though he employed a reasonable caution when talking with her. He had learned that dealing with Hilda Johansson could be dangerous.

Then, when she had gleaned all she could from her two best sources, then—well, then, she supposed, she would have to go and talk to Patrick's cousin Clancy. She didn't look forward to it. He would be angry and upset about his father, as well as contemptuous of her as a Swede. The interview was likely to be unpleasant. And how would Mrs. Malloy react, Mrs. Malloy who had sent someone else to seek her help instead of coming herself?

Hilda lifted her head high. She had not asked for this job. She had not taken it on willingly. But now that she had been coerced into it, she would pursue it with all her energy, all her stubborn intelligence. The Malloy family, however reluctantly, had asked for help. Very well, they would learn how uncompromising that help could be.

Patrick was at the station, lounging in a rocking chair on the front porch, with Sam, the firehouse dalmatian, lying beside him. He stood when he saw her; the dog stood, too, and wagged his tail. Hilda sailed up, determined not to let Patrick see her relief. It would have been terrible if he had not been on duty and she had had to seek him out at his home; she had never been there and did not even know where he lived.

"Good day, Patrick," she said coldly. "I have come to return your money. I spent five cents of it for the streetcar."

"No need to give it back," he said gruffly.

She poured the coins from her hand onto the small wicker table next to him. Some of them rolled to the floor. She dusted her hands together with a delicately repudiating gesture.

"I have come also to ask you some questions."

"Well, sit down then. Or do I have to stand here all day?"

She sat in the other chair, making no comment on his rudeness. She was rather pleased to have made him angry, but she had neither the time nor the inclination to pursue the quarrel just now.

"I suppose you've come about me uncle."

"Yes. Your family have asked me—"

"His family. Not mine."

"You know, then. And there are not two families, but one." She dismissed complex family connections with a wave of her hand. "We will not talk about families, not now. Now I need to know everything that happened at the fair."

"An' what're you doin' here at this time of a Thursday afternoon, anyway? Did you make up somethin' to tell that butler of yours?"

"Colonel George has given me a week away from my regular duties to learn the truth. A week only, Patrick, and we waste time! Tell me what you know."

She set her jaw in a way that was all too familiar to Patrick. He might as well give in. The only way to get rid of her now, unless a fire alarm came in, would be to give her the information she wanted. And he wanted to get rid of her as quickly as possible. Yes, he did. His family was right. It was foolish to get mixed up with Protestants.

"Patrick!"

"I'm thinkin'." He drew a long breath, trying to organize his thoughts into the shortest possible narrative. "Clancy came to fetch me. You know about that part."

"I do not know why he came. He said only that your uncle needed you. Your uncle, he is Clancy's father, yes?"

"Yes. Uncle Dan's me mother's oldest brother, but Clancy's his youngest son, so he's not a lot older than me. He's a bully, though, always has been. Used to pick fights with me when we was boys. I always licked him, though, and I could have yesterday, too, but I didn't want to make a ruckus in front of you."

"Yes. Go on."

"So I went with him, and he said Uncle Dan had a problem. Real worried, he was, or at least that's what Clancy said, and needed some help."

"But what was the problem? With what did he need help?"

"He wouldn't say. Said Uncle Dan'd tell me himself. But we looked and looked for him, and all we found was . . ." Patrick swallowed as he remembered what they had found.

"Where did you look? Where had Clancy left your uncle?"

"Under the grandstand, waitin' for the race to be over so he could go in and make his speech and have the greased-pig race. He'd been standin' there talking to Mr. Bishop and some other men, Clancy said, and then Bishop went away, and a little later Uncle Dan started lookin' upset and sent him—Clancy—to find me."

"Patrick! He was talking to Mr. Bishop? Yoost before Mr. Bishop was killed? That is bad!"

"It's not so good," he admitted.

"Do the police know this?"

"I didn't tell 'em. Didn't see as I needed to, since I didn't watch it happen. Don't know if Clancy told."

"Does he tell the truth, your cousin Clancy?"

Hilda had forgotten her quarrel with Patrick in her sympathetic distress, and so had Patrick. Now, however, he was ready to infer an insult.

"Ye think the Irish are all liars, is that it?"

Hilda stood, her sympathy instantly shattered. "I think the Irish have bad tempers and do not know when someone tries to be of help!"

She swept off with never a backward glance. Patrick aimed a kick at Sam and went into the firehouse, banging the screen door.

Hilda's next stop was the police station a few doors away. It was not a place she would have gone to willingly. The floor was filthy with tobacco juice that had missed the spittoons, and the air was full of its smell. And the policemen were apt to make rude remarks to her, not only because she was an extremely pretty girl, but because she had the effrontery to think she could solve crimes. She usually liked to have Patrick as escort when she absolutely had to enter the station. Today, she told herself, she would have preferred Sam's company to Patrick's.

She set her face in its most severe expression and stepped briskly up to the desk. "I wish please to speak to Patrolman Lefkowicz." She pronounced the name, as nearly as she could, the proper Polish way: Lef-KO-vich. She hated it when people mispronounced her name, which should be YO-hahn-son. Accordingly, she tried hard to get other names right, even the difficult ones.

"Who?" said the policeman at the desk.

"She means Lefkowitz," said a passing policeman. "He's in back. I'll get him. You wait here." The last remark was addressed, with scant courtesy, to Hilda.

She gritted her teeth. "Thank you, I shall wait outside. I do not like the way this place smells."

When Patrolman Lefkowicz joined her, he was, as usual, somewhat apologetic. "I am sorry, Miss Johansson. He is not so polite, always, Patrolman Hanrahan, but he does not mean—"

Hilda waved aside extraneous matters. "It does not matter. Mr. Lefkowicz, I must know what action the police take about Mr. Malloy. They—you—have not yet found him?"

"No, and we are looking for him very hard. The superintendent does not like to have a murderer walking around free."

"I do not think he killed Mr. Bishop." A touch of frost entered her voice.

Lefkowicz shook his head. "You are mistaken, Miss Johansson. This time you are mistaken. There is no doubt about Mr. Malloy's guilt."

"How can you say that?" Hilda was trying hard to keep her temper. "Did someone see him do it?"

"Yes."

She was shaken. She tried hard not to show it, but if this was true . . .

"Who saw him? How do you know the person tells the truth about what he saw?"

Lefkowicz's voice was gentle. "Miss Johansson, I said that there was no doubt. It was his parish priest, Father Faherty. He had come looking for Mr. Malloy, to encourage him before his speech, I suppose. Someone pointed out where Malloy was, under the grandstand, and Father Faherty came up just in time to see Malloy strike several blows and then run away."

# 6

For now we see as in a glass, darkly; but then face to face. . .
—the apostle Paul, the First Epistle to the Corinthians

A wave of something that was nearly nausea swept over Hilda. Lefkowicz, seeing the color drain from her face, put his hand under her elbow.

"Here, sit down on the bench. Are you all right, Miss Johansson? Shall I get you a glass of water?"

"No," she whispered. "I am all right. I will be all right," she corrected herself. "If you will stay here for a little?"

"Of course," he assured her. Nevertheless, he glanced nervously toward the station-house door. He was too new an immigrant, and too Polish, to be in full favor with his superintendent. He knew he had to watch his step.

Hilda saw the glance, and something about his anxiety steadied her. He, too, was a pawn in the hands of hostile authority. She was warmed a little by the thought of the two of them fighting injustice and oppression together, alongside the other immigrants who were building this country with their muscles and their brains and, all too often, their blood.

Of the dozens of questions whirling in her mind, she focused on the one that worried her most at this moment.

"Does the family know this?"

"I do not know. Maybe not. Father Faherty came to us only an hour ago, or a little more."

Hilda almost gasped with relief. Then they had not sent her out knowing she was to receive this blow. Patrick had not sent her out . . .

Patrolman Lefkowicz was still talking. "He had to struggle with his conscience, the priest, to know whether or not he should tell us this about his parishioner. Or so he said." There was a faint hint of skepticism in his voice.

Hilda not only heard the skepticism, she felt it like a dash of cold water in her face. Her rosy image of unity vanished. Lefkowicz, a Catholic, did not entirely trust even a priest of his own religion because that priest was Irish. Probably he did not entirely trust her, either, because she was Swedish. She shook her head sadly. "Mr. Lefkowicz, we who are new to this country have only each other. We must not quarrel among ourselves or we have nothing."

He was not as adept as she at reading thoughts, and had no idea what she was talking about. He stared at her.

She rose, nodded gravely, and was gone.

No one was on the porch of the firehouse when she returned. She knocked at the door; women were not allowed to enter the station, which was also the firemen's dormitory during duty hours.

The door was answered by a bark from Sam and then by a fireman Hilda did not know.

"I am Miss Johansson. I must see Mr. Cavanaugh, please. It is important."

The man frowned. "I reckoned who you were. Pat's not too pleased with you, and he's taking a nap. I expect I'd better not bother him."

Hilda's deep distress lent her a new patience. "I have been gone only a few minutes. He cannot be asleep yet. I would not ask if it were not"—she hesitated, groping for the proper English phrase—"if it were not a matter of life and death. Please tell him that, and say that I am sorry I made him angry, but I *must* talk to him. Please tell him."

She didn't know if her cause was better served by the urgency she had tried to convey, or by the apology, but Patrick came to the door in a few moments. His blue tunic was not completely buttoned; he wore no cap.

"Well? What is it this time?"

"Patrick, come outside, please," she said in a low tone. "You will not want everyone to hear what I must tell you. I have come with very, very bad news."

"What? They haven't found—he's not—"

Hilda opened the screen door and took Patrick's arm, gently drawing him outside. Still speaking very softly, she said, "No, it is not that, but almost it is worse. I have talked with Mr. Lefkowicz, Patrick. He says that the police look very hard for your uncle because they know he is the murderer."

"What do you mean, *know*? They can't know that!"

"Hush! Patrick, someone saw the murder as it happened, and says that it was your uncle who struck the blows."

Patrick paled and sat down hard on a porch chair, and Hilda sat down beside him. He took a few hard breaths before he was able to ask, "Who? Who says such a thing? He's lyin', he must be, he—"

"Father Faherty."

For a moment Patrick was simply unable to take it in. What Hilda was saying made no sense. He stared at her, and the shock and bewilderment in his blue eyes brought tears to her own.

"I must go and talk to him, Patrick. Will you go with me?"

"Go with you?" He still looked dazed.

"To talk to Father Faherty," she said patiently. "When does your duty end?"

"My duty? Oh, when do I go off duty, you mean. Not till ten. We can't go and see a priest then."

She took a deep breath. "Then I go to see him now. I must know yoost what he saw, and when. There is somehow a mistake. I must learn what it is."

"You mean you don't believe—"

"Of course I do not believe your uncle killed Mr. Bishop. But I do not believe your priest lies, either, Patrick. I do not know what has happened, but I must know if I am to find your uncle." She took a deep breath again and looked him squarely in the eye. "And, Patrick, I am sorry that I became angry with you. We must not—that must not happen again. If I will try to keep my temper, will you also try?"

There was something in her voice that penetrated the cloud of his confusion and misery, and something in her face that made his heart beat raggedly, even now when he was nearly distracted with worry. He reached out his hand, and she took it.

"I'll try, me girl."

That was all. She loosed his hand and stood, and he, after a bemused moment, recovered his manners and stood, too. But in that brief, simple gesture a covenant had been sealed between them. Both knew it, though neither could have said exactly what it meant.

"I go now to see your priest, Patrick. He lives in the house next to St. Patrick's, yes?"

"Yes." He gazed at her.

"And, Patrick, I am embarrassed to ask, but where do you live? Because I must talk also to your family, and to others who know your uncle well."

"I'll take you 'round to me mother tomorrow, first thing. That's if you really have the time off?"

"Colonel George has said so. I will see you tomorrow, then, whenever you wish to come. Good-bye, Patrick, and try not to worry too much. The *Herre Gud* will look after us all."

As Hilda approached St. Patrick's church and the rectory, her heart was beating as raggedly as Patrick's had a few minutes before, but for a far different reason. From the time she was a child, Hilda had been taught to fear Catholics, and especially Catholic priests and nuns. She had never, truth to tell, come into contact with any of these fearsome papists until she had come to America and gone to work at Tippecanoe Place. There, her daily work next to an Irish cook and an Irish waitress had taught her that they were people just like other people, and at least as devout in their religion as she was in hers. Norah, indeed, had become her best friend, and it was through Norah that she had met Norah's cousin Patrick.

An experience at the University of Notre Dame a couple of summers before had taught Hilda a thing or two about priests and nuns, as well, and she was no longer quite so terrified of them as she had been. But never had she set foot in a Catholic church, except the basement storage space, and that had been stretching a point. And never had she deliberately called upon a priest. She wasn't even sure if they allowed women inside their houses. It took considerable courage to go up the steps of the tan brick house and ring the bell.

The housekeeper who came to the door settled the question about women in the house. Middle-aged, gray of hair, and stout of figure, she had no allure, but she was definitely a woman.

"I wish to see Father Faherty, please, if he is here," she said. Her voice was as firm as she could make it, though her knees shook a little.

The woman made no objection, but gestured her inside to a small parlor. "And who shall I say is callin'?"

"My name is Miss Johansson."

That did startle the housekeeper a little, but she said nothing except, "Sit down, then, and I'll tell him you're here."

Fortunately for her peace of mind, Hilda was not left to wait for more than a minute before an elderly man in a clerical collar appeared in the doorway. "Miss Johansson? I'm Father Faherty. You'll have come about the terrible Malloy matter, I'm thinking."

She stood and curtsied. "Yes, sir. How did you know?"

He made a weary gesture and pushed back his thick glasses. "Sit down, sit down." He did the same. "Clancy Malloy came to me this afternoon to talk to me about where his father might be, and told me that his mother had set you to work on the problem. It was then I had to tell him what I'd seen, and that I had decided it was my duty to tell the police." He pushed his glasses into place again and sighed. "I'm sorry, child, that you've been set such a task, for I must tell you plainly you've no hope of success. It might be better, in a way, if Dan Malloy were not found. I've no doubt he ran away in horror at what he'd done, and if he's found there's only one end to the story."

Hilda clasped her hands tightly together, the knuckles showing white. "Sir, I think there is somehow a mistake. I do not believe Mr. Malloy killed Mr. Bishop."

The old priest shook his head sadly. "Child, I know what I saw. I will never forget that terrible moment, though I wish that I could."

"Will you tell me what you saw, sir?"

"It's not a tale to tell to a girl."

That smarted. "Sir, I am a woman grown, and I wish to hear it. I know it will not be pleasant, but I *must* know if I am to help the family." A little of her stubbornness had returned, and with it a modicum of courage. "Sir, I do not know if your Bible is the same as mine, but in mine it says that the truth will make us free."

Father Faherty's glasses had slipped again. He looked at her sharply over the top of them. "Mine says the same, or near enough. Very well. I see you're determined to worm it out of me. Never say I didn't warn you.

"I went to the fair that afternoon to listen to Dan Malloy speak. He's a powerful speaker and likely to win the election—or he was." The priest sighed heavily. "I wanted to encourage him. Dear, dear, to think . . . anyway, I couldn't find him where I thought he'd be, near where he was to go into the arena, so I asked a couple of men I saw there."

"What men? Who were they, do you know?"

"No, I'd never met them. No idea who they were, but they said they'd seen Mr. Malloy just a moment or two before, and that they thought he'd gone to another part of the place. We were under the grandstand, you'll realize, under the actual seats."

Hilda nodded, intent on the narrative.

"The men were very helpful. They were in a hurry to be off somewhere, but they showed me where they'd last seen him, and pointed to where they thought he might have gone, just 'round a corner. When I turned the corner, I could see that there was a sort of room just a little ways away, with a door on the one side, the side nearest me. Of course the roof—under the seats, you'll understand"—Hilda nodded—"it sloped down pretty sharp, so the room wasn't very big, not much more than a good-size closet, but it was big enough to—" He shuddered and stopped.

Hilda's eyes never left his face. She leaned forward, her chin in her hands.

"The door was open, and inside I could see Dan Malloy bending over another man, beating him savagely with a club of some sort. I stopped. I think I cried out, but I felt faint and dizzy. Indeed, I think I nearly lost consciousness for a moment or two. When I came to my senses, I thought I should go for help, and looked around, but the two men who had been helpful had gone, and no one else seemed to be nearby.

"Well, it came down to just me, so I looked back. But Mr. Malloy was not there, and the other poor man was lying on the floor. I went to him, of course, to see if I could be of some help, but he—he was dead, poor chap. I could see then that he was Mr. Bishop."

The priest took a handkerchief from his pocket and mopped his brow.

"For a moment I couldn't think what to do. I've not seen much violence in my life, and I felt sick. If only I'd not been such a foolish coward—if I'd tried to stop it—but I was shocked straight out of my wits to think that Dan Malloy could do such a thing! I'd never have believed it if I hadn't seen it with my own eyes. And then there was a great deal of— That is to say, the scene was horrifying.

"I said my prayers, of course, and then I realized after a time—it seemed a long time, but it could have been no more than a minute or two, I suppose—that I must find someone, tell someone, do something. I didn't like to leave the poor man, but of course I could do him no good, so I went to find help. It took me quite a time; I bumbled about like a fool, hardly knowing where I was going.

"When I finally saw a policeman, I saw that he was running toward the grandstand, and others with him. It was apparent that others had found poor Mr. Bishop and I was not needed, so I went home to try to think what to do. That was foolish, too, I suppose. I should have stopped to talk to the police, but I didn't think about that then. I could only think of the terrible thing Mr. Malloy had done. I did not sleep at all last night."

He made the last statement very simply. Hilda could see that he was not asking for sympathy, merely reporting a fact. She pressed on.

"Sir, what did he wear? Mr. Malloy, I mean. I must know if I am to look for him."

"Child, I told you—" The look on Hilda's face stopped him. He sighed again. "He was wearing what he always wore for political speeches—the black-and-white-checked coat and the green porkpie hat."

"His trousers were black?"

"Dark. Probably black."

"And his shirt and tie?"

"My dear, I saw him for a few seconds. He was beating a man to death! How can you expect me to have noticed his shirt and tie?"

"And what does he look like?"

"You've seen him, surely!"

Hilda shook her head. "I have seen only cartoons in the newspaper. I am not allowed to attend political meetings."

The priest nodded. Very few men allowed their womenfolk to take any interest in politics. There was little point, since women could not vote, nor could they, the men were convinced, understand the issues. "Yes, of course. Well, Mr. Malloy is not a tall man. He— I'd say he looks much like anyone else." He spread his hands helplessly. "I'm not good at descriptions."

She held on to her patience. "What color is his hair?"

"His hair." Father Faherty squinted, as if seeing Dan Malloy before him. "Going to gray a bit, now, but it used to be red."

"And he is Irish; his eyes are blue."

"Goodness, child, I suppose so. I never noticed his eyes."

"He is not tall, you said. Is he fat or thin?"

"Not thin. He is a well-to-do man, and he enjoys his food and drink."

Fat, Hilda thought. Or portly, at the very least. She would have to ask the family for details.

She stood. "Thank you, sir. If I need to talk to you more, may I come again?"

The old priest struggled to his feet. "Child, my door is open to anyone who needs me. I will tell Mrs. O'Hanlon she is to admit you at any time. But I say again what I have said before. It would be better for Dan Malloy's family, better for him, better for the whole community if he were never found."

Hilda curtsied politely, but she had the last word. "It would not be better for the truth, sir."

He had not accepted her belief in Mr. Malloy's innocence, she thought as she sped to her next destination, but it did not matter. She had learned some things that she needed to know, and a vague idea was beginning to form in her mind. Before the afternoon was spent, she hoped, she would learn more.

She knew where the First National Bank was, though she had never been inside. Her family's bank had always been the wooden box under her brother Sven's bed. There Hilda and her siblings, week by week, had put everything they could manage to eke out of their small wages. It had meant going without luxuries, and sometimes, especially near the beginning, without necessities. And there had been times when they had had to use some of their carefully hoarded money, once when Studebaker's had laid men off for a week or two and Sven had had no work, and one terrible summer when Gudrun had nearly died of a fever.

Real banks like First National were rich people's bastions, large, intimidating marble temples where people with far more wealth than they needed hid it away from people like Hilda.

Her heart was pounding again. Taking long, deep breaths she willed it to slow down. There was no need for her to be afraid of a bank or of bankers. She rounded the corner of Washington Street onto Main Street and marched up to the door of the bank.

It was locked.

She tried it again, shook the knob. The heavy, solid door would not yield.

"Here, what're you doing?"

It was a helmeted patrolman, his billy club hanging casually from one hand.

"I wish to see Mr. Murphy," said Hilda haughtily. "Or Mr. Leahy. They work here. I have business with them."

"Huh! Likely story. It's four-thirty. Don't you know banks close at three, greenhorn?"

Greenhorn! The insult cast at all immigrants. Hilda's temper rose. "I am not a greenhorn! Nearly six years I am in this country. I work for the Studebakers!"

"So do half the furriners in this town."

"Not at the factory, at Mr. Clem's—"

"I don't care who you work for, you got no business at this bank. So just move on like a good little dumb Swede."

She had no choice. People were beginning to stare. She glared furiously at the patrolman, who smiled broadly, showing bad teeth.

She turned on her heel and strode away.

# 7

It would be an endless task to trace the variety of mean-
nesses, cares, and sorrows into which women are plunged
by the prevailing opinion that they were created to feel
rather than reason. . . .

—Mary Wollstonecraft, *A Vindication
of the Rights of Women*, 1792

NOW what was she to do?

The sun shone mercilessly. The temperature was at least
as high as yesterday's, the humidity, Hilda thought, even
higher. She could not walk the streets indefinitely, but she did
not want to go back to Tippecanoe Place. There was always the
chance that Mr. Williams might find jobs for her, or that Colonel George would decide her intervention in the matter was no
longer needed now that Dan Malloy's guilt was so clearly established.

No, she must find Mr. Malloy's home, talk to his family, and
then she must talk to Patrolman Lefkowicz and try to make him
believe what she had to say.

She could go back to St. Patrick's. Father Faherty would
know where the Malloys lived. But it was a long walk and her
feet in their tight boots were swollen and aching.

She dropped down on a stone bench in front of a gray stone
building. It was on the west side of the street, shady at this time
of day.

She leaned back for just a moment against the cool stone.

Cool, but rough, with points and sharp edges. The building was not old; the stone had not yet weathered. She sat upright once more. A lady should not slump in public, anyway. She looked at the door. Was this a bank, or a place where she might go in for a little while, out of the heat?

The archway over the door said "Public Library."

Of course! The library, donated to the city by the Olivers and the Studebakers and a few other wealthy families. She could not only go in, she could find there the information she needed. How stupid she had been not to notice where she was!

She stood briskly and walked up the steps to the door.

Within, it was shadowy and nearly as cool as she had hoped. The smell of books met her, the smell she loved from the small library at Tippecanoe Place. Books to her meant wealth. Someday, she vowed fiercely, she would own books, many books, and would have the time to read them.

For now, these books in this building were her own, to use as she needed. This was a place for people like her.

She approached the desk with some confidence. "Yes, miss?" said the librarian, with no hint of condescension.

"Please, I wish to see the city directory."

It took Hilda no more than a minute to locate the name. "Daniel Malloy, merchant," with two addresses listed, the department store on South Michigan and also his residence. He lived on West Colfax, which both startled Hilda and dismayed her. She had known the store was doing well, but she hadn't realized the Malloys were quite so rich. For the homes on West Colfax were fine, expensive homes, not mansions like Tippecanoe Place, of course, but homes of the wealthy, all the same. The street was named after Schuyler Colfax, vice president under Grant and one of South Bend's most famous citizens until his death in 1885. His son, Schuyler Colfax Jr., who had until a few days ago been mayor of South Bend, lived on West Colfax still.

She sighed. She would have to go back to Tippecanoe Place after all. She could not, or would not, go calling on West Colfax Street in her maid's uniform. With a wistful glance around the library at all the books, she went back out into the hot afternoon.

The servants' entrance to Tippecanoe Place was left unlocked from early morning until bedtime, for there was always someone in the kitchen area to keep an eye on things. Mrs. Sullivan, about now, would be beginning preparations for dinner. The Studebakers dined well and elaborately, even when they were not entertaining, so dinner was an affair that required concentration and effort on the part of all the servants concerned.

Hilda slipped inside the door very quietly. There was just a bare chance she could get to the back stairs unnoticed—

No such luck. Mrs. Sullivan was just coming out of the kitchen as Hilda began to tiptoe past. The cook stood, hands on ample hips, and looked Hilda up and down.

"So, Miss Hoity-Toity! Too good for the likes of us, are you?"

"No, Mrs. Sullivan. I did not ask for this job. I was told I must do it."

"Hmph! Gettin' too big for your britches, is what I say."

She would have said a great deal more, but Hilda, with a muttered excuse, managed to squeeze past her bulk and run up the stairs.

This was the way it would be, she could see clearly. The other servants would hate her for what they saw as undeserved privileges. The Irish family who had asked for her help would despise her because she was poor and was not of their kind.

She set her jaw. She would prove to everyone that she deserved the responsibility she had been given. Then . . . she shook her head impatiently. She would not worry now about what would happen then.

She bathed her sore feet in the tepid water in her basin, changed quickly into the clothes she had worn to the fair, corset and all, and set out, leaving again by the front door to avoid the servants.

The walk was no more than three short blocks, not long enough for Hilda, who needed to decide on an approach to the Malloy family. They would welcome her presence and her questions with much the same enthusiasm they had shown for her intervention at the fair. The questions had to be asked, however.

Should she present herself at the front door or the back? Was it better to appear humble, a servant begging an audience, or confident, an employee seeking information necessary to the job?

Humility, however sterling a virtue, was not a notable part of Hilda's makeup. She was dressed as a lady. She would call as a lady.

Taking a deep breath, she mounted the impressive front steps and gave the doorbell a firm twist.

It's a fine house, she thought as she waited, but of course nothing like as fine as Tippecanoe Place. *She* lived in the biggest, best, most expensive house in town. Never mind that she lived on the top floor. This was far smaller, no more than five bedrooms, she estimated, and no live-in servants, unless they lived over the garage. Brick, not stone, and of an older style, plainer than many of the Victorian-era houses on the street. She was speculating scornfully on the probable cost of the home—a great deal, but a pittance compared to Mr. Clem's incredible mansion—when the door opened.

A maid, not a butler. Good. In spite of herself, Hilda was intimidated by butlers. And this was little more than a child. Hilda had expected at least a housekeeper of the matronly dragon variety. The Malloy household must be in disarray if a chit of a girl was allowed to answer the door.

"Good afternoon," she said in her haughtiest manner and the best American accent she could manage. "I am Miss Johansson. I wish to see Mrs. Malloy or Mr. Clancy Malloy."

"I don't know, miss," said the maid in an accent Hilda couldn't quite place. "They're not seeing no—anybody."

Hilda's scorn grew. This girl was not properly trained and had no business answering the door to visitors. The phrase was "They are not at home." Everybody knew it meant the same thing, but it was an accepted social lie, intended to preserve the privacy of those who could afford privacy.

"Please tell them that I am here," said Hilda even more imperiously. "I am sure that they will see me."

And that was another lie.

"Yes, miss," said the maid, thoroughly cowed. "If you'd like to have a seat, miss?"

It was as well that Hilda's self-esteem had been bolstered by the maid's attitude, for she needed confidence to deal with Clancy Malloy, who appeared in a few minutes, bushy black eyebrows drawn together in a formidable frown.

"What do you want?" He towered over her.

She remained seated. If Clancy had any manners at all, he'd sit so she wouldn't have to look up at him. She was not about to stand in his presence. To do so would be to acknowledge his superior social position. Given his attitude toward her, she'd die before she'd render him any subservience.

"Mr. Malloy." Her tone was as icy as the one she'd used with the maid. "Your mother has asked for my help. I did not wish to concern myself in the matter of your father's disappearance, but I was asked to do so. I can do nothing without your—" Her English deserted her. What was the word she wanted? "Without your help," she finished lamely. It was not right, but it would have to do.

"Hmph," was Clancy's sole reply.

She gritted her teeth. He was determined to be rude, was he? Very well, she would ask her questions before he could decide to leave.

"I must know several things. First, what does your father look like?"

He barked a laugh at that. "I *told* Mother it was stupid to ask you for help! Imagine trying to find a man when you don't even know what he looks like!"

"That," said Hilda, trying hard to keep her temper in check, "is why I have asked."

He snorted, but pointed to a photograph on the wall of the vestibule. The ornate, gilded frame was the most impressive thing about the picture, which showed the head and shoulders of a fleshy man with a bulbous nose and a luxuriant gray mustache, a man who looked much as Clancy would look with added years and added pounds. His features were set in a solemn expression that, Hilda knew, meant little. Photographs always looked solemn; no one could hold a smile for the time it took the camera to record the image. The lines around Mr. Malloy's eyes, though, showed a man accustomed to fifty years or more of laughter. Unexpectedly, Hilda warmed to him.

"He looks very much like you," she commented. "I wish the picture were not of his face only. Is he a big man?"

Coming on the heels of her comment about Malloy's resemblance to his son, it was not the most tactful of questions. Clancy's scowl deepened.

"About as tall as I am. Maybe a little stouter."

"His eyes?"

"Blue. And what good it's going to do you to know that, I can't imagine. Is that all? My mother needs me."

"Mr. Malloy, I wish to talk to your mother."

"No. She's nearly prostrate. I won't allow it, and it'd do no good, anyway. Go home, girl, and leave matters you don't understand to your betters."

Hilda had kept her temper in check with the greatest difficulty. Now her control snapped. She stood and faced him.

"Mr. Malloy! I try—am trying—to help your family and you do not—do not cooperate!" *That* was the word! "I wish you to tell your mother that I do not believe your father killed Mr. Bishop, and that I have an idea where he might be. You will go and tell her that *now*, please, and she will talk to me, I think!"

She glared at him, her hands on her hips, her face flushed with anger. Malloy moved a step toward her, his fists clenched.

"Clancy? Clancy, what is it?"

At the sound of the gentle voice behind him, Malloy looked extremely put out. "Nothing, Mother. Don't disturb yourself. This person is just leaving." He put a hand to Hilda's shoulder to turn her toward the door, but she twisted out from under his grasp and darted to Mrs. Malloy, who stood in the parlor doorway. Hilda curtsied carefully, the deference of a younger woman to an older, not the bob of a servant to a mistress.

"How do you do, ma'am. I am Miss Johansson and I have come to report to you."

"Oh, Miss Johansson, have you news?"

She started to answer, but Clancy interrupted. "Nothing important, Mother. A few questions, that's all. She was about to go, and you should be resting. I'll deal with it."

Hilda could hear the suppressed fury in his voice. Apparently, his mother could, too.

"Clancy, my dear, how can I rest when your father is in such trouble? Miss Johansson, come in, please, and tell me quickly what you know."

She led the way into the parlor and gestured to an elaborately carved chair, its tufted upholstery a lovely rose damask. Hilda waited until the older woman had seated herself on the matching love seat before sitting down, and the interval gave her a moment for a sidelong look at Clancy, who was helping his mother. He was simmering with impotent rage, and Hilda was puzzled. She had expected a cold reception, even perhaps a rude one, but nothing like this. Surely he was displaying more than just simple pique over her intervention in his family's affairs.

When his mother was comfortably settled, he made one more try. "Mother, I really think you should let me deal with this. You'll only upset yourself."

She was a tiny woman, Mrs. Malloy, at least a head shorter than her son and weighing perhaps a third as much. She wore a black silk gown whose waist was far smaller than Hilda's, with a snowy lace fichu and a beribboned lace cap as fine as the frost on a windowpane. She looked as fragile as frost, too, as though a strong breath might make her fade and disappear. But she sat straight on the love seat, her spine not touching the furniture. The footstool she needed to keep her legs from dangling like a child's added somehow to her regal bearing. She gave Clancy a sharp look, and her voice, though still quiet, had steel in it.

"My dear, you must let me do as I think best. Leave us, please."

He smoldered for a moment and then left the room, muttering under his breath.

"I must apologize, Miss Johansson. My son means well, but

he always thinks he knows best, and he is upset. Perhaps he did not treat you very courteously?"

Hilda bit her lip and said nothing.

"Please try to forgive him. Now, tell me what you have learned. You have learned something, I can see from your face."

The tone of her voice had changed, subtly, to one of expectancy. Hilda hated to have so little to offer her. Still, there was something, maybe something important.

"I do not wish you to think that I know anything for certain yet. But I have talked with Father Faherty, and I think—I *think* only—that I understand why he said what he did."

Mrs. Malloy's face did not change. Hilda would have thought her cold and unresponsive had she not happened to notice the older woman's hands. They tightened, pulled for a moment at a handkerchief, and then relaxed. Hilda could see the act of will that had forced the hands to be still.

When Mrs. Malloy spoke she was in total command of herself again.

"Yes. Father Faherty. We are at a loss to explain what he has said. He's as fine a man and as fine a priest as I've ever known, and he'd never lie, not if the devil himself were offering a bribe."

She spoke with no accent, but the Irish lilt came out in moments of stress. Hilda could sympathize. She herself was at her most Swedish when she was aggravated or distraught.

"Mrs. Malloy, how long has Father Faherty worn spectacles?"

The older woman did respond to that. She looked startled and somewhat annoyed. "Heavens, child, I don't know! As long as I can remember, and we've known him for many years."

"Does he use them for reading?"

"What a very odd question! Now that I think of it, I don't believe he does. At least I know I've seen him reading his breviary, and he always looks over the top. When he looks at people, too."

"Yes, I noticed that, too. And I saw that his spectacles are very thick. I think that he must be badly nearsighted."

The annoyance was more pronounced now. "Miss Johansson, why are we talking about Father Faherty's eyesight?"

"His spectacles do not fit him very well. They slide down his nose and he must push them up. Mrs. Malloy, he does not, I think, see well things that are at a distance. He saw a man dressed in Mr. Malloy's clothes. I believe he would not have been able to see who it was. I do not think that he saw Mr. Malloy at all."

# 8

I had heard my father say that he never knew a piece of land [to] run away or break.
—John Adams, *Autobiography*, 1802–1807

HILDA watched Mrs. Malloy closely. Even a pleasant shock can be disturbing, and the woman was not young. If she swooned, Hilda would have to send for help, which was the last thing she wanted to do. Clancy would be delighted to have a good excuse for throwing Hilda out of the house, and a fainting mother would certainly provide him with one.

Mrs. Malloy had no intention of fainting. She blinked a few times, took a deep breath and released it. "What fools we've been. I knew it could not have been Mr. Malloy, and yet . . ."

"No, not fools," said Hilda warmly. "You have been troubled, and it is no wonder. This has been a terrible thing for you and your family. You have not been able to think properly. But now we can think and talk and I can learn where he might be; only before we do that, the first thing that I must do is to go to the police and tell them what I have guessed—what I have concluded."

"Let us do that, Miss Johansson. We have— They will listen more readily to us, I think."

"You have influence, *ja.*" Hilda nodded. "But the police,

they are eager to blame someone for the death of Mr. Bishop. I do not know if they will listen to you. They did not when Mr. Malloy was accused."

"That," said Mrs. Malloy with a grim face, "is because poor Clancy lost his temper and put their backs up. I will not send him this time. I will go myself, and I will go not to the police but to the mayor. A Fogarty will listen to a Malloy, and I will see that he makes the police superintendent listen to *him*. Mr. Malloy must be found, no matter what the politics of it may be. The superintendent was appointed by Mayor Colfax, of course, but he has a new administration to contend with now, and it's time he learned it. It was a blessed day for us all, the day Edward Fogarty was elected, even if his people do come from County Cork and ours from Kerry.

"But, my dear, you have raised more questions than you have answered. I believe you're right about what Father Faherty saw. It's the only explanation that makes any sense at all, but it doesn't make much. Why would someone dress up in my husband's clothes to kill a man? And what has become of Mr. Malloy?"

This was the part that Hilda didn't really want to talk about, but she must. She took as deep a breath as her corset allowed.

"I think he has been taken away. I think he has been made to appear the villain. I think that someone does not like him at all, someone who did not like Mr. Bishop, either, and who thought that this would be a clever way to be rid of them both."

"But *why*? A man does not kill because he dislikes someone! You have some knowledge of murderers, Miss Johansson. That is why I wished you to help us. You must know that only the strongest of passions will lead to murder. So far as I know, Mr. Bishop had no enemies, or none who hated him enough to—to do what was done. And I *know* that Mr. Malloy has no such enemies."

Nevertheless, Hilda thought darkly, Mr. Bishop was killed, and Mr. Malloy may be dead, too. She didn't speak the thought aloud. She would not argue with Mrs. Malloy, but she was sure that the rich and powerful always had enemies, though sometimes they were too naive to know it. Hilda, unlike many in her class, didn't hate the rich, but she had a low opinion of their shrewdness in anything but business. It seemed to her that the poor knew a great deal more than the rich about life in general. They lived closer to it, without the plush cushioning that wealth provided.

However, this woman before her was certainly not naive, and it was hard to imagine that her husband was, either. For the moment, Hilda would take Mrs. Malloy's statement at face value, mentally file it away, and approach the problem from a different angle.

"I do not know why these things have happened, but I think, if I am to find your husband, I must know more about him. And I still wish to look for him, madam. Me, I do not always trust the police. So tell me, please, what kind of man is he? What does he like to do? What are his interests?"

For the first time, Mrs. Malloy smiled. In part, Hilda thought, she appreciated Hilda's use of the present tense. They both feared that Mr. Malloy might be dead, and both knew of the other's fear. It loomed between them. But it was a fear never to be spoken, never to be acknowledged—unless or until it became impossible to deny. That silent understanding forged a bond between the two women.

Or perhaps Mrs. Malloy simply liked to talk about her husband.

"He is a brave and dedicated man. People who know only his public face don't always know that about him; they see only the clown.

"You need to understand his background. We were all farmers, of course, back in Ireland. His family and mine, I mean, though we didn't know each other then. Most of the Irish were farmers, tenant farmers working the land for the wealthy landowners. Mr. Malloy was born at the very end of the Famine, the first son of his parents. His family was very poor, even poorer than most, and the good Lord knows we none of us had money enough to call our souls our own."

Hilda nodded. She knew all about rural poverty, but even

her family, struggling for subsistence on poor, rocky soil, had not been as badly off as the Irish. They had always had food to eat—never enough, never in great variety, but they hadn't starved. The Irish had. The potato famine had wiped out families, devastated whole counties, created suffering on an almost unimaginable scale.

Mrs. Malloy went on. "My husband's father died when he, Daniel, was ten. The father was still a young man, but he was too tired, he'd starved too long trying to keep his children fed. There were six living children by then; three had died in the bad times. The bad times went on, you know, child, even after the potatoes started growing again. His mother decided to try to take the family to America, but she died, too, before she could work out how to raise the money. Those were terrible times, child."

She sat silent for a moment, remembering, and then shook her head. "Terrible times," she repeated. Too terrible to talk about, Hilda surmised.

"So Daniel Malloy, who was only eleven, went to work to try to keep the family together. An aunt and uncle looked after them, but they had no money to spare, not enough, really, to keep their own children fed, let alone a pack of nieces and nephews. It wasn't easy for grown men to find work in those days in Ireland, let alone a skinny child, but he managed somehow. He's never told me what he did. Some things are best not talked about."

Her hands tightened again. Again she relaxed them with an effort of will. Almost reluctantly, Hilda was beginning both to like and to admire this tiny woman with the ramrod spine and the indomitable strength.

"When he was sixteen he worked his way across to New York. The Civil War in America had been over for a year, and New York was booming. He could find work there easily enough, hard work, backbreaking work for little pay, but he sent money home, all the same, and one by one his brothers and sisters were able to join him. They worked, too, and brought over as many of the family as wanted to come, aunts and uncles and cousins.

"They'd moved west by that time, most of them. Mr. Malloy settled in South Bend in 1873. It wasn't the best of times; there was a panic and jobs were hard to find. But things got better and always he worked hard and had a good time doing it. He works hard and plays hard, my Daniel. He always has.

"My father had moved us here in the sixties and gone to work for the Studebaker brothers. Oh, it wasn't the grand factory that it is now, world famous and all, but they did a good business, all the same, and my father, Mr. O'Brien, did well, refining a new process for the paints and varnishes for the wagons."

Hilda blinked. O'Brien! She knew that name; it was famous in South Bend. If Mrs. Malloy was an O'Brien, it did much to explain the pride and dignity that were so evident in the woman.

"Mr. Malloy went to work in a shop when he came to town, a small dry-goods shop. I met him there one day when I went to buy a new dress for my mother. He sold me the goods—oh yes, he did! He was the handsomest man you've ever seen, with a laughing eye and a quick wit." She laughed a little. "We were married in less than a year. He had even more reason to work hard, then, and he became a partner before Sean was born and bought the shop when Mary was two. That was in seventy-nine. This house was a present for me in eighty-two, when Clancy was born."

She paused a moment and looked around her. "Yes, he's worked hard and done well for his family—all of them, not only me and our children. But I told you he was dedicated. He wants to do more, help all the workingmen and -women, and just hard work and money can't do that. For that we need to change the way things are run, change the laws. And it's politicians who make changes, them and big businessmen. Mr. Malloy reckons he can make things better by getting to Congress, and a small local election is the way to start. That's why he's running for the council, Miss Johansson. That's why he's working so hard and playing the fool to get elected. Oh, he enjoys the fuss and the hullabaloo, and he loves setting people on their ears. But it's more than that. He wants that job, and he means to get it by showing the ordinary man that he's just as ordinary as they are. And we must find him, so he can do that. I will not—I will *not*, Miss Johansson—allow anyone to deprive him of the reward he has so richly earned!"

And even, Hilda thought, if Mrs. Malloy is right and her husband has no enemies, I would be very surprised if she has none. A good many men might well hate and fear so strong and determined a woman.

"I will try to find him, Mrs. Malloy, but I must know where to look. I think that the men who did this will take him to some place where he might go anyway, so that when he is found the police will think he has run away. Is there a place, perhaps out in the country, where he likes to go? Does he fish? Or hunt?"

Mrs. Malloy considered. "There's a lake cottage up in Michigan, just a tiny place near Union Pier, where we used to go sometimes in the summer when the children were little. We haven't been there for years. I expect it's mighty run-down."

"Is there a train to get to it?"

"Gracious, no, we had to take the carriage, and a hard journey it was, too, with the roads so bad. Mr. Malloy talks about going back up and having the place seen to if we buy an automobile, but I don't know. His time is so taken up . . . that is, it was . . ." She bit her lip.

"Is there a closer place? One that he has used recently, that other people might know about?"

"I can't recollect any such place. Oh, there's some land out south of town that he bought about a month ago, thinking about having a farm when he retires from the store. I think he's wanted a farm of his own ever since he was a boy, slaving for half nothing on another man's land. He takes a drive out there now and again to look at it, and he's taken me once or twice. But that's not what you want. There's no house there."

Hilda considered. "Are there any farm buildings?"

"No, the land's never been cleared. It's all woods, but Mr. Malloy says there's rich soil there, good for corn and wheat."

It didn't sound at all promising. If Daniel Malloy had been taken to a piece of forested land, he had not been taken there alive. There would have been no place to hide him, no way to make sure he stayed there and didn't simply return to town. Nevertheless, Hilda pursued the idea, since it was the only one she had.

"Where is this place?"

"About five miles south of where Michigan Street ends. It's all woods," Mrs. Malloy said again. The two women looked at each other, and again the unspoken fear stood palpable between them.

"It is far to walk," said Hilda, half to herself, looking at her boots.

There was silence for a long moment, and then Mrs. Malloy stood and pulled the bell cord. When the maid appeared, Mrs. Malloy said, "Agnes, please ask Mr. Clancy to come here."

Hilda didn't care much for that, but there was nothing she could do but wait. She certainly didn't want to be asking anything important when he came into the room.

He was there in such a short time Hilda wondered if he had been listening outside the door. It was obvious that he was still in a temper. His mother gave him no chance to speak.

"Clancy, my dear, would you order the carriage, please? I would like you to go with Miss Johansson and show her the new farm your father's bought."

"But, Mother, I—"

"At once, please, dear. I will go with you for a little way; I have an errand."

The three rode together as far as Main Street, where Mrs. Malloy alighted at the mayor's office. Clancy tried to protest, but his mother silenced him with a look and walked up the steps. With a curt word to the coachman, Clancy sat back and scowled at Hilda.

"I don't know what you think you're doing, Miss Johansson, but I don't appreciate your butting into our family's troubles."

Hilda did not consider that the remark required a reply.

"I'd think you might have the decency to leave us to our grief. My mother is prostrate; can't you see that?"

"Your mother is not prostrate at all. She is in perfect control

of herself," Hilda snapped. "She is, I think, a very courageous
lady. And she has asked for my help, and I will give it to her
whether you like it or not."

"Hmph! Patrick said you've got the very devil of a temper. I
believe him."

"And he said that you are a bully. I, too, believe him."

After that Clancy sat and sulked.

The road, even after the Michigan Street pavement was left
behind, was in reasonably good condition. The weather had
been dry, so there was no mud, and the ruts weren't deep. There
was dust in plenty, though. Hilda soon wished she had worn her
uniform. Her good clothes would be a wreck by the end of the
day.

The horses were able to keep up a good pace. Not much
more than an hour had elapsed before the driver pulled the carriage to a stop and looked back at Clancy for further direction.

"Wait here." Clancy got out and strode off, not bothering to
offer Hilda assistance. With an apologetic grimace, the coachman handed her down. "You'll have to excuse him, miss," he
whispered. "He's right upset about his father."

Hilda was getting a little tired of being asked to excuse
Clancy.

He stood at the edge of the wood, his hands in his pockets,
looking out at, apparently, nothing in particular. At least there
seemed to be nothing to see. Hilda walked over beside him and
tried to peer through the trees.

The forest was dense. Beech and maple trees grew thick, let-
ting little light through to the floor of the wood. In mid-September, a few leaves were beginning to fall, but there had been
no frost yet, and the scene still looked almost like summer. The
smell that reached Hilda was the rich, moist smell of summer
earth and growth.

Hilda sniffed. Maybe the smell was just a little too rich and
moist.

"There is marshy land here, yes?"

"I don't know what business it is of yours, but yes. A big
patch of it, right in the middle. My father says—" He broke off.

"What does your father say, Mr. Malloy?" And when Clancy made no reply, "I can ask your mother, but if I do I will also tell her you refused to answer."

"Damned little snoop of a Swede! If you must know, my *father* says the land is rich. My *father* says it was worth spending a lot of money on, says it'll all be mine someday. A swamp! But of course my *father* is always right."

"A swamp can be drained, Mr. Malloy. And the land is then very rich." But her attention was not on her words. A swamp, she thought, can also be used to hide things. If there are bogs—quicksand . . .

"I wish to see the marshy land, please."

"Well, you can't. Look at you, dressed up like you're going to a party! There are snakes in there, my fine lady, and briars, and mosquitoes big enough to bite your head off. I've only been in once, and I wore denim overalls. Looked like a common laborer! If you want to go, go ahead. I'm not coming with you."

She glowered at him, not bothering to disguise her feelings. "Is there another way to the marsh? A road at the back of the land, maybe?"

"No roads. No buildings. Nothing except woods and swamp."

"How far back does your father's property go? And how far down the road?" She was no longer troubling to be polite.

"Thinking about buying it, are you? Got lots of money tucked away, hardworking little Swede that you are? It's small, but not small enough for you to buy. Forty acres, there are. We're at the north end, and that tree down there, the oak with the lightning scar—that's the south end." He pointed about a quarter of a mile down the road. "And it goes back about that far—it's roughly square. And there's not a damned thing in there that anybody could care about, least of all you."

There was also, Hilda thought with a sigh that she kept to herself, no sign that anything larger than a rabbit had pushed through the dense underbrush any time recently. She turned without another word to Clancy, got into the carriage with the coachman's help, and sat waiting to be taken back to town.

# 9

Families, I hate you!
—André Gide, *Fruits of the Earth*, 1897

WHEN the carriage pulled into the drive at Tippecanoe Place, the dusk had nearly turned to full dark, long past the sunset curfew for the Studebaker servants on their days out. Hilda reminded herself that she had not, technically, had a day out. She had been working, pursuing her investigations at the behest, or at least with the permission, of Colonel George—but she was still nervous about what the butler might say.

The coachman, John Bolton, said it first. He was strolling across from the mansion to the carriage house when the Malloy carriage pulled up under the porte cochere to let Hilda out. She jumped down quickly without a word to Clancy, who had likewise spoken not at all on the journey. The crickets and cicadas were keeping up their late-summer symphony, but sluggishly. The temperature was dropping rapidly now that the sun was down.

"About time you got home, Milady," was John's greeting. "You've missed your supper."

"I can get something from Mrs. Sullivan." Hilda was too

tired and too discouraged to spar with John. She had spent a most exhausting afternoon after a night with almost no sleep, and so far as she could see, she'd learned nothing at all about where Dan Malloy might be. She headed for the servants' entrance.

John laid a hand on her arm. "Who was that in the carriage?"

"Mr. Malloy."

"*Malloy!*"

Hilda shook her head wearily. "Mr. Clancy Malloy. His son."

John stepped back and chuckled wickedly. "Getting a bit above ourselves, are we? Consorting not just with the Irish now, but with the *rich* Irish!"

She was in no mood to be teased. "John Bolton, what I do is not your concern! I will go where I wish, with whatever company I wish, and you will not put your nose in my affairs!"

It was an outburst she was to regret bitterly before another day was over.

Her supper was a cold hodgepodge spiced with caustic remarks from the cook, who didn't appreciate preparing meals for people who didn't turn up to eat them, and told Hilda so at some length. After she had eaten and cleaned up after herself, she sought out Norah and found her in the butler's pantry washing the best crystal.

"That is my job."

"And do you think I don't know that? It's makin' more work for all of us, you know, you bein' out o' the house an' free as a bird all day long."

Hilda felt, at the moment, as free as a caged canary. She was fatigued to the point of exhaustion. She was worried and frustrated by her lack of progress, and afraid of new horrors that might await her if her search for Malloy brought her too close to his abductors—who were, presumably, murderers. But she owed Norah better treatment than she had been giving her lately, and besides, she needed her help. Silently she picked up a towel and began to dry the heavy cut-glass tumblers.

"So did you find out anything, all the gallivantin' you did?"

Norah's curiosity overcame her sense of injury.

Hilda sighed and dried another glass. "I learned only a little, and nothing to help. I learned that Father Faherty maybe did not see Mr. Malloy at all."

A glass slipped out of Norah's hand. Fortunately, the dishwater cushioned its fall. "What're you talkin' about? What did Father Faherty see?"

Wearily Hilda explained first about his statement and then about his glasses and her theory of what might have happened. "But it is an idea only, you see. Until I can find Mr. Malloy, I cannot prove anything." She went on to tell about her fruitless expedition to the Malloys' country property.

"What made you think he'd be out there?"

Hilda sighed again. "I do not know. It was a place to look, and I could think of no other place. He will be hidden, I think, in a place where he might go to hide if he were running away. It would be sensible to put him in such a place, so that when he is found the police will think he went there by himself."

"It'd be a whole lot more sensible just to kill him and have done with it," said Norah bluntly.

Hilda shook her head. "You are right, but I cannot think that. I must try to believe he is alive. Do you know any places where he might go?"

Norah picked up the glass again, rinsed it, and put it on the drain board. "I don't really know him. I see him at church sometimes. I know some people who know him, and I can ask them, but it'll be Sunday before I have the time."

There were no more comments about Hilda's freedom. Norah had begun to realize how heavy a burden her friend was carrying.

They finished their job in silence. It wasn't even nine o'clock when Hilda trudged up the steep, narrow back stairs, got out of her good clothes with less care than they deserved, and fell into bed.

She woke the next morning at five-thirty from force of habit. It would have been pleasant to lie abed and revel in the unaccustomed luxury of being able to stay there as long as she wanted, but her mind, once awake, wouldn't let itself drift back into repose. The duties and problems that lay ahead were too troubling.

At least the day would begin well. Patrick had promised to come and get her "first thing" and take her to meet his family. True, her welcome at the Cavanaugh house was uncertain, but she would be going there on business, not as a friend of Patrick's; that might help. And seeing Patrick again would be worth a little annoyance.

They were going to have to come to terms with their relationship one of these days. One day soon. But, perhaps—Hilda yawned mightily and sat up—perhaps not today. There was much to do today.

Her clothes had to be washed, for one thing. They were her only really nice summer wear, and she couldn't afford anything new. Until the rest of the family were here in America and safely settled, there was no money for fancy clothes, or for anything else one didn't really need.

Waiting until she had heard Norah start down the stairs, she got up and dressed in her black uniform—cap, apron, and all. Her relations with Norah had improved, and she saw no reason to strain them again. It would be prudent to wear her usual clothing and not to flaunt her relaxed schedule.

In fact, after she had washed her clothes and hung them to dry, she decided to do most of her usual early-morning chores. Patrick would hardly arrive before eight, and her nerves wouldn't let her sit idle. She did take a moment, when she found yesterday evening's papers in the library, to glance at the front pages. Mr. Bishop's death was reported in full, of course, with Mr. Malloy under grave suspicion, but the lead stories in both papers were about more violence in the Pennsylvania coal fields. The *Times*, predictably, took a different slant from the *Tribune*. Hilda didn't fully understand the rhetoric; she could see only the harm that had come to everyone, and would continue to come, especially to the little people—the workers, the immigrants.

After breakfast she took off her cap and apron, put on her

old black hat, and slipped out the back door to wait for Patrick.

He had been waiting for her in the carriage house, and the moment Hilda saw his face she knew something was badly wrong.

"So you still want to see my family?"

"Yes, Patrick, I must talk with them about Mr. Malloy. Why do you look—?"

"Come along, then," he said gruffly and strode off down the back drive.

"Patrick, wait! What is it? What is wrong?"

He kept walking.

"Patrick, talk to me! You promised you would try to keep your temper, and I will try to keep mine, but I must know why you are upset."

He stopped and turned. "I suppose you don't know!"

"No! I know nodding—nothing."

He looked at her closely and softened his tone by a fraction. "I suppose you weren't with Clancy Malloy all yesterday afternoon, and into the evenin'!"

"Yes," she said, perplexed. "Well, for most of the afternoon. We went to see his father's land, in the country. I thought Mr. Malloy might be—"

"That's not the way he tells it!"

For a moment Hilda didn't grasp his meaning, and then the light dawned. Her blue eyes turned the color of ice; she took a step backward.

"Patrick! Do you think I would—how can you believe—that is a terrible thing to—"

He held up a hand. "You were goin' to keep your temper, remember? You're sayin' you drove out to that farm or whatever it is, an' drove back, an' that's all there was to it?"

She glared at him. "You dare to think there was something else?"

"Look, all I knew was what Clancy's been sayin'. An' he's me own cousin. An' John Bolton, he says you were none too anxious to talk about what you'd been doin' when you got back last night. Late, he says, nearly dark."

Hilda clenched both fists so hard her nails cut into the palms of her hands. "And you believe them and not me?"

Patrick started walking again, but not as fast as before. "I hadn't heard your side of it. If you say there was nothin', then there was nothin', an' I'll flay the hide off Clancy."

But he wouldn't look at her.

Hilda stalked along behind him, warring within herself. Part of her wanted to defend herself, tell Patrick exactly what she had done yesterday afternoon, citing the Malloys' coachman as witness. Part of her wanted to turn around, go back to Tippecanoe Place, tell Colonel George she had abandoned the investigation, and resume her usual duties. Part of her wanted to let her temper explode in a glorious tirade against Patrick, Clancy, and all the Irish in this or any other country.

She did none of those things. She followed Patrick the few blocks down Taylor Street, past St. Patrick's Church, to a neat little white-frame house with a neat white-picket fence.

Patrick stopped and took a deep breath. "This is where I live. Me mother's home, and two of me brothers. They work at Birdsell's, and they're on short hours with the coal strike. Hilda, I—they've heard Clancy's story, too."

She looked him straight in the eye. Hers were still blue ice. "Do you believe me, or not?"

He swallowed. "I believe you."

"Then I will tell your mother and your brothers that what Clancy Malloy says is a lie. If you tell them the same, they will believe you. And then I can ask them what I need to ask."

Patrick had a feeling it wasn't going to be as simple as that.

# 10

Love, bumping his head blindly against all the obstacles of civilization.

—George Sand, *Indiana*, 1832

ILDA'S first meeting with Patrick's family was a disaster, a nightmare she was to remember for years to come.

Mrs. Cavanaugh met her at the door and ushered her, with icy courtesy, into the parlor. The two brothers, Kevin and Brian, rose at her entrance, but spoke no word.

They seated her in the best chair. And then the Cavanaughs sat in their overcrowded parlor, surrounded by stiff family portraits and holy pictures, and waited for Hilda to speak her piece. No matter what it was, they knew in advance that they were implacably opposed, and they didn't bother to hide it.

Patrick? Yesterday Hilda would have felt he was certainly on her side, that she could rely on him to smooth over the situation. Today, the way he was acting, she wasn't any too sure even about him.

She had prepared a careful speech. How happy she was to meet Patrick's family, but sorry that such a sad event had brought her here. How she hoped that they could help her find Mr. Malloy who, she was sure, had been unjustly accused.

She forgot every word of it. She forgot her intended rebuttal of Clancy's tale. She sat there in the scratchy plush chair, smiling until her face ached, trying to make her mind function. The clock on the mantel ticked.

Patrick, who was standing by the cold fireplace, acted at last. He cleared his throat. "Ye wanted to ask about Uncle Dan?" he prompted.

"Yes. Yes, please. I am sorry to bother you, Mrs. Cavanaugh, but as you know, I look—am looking for Mr. Malloy. I thought you might know some places I could look."

Put baldly like that, the question sounded idiotic. Mrs. Cavanaugh shook her head briefly. "I'd not be havin' any idea." Kevin and Brian glowered. The silence thickened.

Hilda tried again. "I think he must be hidden somewhere. I believe that the men who killed Mr. Bishop have taken him away. Does he have any enemies, do you know?"

"My brother is not a man to make enemies, Miss Johansson." Mrs. Cavanaugh smiled frostily.

Kevin and Brian continued to glower.

Hilda endured it for five more minutes and then stood, extending her hand to Mrs. Cavanaugh, who barely touched Hilda's fingertips. Kevin and Brian got to their feet. The glowers had changed to scowls.

"Thank you very much. I am happy I could meet you. Please excuse me; I must go now and see Mrs. Malloy."

"And her son will maybe be there, too?"

It was said very quietly as Mrs. Cavanaugh moved toward the door.

Hilda was shaking as she walked back to Tippecanoe Place, and she could not have said whether it was with anger or some more treacherous emotion.

Patrick didn't try to talk to her until they reached the basement stairs.

"Hilda, I'm sorry. I knew they'd not be greetin' you with open arms, but I didn't think—"

She put out a hand. "Patrick, stop. It is not your fault. Maybe it is not even their fault. It is the way the world is. I think"—she stopped and took a deep breath, trying to steady her voice—"I think I will not see you for a few days. I must try to find Mr. Malloy and not disturb myself about other things. I cannot—"

She stopped again. *I cannot bear it that your family hates me*, she wanted to say. *I cannot concentrate on anything else if I worry, now, about what is to become of us.* She said nothing; she stared at her boots.

Patrick scuffed his feet and licked his lips. "All right," he said at last. "Leave a message at the firehouse if you need me."

And he was gone.

Drearily, Hilda descended the steps and went into the house.

It was still early. The family had probably not yet finished their breakfast. Hilda managed to get to her room without being seen, and sank down upon her bed.

She wanted to throw herself on her pillow and cry and cry. She wanted to forget all her responsibilities. She wanted to turn back the calendar, make it be last week when none of these awful things had happened.

Crying would only give her a headache. Her responsibilities wouldn't go away. She would have to face them.

She washed her face in cold water and thought about her next step.

She would have to see Mr. Malloy's associates, and that meant starting with Mr. Murphy and Mr. Leahy at the bank. She glanced at the clock. It was just past eight-thirty. That excruciating ordeal at the Cavanaughs' had taken much less than half an hour. She wasn't sure when banks opened, but surely not before nine. That meant that she had time for one other errand first.

It was far too early to make a call, but she was past caring about social niceties. She was going to go and give Clancy Malloy a piece of her mind.

She left on her uniform and dreary hat. Today was not a regular laundry day, so Mrs. Czeszewski would not be here and the sad irons would not be heating. She didn't feel like taking the time to build up the laundry fires, heat the irons, and press her

good clothes. Anyway, plain black was good enough for a—a—
Her Lutheran upbringing would not allow her to find a word to
describe Clancy.

She would find plenty of words to say *to* him, however. She
sailed downstairs and out the door, all her pent-up emotions dis-
tilling into pure, glorious anger.

The anger was fanned a little hotter when the door at the
Malloys' house was answered by a butler. Evidently, yesterday's
untrained maid had been a temporary expedient. Hilda had despised Agnes, but she at least had not been supercilious. The
look now on the butler's face suggested that Hilda was some
species of verminous insect.

"Tradesmen and domestics, rear door." He started to close
the door.

She pushed it open again before the latch caught and glared
at him. "My name is Miss Johansson. I have business with Mr.
Clancy Malloy."

The expression now was intended to exterminate the insect.
"Mr. Clancy is not at home."

"I will wait."

"I cannot say when Mr. Clancy might be at home."

"I have time."

"He may be away for some days."

That improvisation was the last straw. "His father is missing
and he has left town? I do not think that is the truth. I wish to
speak to Mrs. Malloy."

"Mrs. Malloy is not at—"

"Then I sit here and I wait until someone will talk to me!"

Hilda pushed past the butler and plumped herself down on
one of the chairs in the hall. "You will please tell Mrs. Malloy
and Mr. Clancy that I am here. And do not tell me again that
they are not at home. I am a maid. Most of the time I am a
maid," she corrected herself. "I know what it means, 'not at
home.' It is too early for them to be out. If they have told you
they will not talk to me, go and tell them that I will not go away
until they do!"

"You are impertinent! I will do no such thing! You will leave at once, and I will see to it that Mr. Williams hears of this! You come barging in here without an invitation—"

"I did *not* come without an invitation! I been—have been—invited to find Mr. Malloy! I have been *invited* to try to learn what has happened! You know who I am, so you know that what I say is true, and you will not pretend—"

"Miss Johansson?"

Mrs. Malloy seemed to specialize in appearing out of nowhere, but this time there was nothing gentle about her voice or her manner.

"You were shouting, Miss Johansson. Is there some trouble?"

Hilda got herself under control with some difficulty, stood and curtsied. "Your butler will not allow me to talk to you, or to Mr. Clancy."

"And why do you wish to talk to us? Do you have news? I don't think you do, or you would have told Riggs."

"I told the butler—that is Mr. Riggs?"

Mrs. Malloy gave a frigid nod.

"I told Mr. Riggs I wished to see Mr. Clancy. There are . . ." Hilda paused. She would have to put this very carefully. "There are some things I wish to say to Mr. Clancy."

"I can't imagine anything you'd want to be saying to my son."

"Then maybe," Hilda replied, the raw edge of her temper beginning to show again under the garment of civility, "maybe you do not know the things he has said about me. Things that are not true!"

"Miss Johansson, are you calling my son a liar?"

There could be no backing down now. "Mrs. Malloy, I do not wish to offend you. I know only that Mr. Clancy has said things to my friend Mr. Cavanaugh—your nephew, Mrs. Malloy —that Mr. Cavanaugh did not like, and that I do not like, either. I am a servant, Mrs. Malloy, and I am an immigrant, but first I am a woman like you, and my reputation is as important to me as yours is to you. I wish to ask Mr. Clancy why he has said such things, for I think that he has said them to you, also, and I wish you to know that *they are not true!*"

Mrs. Malloy compressed her lips. "You may go, Riggs."

"Please, madam, I would like him to stay. He is a servant, too, like me." (Riggs looked mortally offended.) "Yes, he is more important than me, but he knows the people I know, and I want him to know the truth."

Riggs looked at Mrs. Malloy, who shrugged delicately.

The butler stayed.

"You asked Mr. Clancy to drive with me to Mr. Malloy's piece of land. We did that. We looked at it a little, not much because there was not much to see and I could not go in dressed as I was. It is very overgrown. And then we came back to town, and Mr. Clancy drove me to Tippecanoe Place. And that is all. Mr. Clancy became angry with me, I do not know why. I do not think he likes it that you have asked me to investigate Mr. Malloy's disappearance. But that is all that happened! If you do not believe me, you may ask the coachman. He will say that what I say is true, and that Mr. Clancy was not—I am sorry, madam—was not even polite to me."

"My son is upset about his father."

"I know that, madam, and I am sorry, but I try—am trying—to find Mr. Malloy and discover what has happened. I do not think Mr. Clancy should treat me like a—a busybody." It was a new word for her; she hoped she had used it correctly. "And please, I do not think he should say things about me that are not true."

Again Mrs. Malloy compressed her lips. She stood, Hilda guessed, less than five feet tall. Hilda had never encountered anyone with a more formidable manner, but for some reason she trusted the older woman's sense of justice.

There was a long silence. Finally Mrs. Malloy sighed. "Very well. I will speak to Clancy. And you, Miss Johansson. Have you any progress to report?"

"No, madam. I am sorry, madam. No one can think of a place where Mr. Malloy might be. But, madam, I believe I will find him."

"Why?" Some of the fire in Mrs. Malloy's eyes had died. "Miss Johansson, we can at least be truthful with one another. It has been two days now. It is very likely that my husband is—that he will never be found alive."

"No, Mrs. Malloy, I do not believe that!" Hilda spoke with all the passion of her nature. "Someone killed Mr. Bishop. We know that it was not Mr. Malloy. If he, too, is found—is not found alive, the police will know that someone else is the murderer. They have taken him away so that he will seem to be guilty."

"And if he is found—I must say it—if he is found dead, and as if by his own hand?"

This was a possibility that Hilda had not allowed herself to consider. She did so now, and her face was very sober as she replied.

"I hope that will not happen. But if it does, then, madam, I will never stop until I have found the men who would do such a thing."

Mrs. Malloy drew a long breath. "You're a fighter, child, I'll say that for you. Very well. You may continue with your search. Have you any money, by the way? I am not very well informed about these things, but I believe there is sometimes some expense involved in an investigation."

"I have money, madam. Colonel George gave me enough for a long time."

A brief, wintry smile crossed the older woman's face. "That was very kind of him, but Malloys pay their own bills." She reached into her chatelaine bag and handed Hilda a ten-dollar bill. "Here is enough, I'd think, to take care of both your expenses and a week of your time. If you have discovered nothing in that time . . ."

"I will, madam. But, madam, this is too much. I earn only four dollars a week, and my room and board."

"You are paid four dollars a week to dust and scrub. I am asking you to do something far more difficult and, perhaps, dangerous. The laborer is worthy of her hire, Miss Johansson. And I'm sure you can find something to do with the money."

"Oh, yes, madam! My family, they come soon from Sweden, and there will be much that they need. But, madam, I will pay you back if I fail."

"There is no need for that. I know you will do your best, and I'm sorry if I misjudged you. Now go, child. Clancy will be down for his breakfast soon, and I think the two of you had best not meet just now."

Hilda couldn't have agreed more.

# 11

'Tis known by the name of perseverence in a good cause—
and of obstinacy in a bad one.
— Laurence Sterne, *Tristram Shandy,* 1760

FEELING a little better, though not much, Hilda went on to
her next chore of the day. She was full of trepidation. She
had been thoroughly snubbed when she tried to go to the
bank the day before, and she was afraid today's reception would
be no better.

The twelve dollars in her pocket gave her a certain amount
of confidence, however. It was not wealth, not in bankers'
terms, and two dollars of it would have to be given back to Colonel George, but it was still more money than she had ever before had all at once.

It was kind of Mrs. Malloy to have thought of the money.
That was the difference between the Malloys and the present
generation of Studebakers, Colonel George and his siblings and
cousins. The Malloys still remembered what poverty was. Mrs.
Malloy had, in fact, behaved throughout this crisis with far
more consideration than Hilda had expected.

Clancy was another story, but so long as she treated Mrs.
Malloy with respect, she felt she didn't have to worry too much

about Clancy. He was a spoiled brat, that was the trouble. Mrs. Malloy had mentioned only three children, an unusually small number. Had there been others, perhaps, who had died in infancy, or even before they were born? If Clancy had come after a series of such tragedies, not uncommon even among the wealthy, no wonder his parents had coddled him. Hilda would have to remember to ask Patrick about the family history.

At the thought of Patrick, Hilda's eyes swam. She blinked furiously. She must not think about her troubles just now, and she must *not* weep in public!

The solid oak doors of the First National Bank stood open today, only the glass-paned inner doors serving as barrier to the outside world. Hilda took a deep breath and walked in with as much assurance as she could muster.

"Yes, miss?" The guard glanced at her clothes and assessed her as a person of no importance.

Hilda almost wished she was wearing her corset. One could not help having a regal bearing in a corset. Without it, she was showing a lamentable tendency to give way to her discouragement, to slump and cower.

"I wish to see Mr. Murphy or Mr. Leahy, please."

He tried not to show his surprise. "Yes, miss. Second floor, miss. The stairway's over there."

It was an imposing marble staircase. Hilda climbed it, willing her heart to stop thumping so hard. They were only men. They couldn't eat her. Mr. Leahy had said so, in those exact words.

The second floor of the bank consisted of a long hallway that stretched in both directions from the head of the stairs. Doors lined the hallway, doors whose etched-glass upper panels bore names. There was no human being in sight; the hall was very quiet.

Lightly as Hilda tried to step, her footsteps echoed on the bare wooden floor as she moved from door to door, trying to find one that said "Murphy" or "Leahy."

The door in front of her opened abruptly, nearly giving Hilda palpitations. Maybe it was a good thing she wasn't wearing her corset, after all. Regaining one's breath was easier without it.

"Help you?" said the young man who came out. There was a smudge of ink on his chin; he was in shirt sleeves. "Sorry," he added, referring either to his informal dress or his near collision with Hilda; she wasn't sure which.

She drew her first deep breath since she had entered the bank. "I look—I am looking—for Mr. Murphy or Mr. Leahy."

"Wrong direction—they're at the other end of the hall. You got an appointment?"

"No . . . but I think they will see me."

"Good luck!" The young man flashed a grin and hurried off, leaving Hilda feeling a little better for a friendly human encounter, however brief.

The two names were on adjoining doors, the last two at the end of the hall. Mr. Leahy's was first, and Hilda had liked him better.

Should she knock?

No well-trained maid knocks at doors, but this was not Tippecanoe Place. She hesitated, then drew herself up. She was not a maid begging for an audience from an important banker, not today. She was an investigator looking into a matter that had baffled the police. The idea pleased her. Firmly she opened the door and stepped inside.

A middle-aged woman sat at a desk just inside the door, working at what Hilda supposed was one of those typewriting machines. If she was pleased to see Hilda, she certainly didn't show it. She looked up from her work with a frown. "This is Mr. Leahy and Mr. Murphy's office, young woman. Have you lost your way?"

"No," said Hilda, her chin lifting. "My name is Miss Johansson and I am here to talk to Mr. Leahy, if he is in."

"You don't have an appointment." It was not a question.

"No, but if you will please tell him I am here, I think he will talk to me. Say that it is about Mr. Malloy."

The woman's attitude changed subtly. Her brows were still furrowed, but she stood and went to the other door in the room. After a moment behind it, she returned.

"You can go in." She was frowning still. Hilda wondered if she always looked that way.

Mr. Leahy, despite the heat of the day, was impeccably dressed in black suit, waistcoat, collar, and tie. His watch chain stretched across his ample torso. His silk topper hung on the hat rack in the corner. He looked every inch the important banker, and he made Hilda feel every inch the insignificant servant.

He stood when she entered, though. He was gentleman enough to do that.

"How may I help you, Miss Johnson?"

She didn't dare correct him, but came straight to the point. "Mr. Leahy, I am sorry to bother you, but I need your help. You are friends with Mr. Malloy, yes?"

He paused to consider. Street noises came through the open window: the snort of a horse, the clop of dozens of hooves, conversations between women shoppers. "We were business associates, but friendly ones. We met at church, of course, and socially at the affairs where everyone meets. You know the sort of thing." He paused, then, looking a little uncertain, but Hilda nodded. She did know the sort of thing. She had helped serve at enough "business" parties at Tippecanoe Place to know exactly how tedious they were.

She had also noticed Leahy's use of the past tense. "Sir, I believe that Mr. Malloy is alive."

Leahy looked at her pityingly and shook his head. "Hope is an admirable virtue, Miss Johnson, but in this case . . ."

"I believe he is alive," she insisted. "But I do not know where to look for him. I believe they may have taken him to a place where he might go by himself." She reiterated her theory.

Mr. Leahy was not impressed. "Hmm. An interesting idea, but not very likely, I'm afraid. However, you still haven't told me why you thought I might be of help."

Hilda no longer thought he would be. He didn't know Malloy well enough to know his favorite lairs, and anyway, his mind was closed. He had decided Malloy was dead. However, she launched into the rest of her speech on the chance that her judgment might be wrong.

Leahy shook his head. "I'd have no idea where he'd be. My word, I don't know where the man liked to spend his leisure time. You'd do better to talk to his family."

There was no point in telling him about her relations with Malloy's family. She stood.

"Thank you. I wonder if Mr. Murphy—"

"Murphy's out of town. Some business in Chicago. Won't be back till late tomorrow. I'm sorry I couldn't help you, Miss Johnson, but frankly, I think you're on a wild-goose chase. That is—"

"Thank you, sir. I know what it means, to chase the wild goose."

Leahy laughed. It did not, to Hilda, sound like a sympathetic laugh. "Yes, well . . . at any rate, I don't see how I can help, and I don't really see you helping anyone, either. Why the Malloys thought . . . however. Sorry, Miss Johnson."

"I am sorry, too, sir. And my name, sir, is Johansson."

Head held high, she nodded coldly and escaped from the office.

Once outside the bank, her footsteps slowed and she allowed herself to slump. She had learned nothing. She had no idea where to go now. She knew no other associates of Mr. Malloy. She knew of no other place to look. He could be anywhere, in any of the thousands of houses or public buildings, in a closet somewhere . . . in the river, she finally made herself admit. There was no point in an aimless search.

His store? The police would have looked there. They would have talked to his political associates. They had, of course, searched his home. They had probably even sent someone to the lake cottage, so inaccessible to Hilda but so easy to reach for anyone with the use of a horse and a conveyance of some kind.

They had, in short, undoubtedly looked in all the obvious places, the places he frequented—his home, his business—

She stopped dead in the middle of the sidewalk. She had reached a quiet section of Washington Street by that time or she would have impeded foot traffic considerably. They had looked for him at home, at the store. Had they thought of the other place he visited regularly?

What had Mr. Leahy said? "I see him at church . . ." Something like that.

Had they tried St. Patrick's?

There would be no place to hide in the church itself, of course. At least Hilda couldn't imagine that there would be. She had never set foot in a Catholic church, but her own church was a big, open space with no place to hide save under the pews or behind the altar. Fine for a child playing hide-and-seek perhaps, at least a child who wasn't afraid of desecrating a holy place, but hardly for a grown man.

She had heard of things called confessionals, wooden wardrobelike things. Maybe someone could hide in there, but it would be so obvious.

So would the rectory, and she couldn't imagine Father Faherty allowing such a thing anyway.

But the basement . . .

Hilda had been in the basement of St. Patrick's once. She'd been helping Norah with a rummage sale, and some of the more durable items for the sale had been stored temporarily in the basement. It was more of a cellar, really, and rather a peculiar shape. There was an area in the middle, perhaps ten by twenty feet, that was paved with stone. Here the ceiling was reasonably high; a person could stand upright. That was where the rummage-sale items had been stored. The walls on either side of the central area, however, were only chest high, and beyond those walls dark, gloomy spaces loomed. The cramped holes were only three or four feet high from dirt floor to low ceiling, but they stretched many feet back into darkness. They were used, as far as Hilda had been able to tell in that brief visit, for storage, though that was a polite word for it. Really they were the last stopping place for those things that no one could quite bring himself to throw away, but that would never again see the light of day.

For, perhaps, a man who might never again see the light of day?

Hilda shuddered despite the warmth of the day, and hurried toward St. Patrick's rectory.

# 12

I have a good eye, uncle; I can see a church by daylight.
—William Shakespeare, *Much Ado about Nothing,*
1598–99

"SURELY not! In his own church? *My* church?"
Father Faherty was scandalized. Hilda tried again.
"Please, sir, may we please yoost go and see? If he is not there, it will take only a little minute, and if he is . . ."

"Young woman, that door is kept locked. There is no possibility that Mr. Malloy is there. The very idea!"

It took another five minutes, agonizing minutes for Hilda, who was becoming more and more convinced that Mr. Malloy *was* there and might even now be dying. In the end Hilda's Swedish stubbornness won out over Father Faherty's Irish version. Grumbling, he got a key from his desk and led Hilda outside to the basement door of the church.

The key wasn't needed.

"Look, sir!" Hilda's voice rose in excitement.

"Jesus, Mary, and Joseph!" The padlock, looking very solid and secure, was nevertheless useless. It dangled from a hasp that had been wrenched away from the frame. The door, a little warped from damp, fit tightly and was still shut, but a pull on the handle opened it easily.

The stone stairs were steep and narrow. Father Faherty led the way, peering down into the gloom.

"I see no one," he said, but he didn't sound at all certain that no one was there. The broken lock had shaken him badly. Moreover, there was an unpleasant smell coming from the cellar.

"Have you a candle, sir? Or a lantern?"

"Yes, of course." They had reached the bottom of the stairs. "There's a lantern here, if I can only put my hand on it—ah, here it is." The priest scrabbled in his pockets for a box of matches. His hands trembled as he tried to light the lantern.

At last light shone out, but it couldn't penetrate the deep recesses on either side of the central room.

"I still don't—"

That was when they heard the moan.

Hilda had, in her twenty-one years, experienced a good many horrors. Nothing had ever terrified her quite like that low moan from out of the depths of that dim cellar. She screamed.

Father Faherty dropped the lantern.

Hilda picked it up before it could start a fire, lifted it high, and shone it now toward one pocket of darkness, now another. It took only a moment to find the source of the moaning.

The man lay in a pathetic little heap in the farthest corner. His clothes were crumpled and filthy. He made no further sound except that of labored, raspy breathing, made no move toward them. Hilda's nerves tightened another notch.

Father Faherty was actually wringing his hands. Hilda had heard of people doing that, but she had never seen it. "Oh dear! This is terrible! Do you suppose he is . . . ?"

"He is alive," snapped Hilda. "We must get help if he is to stay that way. I do not think I can get him out by myself."

"No, no!" The elderly priest pulled himself together. "I'll help you."

"You will get very dirty." Hilda eyed his black cassock and spotless white collar.

"My dear, so will you. And he is my parishioner."

Hilda smiled briefly. Father Faherty might be ineffectual in some ways, but he seemed to care about his flock. Accepting his assistance, she climbed up on a box and then scrambled up to the dirt floor of the storage area.

It was a slow, dirty, awkward business, even though they had only about ten feet to traverse. The low ceiling meant they had to crawl, and both were hampered by their long skirts. And when they reached Mr. Malloy, he was not able to help himself at all. Frightened that they might be hurting him, but unable in the close quarters to handle him any more gently, they managed to straighten him out and get hold of his arms and legs. They knocked over a pitcher of water in the process. It was nearly empty, but the little water it had held was enough to turn that patch of floor to mud.

Between the two of them they managed to drag him to the edge of the storage area, but there they had to give up.

"He's a heavy man and no mistake about it," said Father Faherty with a grunt, sitting back on his heels and wiping sweat out of his eyes with the back of a grimy hand. "I don't see how we can lift him down."

"We cannot," said Hilda flatly. She had ripped a sleeve and pulled out several inches of hem, but her chief concern was Mr. Malloy. Beyond a groan or two as they had manhandled him, he had made no response to their attentions. "We must get a doctor."

"Yes, at once. There is a telephone at the rectory. I will go, if you will be all right here?"

"Yes, but hurry, please."

Father Faherty jumped stiffly to the floor of the central part of the basement, fell, righted himself, and limped up the stairs as fast as he could.

Left to herself, Hilda sat on the floor, her legs hanging over the edge of the wall. Mr. Malloy was now breathing heavily, stertorously, and she was anxious about his condition, though there was little enough she could do. She wished there were still water in the jug; she might have moistened his face.

As the moments passed, however, and she saw no change in him, she had time to become somewhat anxious about herself. Her dress, her *uniform* dress, was probably ruined, stained as well as torn. Her braids had come unpinned and hung heavily down her back. She badly needed a bath, but it was only Friday; servants' baths were on Saturday night. She was glad she could not see herself, but she could imagine all too well how she must look. How was she to get back to Tippecanoe Place in this condition? And what would Mr. Williams say if he saw her?

She knew the answer to the last question, in substance if not in detail. She sighed. This assignment was proving even more troublesome than she had expected, and she hadn't expected anything good.

Father Faherty returned fairly quickly, bringing the doctor with him. They helped Hilda down and suggested she leave them while the doctor examined his patient.

"You might," said the priest, clearing his throat in some embarrassment, "see Mrs. O'Hanlon, my housekeeper. Perhaps she can help you—er . . ."

Hilda accepted with demure gratitude and slipped away.

She made the most of the facilities offered her, and half an hour later she looked and felt better. She had sponge-bathed in cold water, brushed her hair and tidied it, done a quick job of repairing her clothes, and brushed the worst of the dirt off them. There were hours of work still to be done before the uniform was presentable, and she still looked forward to a hot bath, but at least she could go back home without disgracing the entire household.

Meanwhile, Mr. Malloy, with the help of the doctor, had been transferred to a guest bedroom in the rectory. As soon as Mrs. O'Hanlon had dealt with Hilda's immediate needs, she bustled away to help the doctor with his patient. Hilda found Father Faherty having a restorative glass of sherry in his study.

Hilda knocked on the open door.

"Come in, my dear, come in!" He gestured to the decanter. "I don't suppose you . . . ?"

"No, thank you, sir, but I would like a glass of water, please, if you will show me the kitchen."

He put his hands on the arms of his chair and began the complicated process of rising. Unaccustomed exercise had aggravated the usual aches and pains of age. Hilda put out a hand.

"No, sir. You are tired and worried. I will go."

He settled back, smiled wearily, and pointed. "The last door at the end of the hall."

She returned with a pitcher of water and two glasses. "I thought you might like some too, sir."

They sat for a moment in silence. Both were tired, as much from shock as from exertion.

Hilda spoke first. "Is Mr. Malloy— What did the doctor say?"

The priest sighed. "He seems to be suffering only from the effects of two days and nights in that fearful hole. Some dehydration, of course, and he will probably be famished when he wakes."

"He has not yet awakened? But, sir—"

"He is under the influence of a drug, the doctor says. Probably only laudanum."

"Then that is why—I wondered why he had not escaped, when the door was open and he had only to leave. But he was drugged."

"My dear child." The priest let his glasses slip down his nose and looked at her with compassion in his old eyes. "The poor man was hiding there until he could think of a way to escape for good."

"Then why did he take laudanum?"

"To dull his mind, to ward off the terrible knowledge of what he had done, to ease his rheumatism—how should I know? I know only that we must tell the police he is here."

"No, sir, please!" The mayor might have believed Mrs. Malloy's story and called off the police, or he might not. Whatever the case, Hilda did not want Mr. Malloy in the hands of the police.

"Father Faherty, please listen to me." She was uncomfortable with the title, but she would use a Popish name for a preacher if it would make him pay attention to her.

"Father, I believe that you were mistaken in what you saw at the fair. Let me tell you why, and what I think happened."

She went carefully through her theory, the assault on Mr. Bishop, the idea of casting the blame on Mr. Malloy. "And if you, sir, do not see very well . . ." She let the sentence trail off discreetly.

"Hmm. It's true enough that my eyes aren't much good except for reading and the like, and I'd misplaced my spectacles that day. But his clothes, child. When the doctor and I got him out of them just now, they weren't only dirty, but—it's sorry I am to say it—but bloodstained, as well."

"They would be, would they not? No matter who was wearing them to kill Mr. Bishop."

"I suppose they would. Have you told the police all this? What do they think of your theory?"

"Mrs. Malloy went to the mayor and told him. I do not know what the police think. But, sir, would it not be better to tell Mrs. Malloy now that he has been found, but wait a little before telling the police? When he is better, we can hear what he has to tell us. If you are there, sir, he will tell the truth." She paused artfully.

The old priest sat in silence for several long moments. Finally, he looked up at Hilda, his faded eyes troubled. "Very well, I will do nothing for now, child, and I will ask the doctor to be discreet as well. As for Mrs. O'Hanlon, she never talks about anything she sees or hears here; that's as it must be, in a priest's home. You may tell Mrs. Malloy, and let her decide what to do. But I'll do nothing that is against the law, you must understand that. I have duties to Caesar as well as to God."

"Oh, sir, thank you! I go now, this minute. She is so worried, I cannot wait to give her the news." Hilda curtsied deeply before she turned to leave. This old man might not be a parson of her persuasion, but he was a good man.

She encountered less antagonism from Riggs, the Malloys' butler, than she had earlier in the day. He would never approve of her, but he had evidently received orders that she was to be admitted and treated with courtesy. Hilda was very conscious, as she sat waiting in the hall, of her disheveled appearance.

"Why, Miss Johansson, what *have* you been doing?"

She was by now used to Mrs. Malloy's noiseless entrances. She stood and curtsied.

"I find—I have been finding—your husband, Mrs. Malloy, alive and nearly well."

The next moment she was very glad that Clancy was not in the room, for the good news undid Mrs. Malloy as no bad news had been able to do. She very nearly collapsed in Hilda's arms.

"I was so afraid, so afraid," she kept repeating as Hilda gently lowered her to a chair.

"Yes. I, too, was afraid."

Hilda offered no further word of sympathy lest Mrs. Malloy break down altogether. She would not want Hilda to see her in tears, and Hilda herself didn't want to see this strong, proud woman lose her self-control.

Mrs. Malloy sat in absolute silence for a few seconds, her eyes closed, not even visibly breathing. Then she sat up straight and smoothed her skirt. "Forgive me, Miss Johansson. I have not thanked you."

Hilda nodded acknowledgment.

"Where is Mr. Malloy? I must go to see him at once."

"He is at the rectory of St. Patrick's. He was in the church cellar."

Mrs. Malloy stood and rang the bell.

"Mrs. Malloy . . . before you go . . ."

"What?" She was all anxiety in an instant. "What have you not told me?"

"Only that he is not awake." Hilda used her most soothing voice. "They—his captors—have given him a drug. When it loses its effect, he will wake."

"Will he be all right?"

"I have not talked with the doctor. Father Faherty says he will be fine. But, Mrs. Malloy, you must decide what you want to do. Please—"

Riggs appeared. "Yes, madam?"

Hilda gave Mrs. Malloy a look of mute appeal.

"Would you bring us some coffee, please, Riggs? We will be in the front parlor."

When he had left, Mrs. Malloy stood, led Hilda into the room, and shut the door. "Yes?"

Hilda took a deep breath. She had only a few minutes before Riggs came back with the coffee. And where was Clancy? Might he burst in on them?

"Madam, I have asked Father Faherty to say nothing to the police, and he has agreed, for now. Until Mr. Malloy can tell us what happened. But do you not think, if you go to see him now, many people will see your carriage arrive at the rectory, and they will wonder, and . . . would it not, perhaps, be better for you to wait until it is dark? He cannot talk to you now, anyway. If you wait, you can, if you are careful, bring him back here, and no one will know."

Mrs. Malloy closed her eyes again, and when she opened them and spoke, her voice was taut. "You don't know what you're asking, child. Perhaps I can make you understand. If Mr. Cavanaugh were hurt, if he had been missing and perhaps dead, could you stay away when he was found?"

It took Hilda's breath away. If Patrick . . . and oh, *Herre Gud*, Mrs. Malloy knew! She had tried so hard to hide her feelings, from Patrick, even from herself, but this woman . . . she tried to steady herself and concentrate on the issue at hand.

"It is true . . ." Her voice came out in a whisper. She cleared her throat and tried again. "It is true that if someone I—I cared about were in danger, I—would find it hard to stay away. But if I would maybe put him in more danger, I could maybe—I do not know. I do not know if I am strong enough."

She was not consciously manipulating Mrs. Malloy. But she had chosen the word, perhaps the only word, that might influence her.

"You believe that strength is called for?" Mrs. Malloy pursed her lips and then nodded, with a heavy sigh. "I suppose you're right. You give your word that he is not able to speak to me now?"

"My word, madam."

"Very well. Ah, here is our coffee. Thank you, Riggs." There was no quiver in her voice.

The butler set the tray down. "Will there be anything else, madam?"

"Yes, send Agnes to me, if you please."

When he had left the room, Mrs. Malloy turned back to Hilda. "You have, I think, had rather a difficult morning, Miss Johansson. Your clothing—"

"Yes, I am sorry, Mrs. Malloy. It is dirty, the church cellar, and I have had little time—"

"I understand, but I thought perhaps you might enjoy the chance to refresh yourself without a great many explanations to your butler. I believe Agnes has a spare uniform that will fit you well enough, until yours can be washed and mended. My laundress will look after that for you. And perhaps a bath . . ." She said no more, but her nose wrinkled slightly.

Hilda colored. "Thank you, madam, but I could not—"

"Ah, Agnes. Miss Johansson had an unfortunate accident this morning. Would you draw a bath for her, please? And find her something to wear, there's a good girl."

The maid looked askance at Hilda. "I've two fresh uniforms, madam. I can let her have one. But I've only one clean set of undergarments."

"Very well, she may use some of mine, though the petticoat will be very short for her."

The maid curtsied and left.

"My dear girl, I owe you my husband's life. A bath and a petticoat are a small price to pay."

# 13

The unexpected always happens.

—Anonymous

C LEAN and decent once more, Hilda returned to the rectory to keep vigil. Mrs. Malloy had extracted a promise that a message would be sent the moment Mr. Malloy was awake.

It was a long wait. Mr. Malloy, the doctor had said, had apparently taken a great deal of laudanum. *Someone gave it to him,* Hilda had wanted to say, but she had kept quiet. There was no telling when he would wake up, but when he did, he should be kept awake, if possible, and given broth if he would take it. No solid food at first; it would make him sick after two days without eating. "If he didn't eat," the doctor had added.

Hilda didn't think he had eaten. She thought he had been meant to die there in that dirty corner of the cellar. But in that case, why had he been given water?

She gave it up. Time enough to think about why. Right now she just wanted Mr. Malloy to talk, to tell them *what* had happened.

Hilda had forgotten about her own lunch, but Mrs. O'Hanlon sent up some food and Hilda ate it, only realizing how hungry she was when the food was before her.

The day passed. Several times Hilda was sure Mr. Malloy was waking. His eyes opened, he made noises, but she could make no sense of what he said, if in fact he was trying to talk. She tried to give him water, but he closed his eyes again before he could drink.

Evening fell. Hilda lit the candle by the bed. Father Faherty came up to see how his awkward guest was getting along and to bring Hilda some more sandwiches. She ate them and drank the coffee that was offered along with them, though to a Swede it tasted like dishwater.

She was about to give up and go home when Mr. Malloy's eyes opened and stayed that way. He looked at Hilda without interest, but she was at his bedside in an instant. "Mr. Malloy! Mr. Malloy, are you awake?"

He croaked something, cleared his throat, tried again. "Who?" he said weakly.

"My name is Johansson. I am a maid. That does not matter. How do you feel? Do you want the doctor to come back?"

"Doctor?" He closed his eyes again, raised a hand to cover them, and moaned.

"Mr. Malloy, please do not go back to sleep!"

He moaned again. "Light . . . hurts . . ."

She moved the candle to the mantel and returned. "Mr. Malloy, talk to me, please! Would you like some broth?"

He tried to shake his head and moaned again. "Water."

She gave him a few sips, but the effort of drinking exhausted him and he sank back, closing his eyes again.

"You must not go back to sleep, sir. The doctor said so."

"What's doctor know?" It was slurred, but at least it was a complete sentence, and pronounced with a tiny amount of energy. "Sleep. Feel wretched. What's matter?"

"You have been drugged, sir. No, *please* do not close your eyes!"

He lifted a hand in what looked like irritation, but he opened his eyes and moved them—left, right, up, down. "Where?"

"You are at the rectory. St. Patrick's rectory. Here, take some more water."

She piled some pillows behind his head and shoulders. This time he drank more easily.

"Why?"

"Why are you here?"

He nodded and winced.

Hilda, uncertain of what to tell him, finally hit on an evasive answer that wasn't an outright lie. "You fell ill, in the church. Father Faherty brought you here so you could be looked after."

He frowned. "Want to go home. Want my wife."

Hilda had hoped that she could ask him some questions before Mrs. Malloy arrived on the scene, but the man was plainly too ill to make a great deal of sense. She sighed and got up to open the door. "Mrs. O'Hanlon!" she called. There were no bells in the rectory; this was not like a wealthy household with servants. When the housekeeper came to the foot of the stairs, Hilda said, "Mr. Malloy is awake. Please tell Father Faherty, and do you have some broth ready?"

"I do," said the housekeeper, and bustled off to get it.

When Hilda turned back to the bed, Mr. Malloy had closed his eyes again.

As soon as Father Faherty and Mrs. O'Hanlon had taken charge, Hilda slipped away to bring Mrs. Malloy to the rectory. Ramrod straight as always, the older woman nevertheless trembled getting into her carriage, trembled as she entered her husband's bedroom, leaning on Hilda's arm. Hilda gave the priest and the housekeeper a meaningful look and the three of them slipped out of the room to give husband and wife an interval of privacy.

When Hilda and Father Faherty reentered some minutes later, Mr. Malloy seemed to be feeling a good deal better. He had drunk his broth, though reluctantly, Mrs. Malloy said. At any rate, it was apparent that he was well enough to be angry. He was sitting up in bed, his gray hair and mustache in wild disarray and a scowl on his face.

"All right, young woman," he growled. "I understand from my wife that you were the one who found me. In the church cellar, of all places."

"Yes, sir." Hilda felt a little timid. This commanding man seemed a far different person from the pathetic one she had rescued.

"And how did you know where I was, eh?"

"I used my head, sir."

"Hmph! Fairly good head, I'd say. Better than mine at the moment." He massaged his temples. "Mrs. Malloy, would you be good enough to move that da—that miserable candle? It gets in me eyes, and I've got the father and mother of all headaches."

His wife moved the candle to the farthest corner of the room. Flickering shadows fell across the bed. Mrs. Malloy dampened the towel on the washstand in the cool water and folded it across her husband's brow. He grasped her hand for a moment and then scowled at Hilda.

"I suppose, young woman, you'd like to know how I got there, would you?"

"Yes, sir."

"And so would I! The last I remember, I was in some damn-fool wagon or whatnot, with a blanket over my head!"

"This was at the fair, sir?"

"Yes, a few hours ago."

Hilda and Mrs. Malloy looked at each other. "It was two days ago, Mr. Malloy," his wife said softly, taking his hand again. "You were missing for two days."

"You're not telling me, Mrs. Malloy!"

"Indeed, my dear." No tremor in her voice, even now, but she held her husband's hand as if she would never let go.

"Maybe if you would tell us from the beginning," suggested Hilda.

"And where's the beginning? Suppose you tell me that, young woman!"

"I think—I think it must have something to do with Mr. Bishop, sir."

"Well, you'll have to ask Bishop about that. I don't know what was going on, only that it was nothing good."

He pushed himself up a little farther in the bed. Hilda arranged his pillows more comfortably and gave him a glass of water. She got a grunt of thanks.

"The beginning, eh? Well, it was at the fair, as you say. We were waiting around to make our speeches, or I was. I'd been talking to Bishop, earlier, but I hadn't seen him for a few minutes. It was getting fairly close to the time for us to begin, so I was looking for him, and then I heard his voice.

"He was in his carriage, just outside the grandstand—or *a* carriage, don't know if it was his. And there were some men with him. Don't know who they were, but they were going at it."

"Fighting?" asked Hilda.

"Arguing, but something fierce. I thought it sounded serious, so I went to Clancy. Wanted his help if I was going to interfere. He thought it'd be a good idea to get Patrick, for reinforcement, so he went off. And the next thing I know, I'm wrapped up in a blanket with a head like a three-day wake and jouncing around in some kind of buggy or whatnot.

"They drove me for hours, seems like. It was hot as Tophet under that blanket, I can tell you. They'd tied me up, too, and stuffed some kind of rag in me mouth, and me clothes were stiff and itchy and me head ached like nobody's business. And that's the last I know, until I woke up here. And you say I was in the cellar? Why did it take so long for them to get me there?"

It was exactly what Hilda had thought! She felt a small moment of triumph. "They maybe drove you around for a long time to confuse you, sir, and so that it would be night, and dark, when they brought you here. Then they gave you laudanum to make you sleep and stay there. I think, I do not know, but I think, that they gave you a jug of water to drink, and put laudanum in it, too, so that you would stay asleep for a long time."

"And who were these villains?" he growled.

Hilda's heart sank. "Do you not know, sir?"

"How would I know? Never saw 'em. Never heard 'em say a word."

She thought furiously. "Could they be the same men you heard talking to Mr. Bishop?"

"Don't know, I tell you."

"What did they say, these men you heard talking and arguing?"

"Couldn't hear many words, just the tone of voice. They

were hoppin' mad, all of 'em, but they were keeping their voices low. Ask Bishop!"

"Did you hear nothing, sir?" Hilda insisted.

Mr. Malloy frowned. "Seems like I heard the word 'explosion,' or 'blowup.' Yes, 'mine explosion,' that was it. But why on earth don't you talk to the man who was there?"

There was a strained silence. Mrs. Malloy looked at Hilda. Hilda looked at Father Faherty.

"Well, speak up, can't you? Something's wrong. What?"

Father Faherty accepted the responsibility. "We can't ask Mr. Bishop, I'm afraid. Mr. Bishop was murdered two days ago."

They had to send for the doctor. Mr. Malloy had turned pale and started to cough, and Mrs. Malloy feared for his health. The doctor, when he came, rounded on them thoroughly for giving a man in his state such a shock, and said that, though he hadn't had a heart attack, he'd best be taken home. "Where," he added, "there'll be nobody to pester him!" He'd given Hilda a pointed look, which she had ignored as she prepared to go home herself.

*Mine explosion!* What on earth, Hilda wondered as she plodded at last toward Tippecanoe Place, did that mean? She wondered also about her reception at the mansion. She was out far later than she had ever been before—at least while on legitimate business. She only hoped she could get in. She had thought for a moment about telephoning to Mr. Williams—but only for a moment. He would be asleep. He would also be so scandalized at the idea of her using the telephone—a *servant*, the *telephone*—that she would be lucky not to be discharged. No, if the back door was locked, she could try to wake Norah, or perhaps sleep on the porch, or if all else failed, a window would be open somewhere, in this heat. She had climbed in windows before.

She was very tired. It had been a long day. Maybe that was why she was less alert than usual. For whatever reason, she didn't hear the footsteps until they were close behind her.

She whirled and gasped just as something soft and heavy and smothering descended over her head.

# 14

... all good to me is lost ...
—John Milton, *Paradise Lost,* 1667

NORAH was restless. It was hot. She had already thrown off the sheet that was her sole bedcovering and wished rebelliously that she could take off her long, voluminous nightdress.

At last she got up and washed her face. The water in the pitcher was almost body temperature, but it cooled her for a little while.

The clock on her bedside table had hands and numbers that glowed in the dark. They were faded now, but Norah picked up the clock and held it close to her face. Three o'clock and past. Far too early to get up, but too late to get in much sleep before the alarm rang, unless she got back to sleep at once.

She lay back, but sleep did not come. Troubled thoughts drifted across her mind.

What had become of Dan Malloy? She had had no chance to talk to Hilda all day, indeed had not seen her since early morning, and then only in passing.

Had she made any progress? Had she given up and admitted that Mr. Malloy was dead, as everyone feared?

Norah sighed. No, Hilda probably hadn't given up. Stubborn Swede! She reminded Norah of Mr. Williams's bulldog, Rex. He was a fat, lazy, amiable dog most of the time, but when he sank his teeth into a squirrel or a rat he would never let go until the animal was dead. Hilda treated an unsolved puzzle in the very same way.

Besides, Hilda was enjoying herself. Norah punched her pillow viciously. It was all very well for *her*, being able to come and go as she pleased and leave her work for other people to do. Mr. Williams had called in a daily to take her place, but it wasn't the same. The woman didn't know the routine, didn't know where anything was, kept asking stupid questions of anyone who was handy. Norah, after a couple of hours of playing nursemaid to the little idiot, had taken care to keep well out of her way.

She sat up again. Would Hilda be awake, too? She hated the heat even worse than Norah did.

She rapped on the wall and listened. No knock came in response. She hadn't heard Hilda come in; perhaps she had been very late and was tired enough to sleep even in discomfort.

Or perhaps she was locked out! Mr. Williams wouldn't have cared whether she was in at dusk or not. He would have locked the doors at the usual time and made her ring the bell, so he could scold her. And she might have preferred sleep on the porch to a dressing-down by a wakened, irascible butler.

There was one way to find out. Scorning her robe, Norah eased her door open, slipped into the hall, and raised a hand to knock on Hilda's door.

The door was open. The bed was empty. By the light that filtered in from the street lamp on the distant corner of the property, Norah could see that the bed was smoothly made and the room in perfect order.

The silly girl! Sleeping out someplace, where anything could happen to her! Well, by the time Norah got done scolding her, Hilda would have done better to brave Mr. Williams's wrath instead.

Barefoot and in her nightdress, Norah stole down the back stairs.

Fifteen minutes later her anger had turned to fear. Hilda wasn't asleep on the porch. That was the first place Norah had looked. Then she had slipped the latch and gone outside, heedless of her state of undress. Not on the bench by the carriage house. Not under the porte cochere. Not propped up against any of the trees, or against any of the doors, or on any of the stairs.

Not on the basement stairs, even, or against the basement door, which—Norah tried it and felt a thrill of fear—was on the latch. Mr. Williams, for once, had trusted Hilda and left the Yale lock unsprung, a thing he had never done before.

Hilda was nowhere on the property.

Trembling, Norah reentered just as the big kitchen clock struck three-thirty.

Three-thirty and Hilda not home!

Norah locked the basement door. At least when Mr. Williams woke, he wouldn't have that to blame on Hilda. Then she went into the dark, deserted servants' room and plumped down on one of the chairs, trying to calm herself. There was no need to get all upset. Hilda was a smart girl who could take care of herself.

But she was chasing a murderer.

No, she was trying to find Mr. Malloy. That was what the family had asked her to do.

And do you think she'll stop at that, the stubborn fool? Not she, who always thinks she knows better than anyone else. She'll go chasin' anybody she thinks might've done for Mr. Bishop, and never give a moment's thought to her own safety.

She might be at the Malloys' house.

A Swede, bein' asked to stay in an Irishman's house?

The Malloys are nice people, except for that pill of a Clancy. She might be there.

Norah sighed and stretched. Undoubtedly, she said to herself firmly, Hilda was at the Malloys', and that other doubting voice in her head could quiet itself. She, Norah, was not going to waste another minute of worry on the heedless girl. She might have let a person know, and not let them worry themself sick in the middle of the night. A thoughtful person would have sent a note.

She trudged up the stairs, righteous indignation shouting loudly enough to still that other small voice.

Her last thought before sleep finally claimed her was, But what if she isn't there?

The household was badly disordered the next morning. The near-useless daily from yesterday didn't show up, and the one Mr. Williams hired after a frantic early-morning telephone call to the agency wasn't much use either. Work schedules were re-arranged, and in all the confusion, Norah was able to spend a good deal of time close to windows and doors, watching for Hilda's return. Instead, a few minutes past eight, she saw Pat-rick. She had gone to the clothesline to hang up the dish towels and was returning to the house when she saw him coming up the back drive.

"Mornin', Norah."

"Good mornin' to you, Cousin Patrick. Looks like rain, saints be praised. Maybe we'll get some relief from the heat."

"Hope so. Norah, is Hilda—has she left for the day yet?"

Norah sniffed. "Left, huh! She never come home last night!"

Patrick's eyes widened. He grabbed Norah by the arm. "What are you sayin'?"

"I'm sayin' she never come home! Stayed the night with one of her fine new friends and never let me know nor nothin'. Not a way to behave to her best friend, I'm thinkin'."

"*Where* did she spend the night?"

"And aren't I tellin' you I don't know? With the Malloys, likely."

Patrick thought about that for a moment. He didn't like it. He didn't like it one bit. If the stories Clancy Malloy was spreading were false, as Hilda insisted, she would rather have spent a night on burning coals than in the same house with him. And if they were true . . . well, either way, he wasn't at all happy. And he didn't mean to let any grass grow under his feet before he found out the truth of the matter.

"I'm off," he said, and tore down the drive as if the devil him-self were after him.

He hadn't intended to come and see Hilda. She'd told him to stay away, but he couldn't help himself. The thought of her angry at him, or unhappy because of his family . . . well, he just couldn't stand it, that was all. They'd had tiffs before, lots of them. They both had a temper. But the occasional spats had been unimportant, even fun. They both enjoyed a good argument.

This time it was different, really serious. She was truly upset.

Or so he had thought. Now, as he pelted down the street toward his uncle Dan's house, the gathering clouds racing overhead, he wasn't so sure. Had she sent him away to give herself time to get to know Clancy better?

His fists clenched. He didn't want to believe it. Hilda had said it wasn't so.

*She can lie in a good cause.*

The thought came unbidden. She'd never lied to him, though.

*Are you sure?*

He slowed his steps a trifle as he neared the house, and tried to catch his breath. He didn't want that stuck-up butler Riggs to see him panting. His breath was still coming a little short, though, when Riggs answered the bell.

"Good morning, Mr. Patrick." Riggs didn't trouble to keep the surprise out of his voice. He was wearing his loose gray jacket, his uniform for his morning chores. The hour was far too early for a call, especially when the master of the house had returned after midnight. But perhaps Mr. Patrick didn't know about that development. "I regret that no one is awake just yet, but perhaps you are calling to inquire about Mr. Malloy?"

"No, I— What about Mr. Malloy? Is there news?"

"Ah. Perhaps you are unaware that Mr. Malloy returned home late last night, sir."

"Returned home! What do you mean, returned home? Just up and walked in, or what?"

"I am not aware of all the circumstances, sir, but the young person, Miss Johansson, came to fetch Mrs. Malloy. It was quite late, well after ten o'clock. They went away and then returned, bringing Mr. Malloy home in the carriage."

Patrick closed his eyes and heaved a long sigh of relief. "So Miss Johansson stayed here for the rest of the night, since it was so late. That's like Aunt Molly, to think of someone else even when she's tired and worried."

"I beg your pardon, sir. I spoke carelessly. Mr. and Mrs. Malloy returned. Of Miss Johansson I have seen nothing since she left here to take Mrs. Malloy to Mr. Malloy."

"You mean she's not here, not at this house?"

"No, sir. Here, Mr. Patrick, you can't go and wake them! Mr. Malloy is a sick man, he needs his rest— Mr. Patrick!"

Patrick, taking the stairs two at a time, paid not the slightest attention.

He hammered on the door of his aunt and uncle's bedroom. It was opened very quickly by his aunt Molly, and she was not pleased. An elegant lace wrapper over her night things, her hair in a pigtail down her back, she was the picture of outraged dignity. She stepped outside the room and closed the door behind her.

"Patrick Cavanaugh, stop making that unholy racket!" She spoke in a furious stage whisper. "Your uncle Dan's not feeling a bit well, and his head aches. If you're so eager to hear what your young woman's accomplished, you can come back at a Christian hour."

She turned to the door, but Patrick put a hand on her arm. "Aunt Molly, I'm sorry, but where's Hilda?"

That stopped her. She turned back to face him. "At home in her bed, I should think. She must have been nearly as late to bed as I was."

"She's not at home! She never came back last night!"

"What nonsense! She left the rectory—"

"Left where?"

"St. Patrick's rectory. It's a long story, but your uncle Dan had been put to bed there. We were just ready to bundle him into the carriage and bring him here, and your Hilda said good night and walked home."

"But she never got there," said Patrick, and turned away. He would not let Aunt Molly see the misery on his face.

# 15

Let us have done with British-Americans and Irish-Americans and German-Americans, and so on, and all be Americans . . .

—Henry Cabot Lodge, address to the New England Society of Brooklyn, 1888

HOME. Aunt Molly had said she walked home. Maybe, since it had been so late, she'd gone to her real home —her brother and sisters' house.

Patrick paced the brick sidewalk, not knowing or caring where he was going. He had to find her. If she was at home—

He stopped. The man behind him bumped into him. Patrick didn't even notice, didn't hear the apology. He'd have to go to her home to see if she was there, and he didn't know where it was.

Aha! He knew her brother's name, though. He could look up the address. He took in his surroundings, realized he was close to the firehouse, and ran all the way there.

"Hey, where's the fire?"

Patrick, rushing into the front room of the firehouse, made no reply to his colleague's stale joke. He probably didn't even hear it. He rummaged frantically through the stack of papers on the desk. "Where's the city directory?"

"On the shelf under the telephone, where it always is. What's the *matter* with you?"

" 'Jenks, Jennings, Jesiorski . . .' " He ran his finger down the list of Js. " 'Joers, Johannes . . . *Johansson, Sven'!*" He grabbed a piece of paper and a pencil, noted down the address, and headed for the door.

"*Wait* a minute!" Joe Luther, the other fireman, blocked the door. "Tell me what's got you so worked up."

"Let me through, Joe, it's in the hurry I am—"

"And you ought to be, for you're due here on duty in half an hour. And if you'd forgotten—and I'd say you had, for you look like a fish, all goggle-eyed and gaspy—then I'm reminding you."

"But I—I can't stay, I have to go and find out—Joe, can you—"

"I'll find someone to cover for you, if that's what you're trying to say. *If* you tell me what's going on."

"But . . ." Patrick sighed. Joe was a big man, and a solid one. He could hardly push him out of the way. And there was no real hurry, he supposed. Five minutes wouldn't change anything. "Miss Johansson is investigating my uncle's disappearance, as you know. Well, not anymore she isn't, for she found him, last night, and he's home."

"You don't say! Where'd she find him? What does he say about Mr. Bishop? Why—"

Patrick waved away the questions like a man batting at mosquitoes. "I don't know, and I don't care. The thing is, Hilda's—Miss Johansson's—missin'. She didn't go back to Tippecanoe Place last night to sleep. So I'm thinkin' maybe she went to her own home, where her brother and sisters live. And I'm goin' there to find out. You're not to say a word about it, mind! She'd not like that. And I'd thank you to get out of me way."

Joe shook his head in commiseration. "Sorry, Pat. That's not so good. Hope you find her. Ever met her family?"

"No, they don't approve of me. And they'll not be home this mornin', they'll be workin', so I'll not meet 'em now, neither. And if you don't mind . . ."

Joe stood aside to let him pass, and then sat down to consider which of the firemen on the roster might not mind a little extra duty on a Saturday morning.

Patrick didn't run to the Johansson house. It was too far away, over two miles, past the Studebaker lumber sheds, past the Swedish Church, and he had no more breath for speed. There was no hurry, he kept telling himself. Hilda would still be sleeping after a late night. He would just assure himself that she was well, and then go away again. He might not even wake her, if by some chance one of her sisters was home and he could inquire without . . .

Without making a fool of yourself, said a jeering inner voice.

The house, when he found it, looked quite a lot like his own. A "factory house," built by the Studebakers for their workers, one of several identical houses on the street. White frame, two stories, small porch in front, small kitchen at the back. All of it neat as a pin, freshly whitewashed, small flower bed neatly weeded.

And the door firmly shut.

He took a deep breath, mounted the steps, and pulled on the bell.

He heard its tinkle from inside the house; one of the windows was open a little at the top. There was no other sound.

She was asleep, of course, just as he'd thought. He rang the bell again, more vigorously, and knocked as well.

Silence.

He had just repeated the sequence once more when the woman next door, who had been washing her front steps and watching him with avid curiosity, abandoned her pail and brush and approached. "There's nobody home this time of day, young man. They're all at work. The girls'll be home after dinner, about two or so. This is their half day. Mr. Johansson won't come back till supper time."

"It's their sister I'm lookin' for—Miss Hilda Johansson."

"Oh, she don't live here. She works for the Studebakers and lives in that fancy house of theirs."

Patrick held on to his patience with difficulty. "I know where she lives. I thought she might've come to spend the night with her family."

The woman shook her head. "Not been here, not that I know of, and I don't miss much. Nothing unusual's happened at all. Say, are you that Irishman she goes around with?"

Patrick was too upset to take offense at the tone, or to deny the relationship. "Yes. When did you say her sisters will be home?"

"Long about two o'clock's their regular time of a Saturday. Are you saying you don't know where she is, Hilda, I mean? She ought to be at the Studebaker place. But you'd know that, wouldn't you? She's not run off, has she?"

Too late, Patrick realized he hadn't meant to imply any such thing. If by some miracle she was off somewhere for reasons of her own, she'd have his skin if he started gossip about her. "Uh—no, of course not! I—I just forgot where I was supposed to meet her, that's all." He tipped his hat. "Thank you, ma'am."

He set a brisk pace down the street, never turning back to see the speculative stare that followed his progress.

His brain was working furiously. He knew something of Hilda's relationship with her family. Sven was fairly indulgent, as brothers went, but it was his job to enforce discipline within the family, and he took his duties seriously. Hilda loved and respected him, but was not apt to confide in him. Gudrun, the elder sister, was a bit of a shrew; one of Hilda's constant problems was to keep Gudrun from finding out about small indiscretions. Freya, on the other hand . . . Freya was the youngest, and Hilda's confidante. Freya, he felt sure, would know all about any jaunt Hilda might have taken.

The trouble was, Patrick couldn't remember where Freya worked. Like Gudrun, she was a maid, and he'd once been told for whom, but the subject hadn't interested him and he'd forgotten. And it was only—Patrick took out his pocket watch—only half-past nine. He couldn't go up and down West Washington Street knocking on well-polished doors. Nor could he bear to cool his heels and do nothing until Freya came home at two and he could question her.

Hilda was all right. Of course she was all right. But the sooner he knew where she was and what she was doing, the sooner he'd be able to settle down to his own work. And he couldn't talk to Gudrun or Freya right now.

On the other hand, he could find Sven easily. Sven worked in the paint department at Studebaker's.

With the greatest reluctance, knowing he'd regret it, Patrick turned his steps toward the great wagon factory a few blocks away.

Like most people in town who didn't actually work at the factory, Patrick had only the vaguest idea of the layout of the place. Two of his brothers worked there, but Patrick himself had never actually set foot on the property. He blundered about for a few minutes, asking directions and getting lost, before he finally followed his nose to the paint shed. The first man he encountered pointed obligingly.

"Sven Johansson? Over there, finishing that wagon."

Sven, a blond giant, stood intent over his work, carefully applying the fine red stripes that made the green farm wagon a work of art. He looked up as Patrick approached, a frown on his face.

"Yes, sir? You wish to speak with me?"

Patrick, six inches shorter than Sven, gulped in spite of himself. "Mr. Johansson, you don't know me, but I need to talk, if you can spare a minute or two. My name is Patrick Cavanaugh."

He held out his hand. Sven turned his back, put his paintbrush in a pot of turpentine, wiped his hands on a rag, and folded his arms. Patrick let his hand drop.

"And what, Mr. Cavanaugh, do you have to say to me that is so important?"

"Do you think we could go somewhere else, maybe?" Patrick was getting tired of craning his neck.

"I do not. I have work to do."

"Well, then, it's sorry I am to be botherin' you, but I thought you might know where I can find Hil—Miss Johansson."

The frown deepened. "If you must find her at all, you will of course go to Tippecanoe Place. Why do you trouble me about it?"

Patrick's temper was rising. He tried to keep it under control, but he knew his face was flushed. "Because she's not there!

I can't find her, and I'm worried about her, and I thought you'd want to help!"

It wasn't possible for Sven to grow taller as he stood there. Patrick knew that, but he stepped back all the same as Sven loomed.

"Why do you worry? What is there to worry you, if she has stepped out to run an errand?"

It had to come out. "Because she wasn't there last night! She never went home at all, and I can't find anybody who knows where she might be. And what with her workin' on the Malloy business—"

"Working on *what?*" Sven's voice had grown very quiet, with a steely edge Patrick didn't care for.

"Mr. Malloy's disappearance. He's me uncle, and the family asked her to look into it, you know . . ." Something in Sven's face told Patrick he had *not* known until that moment, and didn't like it now. "So she got leave to come and go as she liked until it was cleared up. But now me uncle Dan's come home, and Hilda hasn't, and—"

"ENOUGH!" Sven's fist came down on the workbench. A pot of paint danced to the floor, splashing bloodlike drops over both men.

"So. *My* sister has become involved with *your* family in a dangerous affair, and now she is missing. How long have you known this?"

"Not even two hours, Mr. Johansson, I—"

"Two hours. *Two hours.* You do not come to me until *two hours* after you discover that my sister is gone."

"I was trying to find her! I thought she was at the Malloys' house, and then I thought she might have spent the night with her family, but—"

"That will do, Mr. Cavanaugh. You have involved my sister in danger before, but this is intolerable." He spoke slowly, deliberately, spacing out his words and emphasizing them with an icy glare. "You will not try to find her. This is my concern, mine and my family's. I have never approved of Hilda's friendship with you, and now I see that I was right.

"Understand this, Mr. Cavanaugh." The giant's hand reached out and grasped Patrick by the front of his shirt, pulling him almost off his feet. "You will do nothing more in this matter. You will never try to see my sister again. But if she has been hurt, understand that you will see me, whether you wish to or not—and soon."

He let go. Patrick stumbled and nearly fell. Sven, ignoring the pool of red paint that spread over the floor, stalked to the door of the paint shed and was gone.

Hilda opened her eyes. At least, she thought they were open, but they met only inky blackness. They felt scratchy, but she couldn't seem to move her hands to rub them. Her feet, too—they wouldn't move properly. And her mouth—was there something in her mouth? Something dry and rough?

She was terribly thirsty and her head ached horribly. She tried to tell someone so, but she could produce only a kind of moan. She turned her head, staring into the darkness until bright stars and sunbursts seemed to appear, somewhere within her eyeballs.

Trying to see only made her head hurt more, and she feared she might be sick. That would be disastrous, with that thing over her mouth. She had better close her eyes again.

# 16

Politicians [are] a set of men who have interests aside from the interests of the people, and who, to say the most of them, are, taken as a mass, at least one long step removed from honest men.

—Abraham Lincoln, in an 1837 speech

I F Patrick had cherished any hope that Hilda's disappearance could be kept quiet, he was soon disappointed. The woman next door told the neighbors. They told their friends. Sven, indulging in the unusual extravagance of the streetcar, reached the houses where Gudrun and Freya worked only a few minutes after he left Patrick. At each house he had to explain to the butler why he wanted to talk to the maid. The butlers told everyone they knew as soon as they possibly could. By the time word reached the ears of reporters at the South Bend *Tribune* and the South Bend *Times*, it was old news.

Even as wildly inaccurate reports were spreading all over town, the matter was being discussed around the Malloy breakfast table.

Dan Malloy, a headache still lurking somewhere near the base of his skull, his stomach still uncertain about what sort of food it would accept, growled as he reached for a piece of dry toast. "No need to fret, Mrs. Malloy. Girl's gone off on her own somewhere. She's got brains, more than I expected. Found me, didn't she? She'll be all right."

"You may be right, Mr. Malloy," said his wife, decapitating her boiled egg, "but I can't help thinking that they said the same about you. That you'd left of your own free will, to escape the police."

He growled again. Mrs. Malloy soothed.

"Yes, I know, my dear, and of course everyone knows better now."

For the police had been there already, before breakfast. How word of Mr. Malloy's rescue had leaked out, no one was certain. Perhaps Mrs. O'Hanlon at the rectory was not quite as discreet as Father Faherty thought she was, or such a juicy story had proved too great a temptation. At any rate, Superintendent Clarke himself had arrived early this morning, only a few minutes after Patrick had left, and had heard at least a partial account of Malloy's captivity. He had apparently accepted it at face value; at least he'd been polite, which was sometimes an effort for him. Neither he nor Mrs. Malloy had mentioned her conversation with Mayor Fogarty the day before, but she had no doubt whatever that the mayor had relayed certain pointed instructions to the superintendent.

He would be back, of course. The murder of Mr. Bishop was still very much an open case, and Mr. Malloy still very much a part of the investigation. But the superintendent had had the grace to allow Mr. Malloy a little time to recover from his grueling experience before he was questioned more closely.

"But I just wonder," Mrs. Malloy continued. "Hilda is smart, as you say. Suppose the men who abducted you have decided that she's too smart, that she is a danger to them? I fear for her, Mr. Malloy, and I'm not ashamed to say it."

"You worry too much, Mother." Clancy toyed with his bacon and eggs. "That girl can take care of herself. I think Father's right. She'll turn up when she wants to. I, for one, wouldn't be surprised to learn she's gone off with some man."

His mother put down her spoon. "That, young man, is unwarranted. Miss Johansson is a respectable girl, and I'll not have you spreading rumors about her. You tried it once before, and I'll not have it, is that clear?"

Clancy scowled. "I was only having a little fun with Patrick. He's such a stick. Thought I'd liven him up a little. What's the harm?"

"The harm," said Mr. Malloy, throwing the despised toast on his plate and leveling a glare at his son, "is to a woman's reputation. Once it is taken away, she is helpless, cast out of society. A gentleman does not trifle with such things, even when the woman in question is a servant. And this girl, I remind you, is in our employ, and not as a servant but as an investigator." His brows drew together. "Not that I think there's cause for alarm, mind you. If the girl's gone away, it'll be for reasons of her own. She'll be chasing an idea, trying to catch up with the villains who nearly killed me. She saved my life, boy, and you'll say nothing against her, understood?"

"Only a bit of fun," Clancy muttered, and excused himself from the table.

Mrs. Malloy sighed when he had left the room. "It's time Clancy went into the business, Mr. Malloy. We've spoiled him a bit, I fear, but he's a grown man now, and he's not got enough to do. It makes him sulky and restless, and he spends entirely too much time racing that horse of his."

Mr. Malloy grunted. "And gambling on the races, as well. Seems to be winning, I'll give him that, but it's got to stop, all the same." He toyed with his toast and then picked up the bell and rang it violently.

"Sir?" said Riggs when he appeared.

"Take away this damned toast! I want bacon and eggs. And potatoes, and some griddle cakes. No food for days, and the doctors want me to 'go carefully.' Hah! Starve a man to death, that's what they're trying to do."

Riggs allowed his eyes to swivel in the direction of Mrs. Malloy, who lifted her eyebrows and gave the tiniest of shrugs.

"Very good, sir."

It was far too soon for that kind of food, and Mrs. Malloy

knew it. Probably he wouldn't be able to eat a quarter of it. And if he ate it all and it made him sick, well, they'd deal with that when the time came.

Much of her success in managing her family derived from her ability to choose her battles, and just now she preferred to let another matter take precedence over her husband's digestion.

"My dear, I really wish you would make some inquiries about Hilda. I'm truly worried about her. Even if she has chosen to go away, many things can happen to a woman alone."

"Don't know she *is* alone. Ah, this is more like a man's breakfast!"

She waited until Riggs had left and Mr. Malloy had eaten a little before pressing the point. "Of course, I could look into the matter myself, but I really wanted to stay at home for a day or two. I haven't got over the fright of nearly losing you, my dear, and I'd like to make sure you're quite well before I stray far from home."

He smiled at her suddenly. "Looking after me, are you, Molly?"

She looked demurely at her plate. He almost never called her by her first name; it was an intimacy. "It's over twenty-five years now I've been trying to look after you, Daniel, and a hard job it's been, and no mistake. You're a headstrong man, my dear."

"Hah! You're tougher than I am, and you know it, for all a strong wind would blow you away." He shook his head fondly. "You still look like the girl in our wedding picture, Molly. Don't know how you do it, with me to give you trouble all these years, but you've always been a beauty. And you always could twist me 'round your little finger. I'll put the word out about Hilda."

"Thank you, Mr. Malloy. More coffee?"

"No, thank you." He put his fork down; his face had turned pale. "I—um—excuse me!"

He managed to make it to the kitchen sink.


"We find ourselves in a difficult position, gentlemen." The honorable Edward J. Fogarty, the new mayor of South Bend, stood at the head of a polished mahogany table in the old mayor's office, since the fine new city hall wasn't quite finished, and addressed the small group of men seated at the table. "Mr. Bishop's death was, of course, most unfortunate, a tragedy indeed."

Heads nodded, cigars were removed from mouths in momentary respect for the dead man. A Republican, to be sure, but now presumably removed far from the political sphere. They could afford to be generous.

"And certainly we all hope that the police will find his murderer with all possible speed. I am working with Superintendent Clarke myself, to assure that the search is carried out expeditiously."

More nods, but the cigars were replaced and puffed on vigorously. A few uneasy murmurs issued from unidentifiable sources.

"However." The mayor took a deep breath. "I'm sure I don't need, gentlemen, to spell out the problem. I know that all of us in this room have no doubt whatever that Mr. Malloy is entirely guiltless in this matter, and we are of course profoundly grateful that he has been found. He is as much a victim of whatever dastards are responsible for the death as is Mr. Bishop himself, though happily to a lesser degree. But the public, gentlemen." He paused, scowled, and resumed. "Are the members of the public as well informed as we? Are they as convinced as we of Mr. Malloy's innocence?"

"And will they vote for him?" said the banker, Mr. Leahy, from the end of the table. He'd lost his patience with statesmanly rhetoric. "That's the real question here, isn't it?" He punctuated his question with sharp little pokes in the air with his cigar. "Has our firecracker of a sure thing turned into a bomb that could destroy us all?"


Around the corner at Republican headquarters on Colfax, a similar group of men sat around a similar table. The cigar smoke was as thick. The suits and high, starched collars, the vests and watch chains, the carefully groomed mustaches were all much like those sported by their Democratic counterparts. But the mood of the meeting was notably darker. The men sat and smoked, saying little.

"Well," said one finally, scraping back his chair, "it looks to me as though we're in for a drubbing. Bishop wasn't much of a candidate, though I shouldn't speak ill of the dead. But he was the best we could find to run for an office that doesn't amount to a hill of beans, anyway. Now he's gone, and here's Malloy telling this fantastic story about being kidnapped and drugged and I don't know what all. We'll be lucky to get a Republican elected dogcatcher."

"I don't care for your tone, Mr. Goodman." Though there was no obvious chairman of the meeting, the speaker sounded as though he was accustomed to authority. "Mr. Bishop was a friend to many of us, and a good Republican. His death is not to be taken lightly."

There were murmurs of "Hear, hear."

"Didn't say it was, but look here, Nelson. We've already lost the mayor's office. This isn't a good time for Republicans in this county, and that's where everything begins, at the local level. We all know that. Now here's this coal strike going on and on, and it could start to hurt a lot of us if it lasts much longer. That cuts two ways. Reserves won't last forever, and people are starting to worry, but there's a lot of sympathy in this town for the workingman. If the strike lasts until the election, some of the fools out there are going to blame the mine operators just as much as the strikers. Blast it all, we can't have this sort of thing. Disrupts the country, hurts business, doesn't even do the laborer any good in the end."

Goodman's audience grew restive. It was all true, of course, but they'd heard it before.

"All right, then. Who's to blame for the strike? Who's to blame for stirring up the common man? Who's trying to take over this country and spoil it for the real Americans? You all know who. The immigrant, that's who. So now here we are, with an upstart Irishman as mayor of this town and another clown of an Irishman all set to become a county councilman, just on the strength of the sympathy vote. We've had Irishmen in politics in this town for too long, my friends. It's time we did something about it, but after what's happened, I'm blessed if I know what!"

There was an uncomfortable silence. Goodman was known to feel strongly about the immigrant question, but there were men in the room who looked at it from a different angle. Goodman caught a whisper from the corner: "Judge Hagerty..."

He pounded his fist on the table. "I'll give you Hagerty. A good man. But he's been dead a long time now, and a judge isn't a real politician anyway. I'm getting just a little tired of everyone talking about him like he was some kind of saint."

"Mr. Goodman, I'm sure we all understand your position, though we may not all share it," said Mr. Nelson, trying to return to the issues at hand. "It's true that immigrants have caused problems in this country, and immigrant laborers may be disruptive at times, but we'd be hard put to run our businesses without them. However, we have strayed from the point. Our purpose here is, first, to decide on an appropriate memorial for Mr. Bishop, and second, to try to find someone to run in his place."

"Who're we going to find that's fool enough? He'll be eating Malloy's dust all the way," came from a small, rather prissy man in the corner.

"I wouldn't be so sure about that." The man who spoke, a large man with a light brown beard, had been silent for the entire meeting.

"Ah, Mr. Vanderhoof," said Mr. Nelson. "You have a good many dealings with immigrants, in one way and another. Perhaps you have some understanding of the Irish that some of us lack. Would you like to explain your point of view?"

"My dealings with immigrants are neither here nor there. I bring them to this country because we need the labor force, and that's that. I won't bother to defend myself to Mr. Goodman. But this election, gentlemen. Now, we've all backed Mr. Bishop, of course. I tried, especially, to talk some sense into him, teach him a thing or two about politics. Well, now he's gone, but our chances in that race just may not be gone with him."

He leaned in to the table, gesturing with his cigar. "We've been operating under the assumption that Mr. Malloy bears no responsibility for Mr. Bishop's death. I wonder if that assumption will hold water?"

He had their attention. "Gentlemen, if I had just murdered someone, I think I might behave in just such a manner as Mr. Malloy has behaved." There was a shocked intake of breath, but no one spoke. "I would go away, hide someplace where I was bound to be discovered sooner or later, make up a wild tale about kidnapping and drugs— don't you think?"

"The man was nearly dead when he was found," said Mr. Nelson, strong disapproval in his voice.

"So he says. Or so his family says. Some drugs can mimic death very effectively, or so a reading of *Romeo and Juliet* would have us believe. I understand that the cellar door was not actually locked. There would seem to be no reason why Mr. Malloy might not have left of his own free will—if indeed he so willed."

There was dead silence in the room. The cigar smoke rose lazily.

"Think about it. I don't believe the public would be so eager to vote for a murderer—do you?"

# 17

In darkness, and with dangers compass'd round, and solitude.

—John Milton, *Paradise Lost*, 1667

HILDA opened her eyes again. With an effort that made her headache worse, she tried to see something, anything. It was no use. The blackness was absolute.

She sat up and realized, with some surprise, that she had used her hands to do so. Hadn't they been bound earlier? And her feet? Or had that been only a dream?

No. She had been bound. She rubbed her wrists, chafed raw from her bonds. But she was free now. At least— She checked her feet. Yes, she could use them.

She had been gagged, as well, and now she was not. Her mouth was dry and tasted terrible, but it was free. That was a great relief. If the pain in her head made her sick, as it sometimes did, she would at least not choke. But she would not think about being sick. The thought sometimes led to the fact.

And, oh, but she was thirsty.

She forced her mind to work. She was, she thought, underground. The smell of damp earth was strong.

The church basement, where they had put Mr. Malloy?

Her spirits rose slightly at the thought. She reached her

hands overhead, trying to touch the low ceiling, but they met nothing. Cautiously, she stood and stretched her arms as high as she could.

Nothing.

She sat down again and realized that the floor was stone, not earthen. Damp stone.

The center of the church basement was paved with stone, but it was too small, too exposed to view. They'd never have put her there.

A cave, then, perhaps. Were there caves around South Bend? She didn't know, but she could think of no other place that would be so dark.

Unless it was night. How long had she been here?

She shook her head impatiently, and immediately regretted it. When the pain and nausea receded, she tried to think again.

Her first need was for water. Caves often had water. If she were very cautious, going on hands and knees and checking for hidden hazards as she went, she might find a pool or a spring. Water would clear her head.

She felt around her, seeking a direction. Her hand encountered . . .

A pitcher?

Water?

With hands that trembled, she lifted the pitcher. It was heavy. She tried to bring it to her mouth.

She was clumsy. A good deal of water spilled over her face. She set the pitcher down to get a better grip, eagerly licking drops of water off her lips and chin.

It tasted—odd.

She sat back and wept, the tears rolling down her face. She made no attempt to stanch them.

Water, blessed water, at her very lips, and she dared not drink it. Whatever demons had put her here had drugged the water, just as they had drugged Mr. Malloy's. Her only chance of escape lay in a clear head—but how badly she wanted that water!

Surely one mouthful wouldn't hurt.

She lifted the pitcher again. Again her hands shook, but she managed to fill her mouth.

If it hadn't tasted foul, she might have succumbed. But the taste was enough to brace her weakening will.

She rinsed her dry mouth and lips, spat out the water, and then, deliberately, she poured the contents of the pitcher out on the stone floor.

And wept again.

Sven, Gudrun, and Freya sat in their little house staring bleakly at one another.

They had been to the police. They had been told to look in St. Patrick's, where Mr. Malloy had been found. They had looked, but the cellar was devoid of human presence. Now they had come home, sick with worry.

"What must we do?" Gudrun finally asked in Swedish.

No one had an answer. "Perhaps, after all, the police will . . . ," Freya began, tentatively.

"Hah! You heard what that Sergeant Haney said! He did not believe us. He does not like Hilda, has not liked her since they met over that matter of Miss Harper's death. He will do nothing, nothing!" Sven pounded his fists on his knees.

"Then we must find her ourselves," said Gudrun grimly, rising from her chair and pacing. The room was small. Three steps to the fireplace. Three steps back. Her skirt swept the leg of a small table and would have upset it if the potted aspidistra on top had not been so heavy.

Freya reached over to steady the plant. "But how can we find her? She could be anywhere!"

Silence fell again, the silence of despair. Freya was the one to break it this time. "If it were one of us, she would find us! We cannot just sit here—"

"Hush, little one," said Sven. "It is because Hilda is headstrong, because she will not listen to my counsel, will not just sit and wait that she is now in such terrible trouble. Also—" He lifted his hands and sighed. "We are not stupid, any of us, but we have not her kind of mind. It was she, always, who could solve the riddles and the puzzle pictures when we were children. We do not think that way. We will try, of course, to think out where she may be, and who might have done this to her, but, my sisters, I think the best thing we can do is to hope, and to pray."

Patrick was more militant in his approach. His treatment at Sven's hands had roused all his Irish temper, and he was determined to find Hilda or die in the attempt. That'd show him, that bully of a big Swede! He, Patrick Cavanaugh, he'd deliver her to the front door and collapse on the threshold, nearly dead from the beating he'd had at the hands of the villains. Then Sven would beg, beg on his knees, for Patrick to accept his apology. "Anything I have is yours," he'd say. "My house, my money, anything!"

And he'd stand up, Patrick would, stagger to his feet through his pain, and clasp Hilda to his bosom. "I ask only Hilda's hand in marriage."

Patrick shook himself. The daydream had gone a little too far, maybe, but all the same, he was going to rescue Hilda. Her family had been worse than no help. Very well, he'd go to her friends.

He strode up the back drive of Tippecanoe Place with a swagger. He'd have preferred to defy protocol and use the forbidden front drive, but the back was quicker, and he was in a hurry.

He beat a tattoo on the back screen. It was just his luck that Mr. Williams happened to be passing and came to the door himself.

"Hilda is not at home," he informed Patrick in frosty tones.

"And may the good Lord give me strength! Do you think I don't know that? Do you think I haven't been lookin' for her all mornin'? Do you think I'm not half off me head for worryin' about her? I've come to talk to Norah and see if we can't work out where they might've taken her."

"I do not know, Mr. Cavanaugh, that it has been established that anyone 'took her' anywhere. It seems to me that—"

But long before the butler had finished his harangue, Patrick had rolled his eyes, torn open the door, and rushed off in search of Norah.

He found her in the kitchen, washing breakfast pots and pans and muttering under her breath. When she saw him, she dropped the iron skillet back into the water with a splash.

"Have you found her? What's the news?"

"No news."

"Oh." Norah picked up the skillet and scrubbed at it again with something that looked to Patrick (unaccustomed to domestic chores) like a piece of chain mail.

"Look, we've got to find her! Me aunt Molly told me she left the rectory at St. Patrick's somewhere around midnight, on her way home. That's not far, Norah! Only a couple of blocks. And in those two blocks, someone caught her and . . ."

He couldn't finish. Norah looked at him pityingly, then turned quickly back to her work as Mrs. Sullivan came into the kitchen.

"And do you think we've time to waste, with the new girl no more use than a sick headache, which is what we're all going to have if His Nibs catches you, Norah, messin' about when you ought to be workin! And how he thinks you're to wait table, with your hands all red and raw from havin' to be a scullery maid, too, I'm sure I don't know."

Hands on hips, the cook glared impartially at both Patrick and Norah. "And I need that skillet for luncheon, so mind you clean it proper, and don't take all day about it!"

Patrick hastily picked up a towel and began to dry the pots on the drain board. "I came to help, Mrs. Sullivan," he said earnestly.

"Hmph!" She stumped away. Not for any blandishment would she have admitted the soft spot she, a childless woman, had in her heart for Patrick.

"She won't let you stay long," said Norah in an undertone.

"I know. Now look, Norah. You know Hilda better than anybody. Where would she go if she was trying to hide?"

"Here," said Norah flatly. "She'd be safer here than anyplace else. This house is locked up tighter than a bank at night. Well, usually."

Patrick pounced. "What do you mean, usually?"

Norah looked around and lowered her voice still further. "Old Sourpuss left the back door unlocked last night. I guess he meant to lock it after Hilda got in, but I expect he fell asleep in his chair, and when he woke, it was late and he forgot about it. Or somethin'. Anyway, it was unlocked when I went to look for Hilda in the middle of the night. So she could have gotten in if she'd wanted to, Patrick. I don't think she's hiding anywhere. I think they've got her."

Much as he hated to admit it, Patrick thought so, too. "Well, then," he said, banging the pot down on the kitchen table, "we have to figure out where they've taken her. I'm goin' back to Uncle Dan's house to talk to him some more, and maybe to Clancy as well."

"You'll be tellin' me if you're findin' out anything?"

"As soon as I know," he promised. "I may need your help."

"I untied her," said the man.

"And left the pitcher of water?" said the other.

"Right where she can't help but find it. She'll be so thirsty she'll lap it off the floor if she spills it."

"Good. That gives us ample time to consider our position."

"I still think we should have—um—ensured a more permanent solution when we first had her in hand."

"It still may come to that. I'm not sure, though, that we didn't make a mistake in taking her. She knows nothing, because Malloy knows nothing to have told her. How could she have harmed us?"

"She's not stupid. She found Malloy."

The other man waved his hand. "Luck. He was hidden in an obvious place, because we wanted him found. It wouldn't have annoyed me if he'd been found dead, but since he remembers nothing, it amounts to the same thing."

"You don't think she'll be found, do you?"

The man began to laugh. "Do you? I'll venture she'll still be filed away nicely, just where we can find her when we want to. We'll give her a day or two to repent her prying ways, and then . . ."

# 18

... through caverns measureless to man ...
—Samuel Coleridge, *Kubla Khan,* 1798

PATRICK sat in the front parlor of the Malloys' house. Outside, a light rain had begun to fall. Summer was beginning to loosen its grip on September.

An untouched cup of tea sat on the small table at Patrick's side. He had come back after his visit to Tippecanoe Place, and had been catechizing his uncle ever since, learning the details of his abduction. A luncheon that nobody much wanted had been served and cleared away. Now it was Saturday afternoon. As hour succeeded hour, Patrick became more and more anxious for Hilda, his questions more and more urgent. "But you must remember *somethin'*, Uncle Dan!"

"How many times, boy! I heard the men quarreling. I didn't like the sound of it, so I sent Clancy, here, to get you. And then they took me—carried me off like a little lamb, curse 'em!"

"Watch your language, Mr. Malloy," said his wife automatically.

"Sorry, my dear. Well, they took me off. And I don't remember anything else, much, until that young woman of yours found me."

"When did they drug you? Before they took you for the ride, or after they put you in the cellar?"

Dan thought about that. "Must have been in the cellar. I don't remember them takin' me, at first—they must've hit me over the head—but I remember the ride, clear enough. Horrible! Jounced around like a trussed turkey. I thought every bone in my body'd break."

Patrick leapt on that. "Then you weren't in a carriage, but a wagon."

"How do you work that out?"

"A carriage has padded seats. You wouldn't have been comfortable, bound and gagged like that, but you wouldn't have worried about broken bones."

Uncle Dan looked dubious. "It was powerful hot and stuffy. A wagon's hard, but it's right airy."

"Mmm." Patrick thought about that. "A closed delivery truck, maybe? Did it smell of anything in particular?"

"It smelled," said Dan with precision, "of wool blanket."

Patrick thought that might explain the hot and stuffy part as well, but he didn't say so. Dan Malloy, though his favorite uncle, wasn't a man to be trifled with. His chin on his hands, he brooded.

"Patrick, my dear," his aunt Molly said with a small sigh, "I have questioned Mr. Malloy most closely about his experience, and, really, he can remember no more than he has told you. He's not yet a well man, you know."

"I know, Aunt, and it's sorry I am to be badgerin' him. But we have to know what happened, and we have to know soon. Hilda . . ."

He didn't have to continue.

Dan put his hands on his knees, heavily. "Patrick, I've done what I can until I'm properly on my feet again. I've put the word out to all the friends I could reach, asking them to keep an eye open. The police are looking, too. The Lord knows I feel guilty about it all, for whatever's happened to that girl, it's related to what happened to me."

"And to Mr. Bishop," said Patrick, the words almost dragged

out of him. He didn't want to remember that Mr. Bishop was dead, but a fact was a fact. And if you put together the facts of the matter, even the few that they knew so far, it was plain that Hilda wouldn't be safe until she was found.

"Maybe," said Molly Malloy, "we're going about this the wrong way. Maybe we should be wondering who would wish harm to Mr. Bishop, Mr. Malloy, and Miss Johansson. All three."

Dan made an impatient gesture. "It's as plain as the nose on your face, woman. Someone killed Bishop. Then he, or they, thought I might know too much. I was there on the spot, after all. How were they to know I was blind and deaf?" He struck one fist into the palm of the other hand. "A fool I was, and I'm admitting it. But they didn't know that, so they took me away. Somewhere along the way they got the bright idea that they could blame Bishop's death on me, so they left me in that cellar to rot. And when young Hilda found me, they decided she was too smart to—to stay on the scene . . ."

He trailed off, but Patrick knew what he meant.

"They thought," he said bleakly, "that she was too smart to live."

The rain strengthened. From somewhere in the distance they heard the low rumble of thunder.

Thirst had become a pain, a raging need that overwhelmed thought, reason. Hilda could remember pouring a pitcher of water out on the floor, though she could not remember why she had done such a thing. It seemed the act of a madwoman. She no longer cared where she was, or why. Her whole consciousness, her whole being, had shrunk down to the need for water.

There had to be water somewhere. She could smell it, a stronger smell than mere dampness. Could she hear it? Was that dripping sound real, or only a cruel trick of her mind? She had slept a little, and dreamt of water, and wept when she woke to ever more demanding thirst.

Surely the dripping sound was real. She turned her head,

cautiously. It no longer hurt quite so much when she moved it. In fact, it seemed to float a little. That was bad, she thought, but she couldn't remember why it was bad, and she didn't try.

When she turned in one direction, the sound was louder, clearer. She shifted her body a foot or so that way.

Yes, louder, definitely! She tried to stand, but her head floated. Crawl, then.

Clumsily she crept toward the dripping sound until her hand, moving forward over roughness, encountered something cold.

Cold and wet! And a drop of water struck the back of her hand as it lay there!

She put her head to the uneven floor of her prison, to the tiny puddle in a hollow, and drank like an animal.

There wasn't much of it, and it tasted like no water she had ever drunk. It tasted of earth, of grass, of things she didn't care to name.

It tasted like heaven.

The drip was steady and fairly rapid. What could she use for a basin, to catch the water as it fell and give her enough for a real drink?

The pitcher, the despised pitcher she had so foolishly emptied. Where was it?

She lapped up a few more drops of water and then crawled back in search of the pitcher.


"Well, then, who'd want to kill Mr. Bishop? Did he have enemies, Uncle Dan?"

Patrick, desperate for information, persisted. His aunt, realizing the futility of making Dan rest, had gone about her business. Clancy sulked in a corner, taking little part in the conversation.

Dan Malloy smiled a little at Patrick's question. "All politicians have enemies, boy, but Bishop isn't—wasn't—important enough to have many, nor would they have killed him. Politics starts getting nasty when someone stands to gain or lose a great

deal—of money, of power, of influence. The stakes in this election aren't high enough to make a difference to a mosquito."

"Then there must be somethin' else. What about his business? Insurance, isn't it? Could he have made enemies there?"

Malloy laughed outright at that. "In insurance? The only enemies insurance men make are policyholders, when the company won't pay a claim. Besides, Bishop was higher up. Didn't
have much in the way of dealings with customers."

"*What,* then? The man's dead. *Somebody* hated him!"

Malloy shook his head. "I don't think so, boy. He wasn't the
sort you can hate. There just wasn't enough to him. He wasn't
smart enough—no, that isn't right. It wasn't brains he lacked, it
was imagination.

"Oh, he was a decent enough man. Did his job, made good
money, went to the Methodist church, had a nice house and a
pleasant wife and a couple of pretty daughters. Got involved in
community affairs, church work, that sort of thing.

"He ruffled a few feathers now and again, but I can't
imagine that he ever made an enemy in his life. I also doubt he
had any close friends. Knew lots of people, but all of them in a
business way. So far as I know. I didn't know him well, but then
I never met anybody who did."

Patrick groaned. "Then *why?*"

Clancy spoke up. "Dad, the man was a meddler. You know
he was. Always pokin' his nose in where it wasn't wanted. Look
at that business over the Labor Day parade."

Malloy nodded, unperturbed. "That's what I meant about
ruffled feathers. You hear about that, boy?"

Patrick shook his head.

"It was hushed up a bit, I suppose. The bigwig Republicans
didn't want their boy making a fool of himself."

Malloy settled into narrative. "The thing was, he—Bishop
—didn't want the parade to be allowed this year. He had some
fool idea that, what with the coal strike, and the riots and all, we
shouldn't encourage a show of labor solidarity. Of course, with
the Democrats in now, he didn't stand a chance of stopping it,
but he tried almighty hard."

"I'd think all the Republicans would've agreed with him."

"Pat, you never did have an ounce of sense!" said Clancy. "Of course they agreed, but they knew a lost cause when they saw one, and they kept their mouths shut. They shut Bishop up, too, but it took a fight."

"Then—"

Malloy saw the light in Patrick's eye and held up a hand. "No, boy. The bosses were annoyed with Bishop, but it was the way a mother's annoyed with a toddler. She gives him a smack when he's naughty, but she doesn't take him very seriously. Bishop was embarrassing them, so they took him down a peg or two, but they didn't—it's ashamed I am to say it of a dead man, but it's true—they didn't respect him enough to get very worried about it."

Clancy muttered something in a sour tone and turned away. Outside the window trees writhed in the driving wind and rain.

Water. Why had she ever wished for water? The drip had become a steady trickle. She had drunk her fill of the muddy water, had refilled the pitcher, hoping the mud would sink to the bottom and leave cleaner stuff to drink, and then sought out a dry spot to try to sleep away her hunger, her fear, her longing for freedom.

There were no dry spots. At every point the roof of her prison was leaking. Was she under a stream, then, a stream that might break through the roof and flood the cave and drown her?

The easing of her thirst had made her a little stronger, and the ache in her head was a mere annoyance now, a trifle. She got to her feet. She had to know more about her prison. She stretched out her arms to their full extent and felt, on one side of her, wet stone. A wall? She moved to it, explored it with her fingers.

No, not stone. Brick. A regular pattern of bricks and mortar, curving up to, she presumed, a ceiling, though she could not reach that high. Dropping to the floor, she eagerly felt it. Bricks, also. She should have noticed that before, when she was crawling about in search of water.

She was in a cellar of some sort. A man-made structure, at any rate.

And where there are walls and a floor, there will be a door.

She started to feel her way along the wall, and then had a second thought. There had been caves near Björka. She remembered her mother's warnings from her girlhood. She was never to go into a cave alone, she was always to have a lantern or a candle, she must always have a rope to lay down as a guide. People could get lost in caves, could die.

Though this wasn't a cave, it was as dark. Who knew what it was, how big it was? And she was light-headed from hunger and fear. It would be easy to make a mistake.

She needed a rope, some twine, something to lead her back to her first position if she became lost. She had nothing of the kind, nor was there anything to tie it to if she had. She sat down on the floor again. Tears came to her eyes, the tears that flowed so easily when she was afraid and exhausted.

"No!" she said aloud. The word echoed off the walls, frightening her still more, but she said it again—shouted it. "NO! I will not cry and be weak. I will be strong and smart. I am Hilda Johansson, and I will find a way to escape from this place!"

The echoes died. They were only her own voice. There was nothing to be afraid of, so long as she kept her head. What could she use for a rope?

She had once had a dress, her best dress in Sweden, that was decorated with braid. Long strands of braid were looped in fancy patterns. It had taken her mother weeks of painstaking work to make those yards and yards of braid and then sew it into those patterns, and when Hilda had outgrown the dress, her mother had removed the braid and put it on a dress for Freya.

There was no braid on the dress she was wearing; it was a plain maid's uniform. All of her clothing was plain, except—her dulled mind reached for the thought and finally snared it—except for her petticoat.

It wasn't her own petticoat. Her own was being washed at the Malloy house, along with the rest of her muddy things. Mrs. Malloy's maid had lent clothing to her, including Mrs. Malloy's own undergarments. She shuddered at the thought of what these borrowed clothes must look like now. Far worse, she feared, than the ones she had thought so disreputable only— how long ago?

That didn't matter. Nothing mattered except getting out of here. That borrowed petticoat had two generous ruffles, each edged with lace. There was lace on her chemise, as well, and on her underdrawers. Yards and yards of lace, all of it easily removable.

She would have to pay Mrs. Malloy back for the ruined garments, and it would cost her a pretty penny, for they were finely made, by far the nicest Hilda had ever worn. Never mind.

She undressed in the dark, removing all her undergarments and then replacing the outer ones. They were wet and scratchy against her bare skin, and she felt herself blushing, even in the dark, at the idea of going without underwear. No decent woman would think of such a thing.

You can put them back on when you've taken off the lace, she told herself, and set to work removing the long swaths of lace by touch.

In a few minutes she had a serviceable string wound 'round her wrist. She stripped again, resumed the despoiled undergarments, and then put on her outer clothes once more.

Now for something to secure her safety line— Ah, yes! The pitcher, the precious pitcher of water. Full of water, it was heavy enough, and it had a handle. She would have to be careful not to pull hard and turn it over, but it would do.

Everything took much longer than it should have. She groped on the floor, the now disgustingly muddy floor, for an agonizing few minutes before she found the pitcher. Then she had to have a drink. The mud had not settled as much as she had hoped.

Perhaps it would be wise to let the pitcher refill. She found a drip closer, she thought, to where she had spent most of her time in her prison and stood the pitcher under it, carefully making sure it was well balanced on the brick of the floor. Then she had to tie the lace to the handle. Lace is not meant to be tied and her fingers were clumsy with desperation, but eventually the knot was secure.

Carefully, carefully, she groped her way to a wall and stood, making sure the string of lace behind her was slack. Only then could she begin inching along the wall in search of freedom.

# 19

THE RUSH TO AMERICA
... Rules that immigrants must have money in their pouch,
that they must be healthy and free from suspicion of crime,
have no deterrent effect.
—*The New York Times* (editorial), May 4, 1902

IT was nearly dinnertime. Mrs. Malloy had ordered a light
meal, keeping in mind her husband's touchy stomach.
Tomato soup, poached salmon, roast chicken with potatoes
and carrots, lettuce salad, apple cake. Nothing heavy, no rich
gravies, no pastry—just a simple family meal.

The question was whether Patrick was going to share it with
them.

She sat in her chair in the parlor, her feet on her stool, and
contemplated him with some exasperation. They were alone;
her husband was resting upstairs and Clancy was out on business of his own. It was really time Patrick went on his way. "My
dear, are you not on duty this evening?"

He turned from his morose contemplation of the newspapers. They were both full of Hilda's disappearance, with dark
hints that the Bishop-Malloy matter was mixed up in it
somehow. "What? Oh, Aunt Molly. What did you say?"

Patiently she repeated her question.

"No. I don't know. I think Joe Luther got somebody to take
me place." He turned back to the papers in the futile hope that
some reporter might have gotten hold of some useful piece of in-

formation, some tiny clue to Hilda's whereabouts.

"But, Patrick, you mustn't lose your job. Hadn't you best go and find out for sure? It's nearly dinnertime. When would your shift start?"

Something in his aunt's tone of voice penetrated his preoccupation. He stood and held out his hands. "I'm sorry, Aunt Molly. I've been hangin' about all day, haven't I? It's just that I keep thinkin' there must be somethin' Uncle Dan's forgot, somebody I could talk to. I'm nearly beside meself with worry."

"Patrick, my dear, sit down." The tiny woman sat in her low chair and propped her feet up on her stool. She nodded at the chair next to her, and he obediently dropped into it.

"Patrick, you're a sensible boy, always have been. Sometimes I wish Clancy . . . but that doesn't matter now. Have you really thought about what will happen if Miss Johansson is found?"

"*When* she's found."

"When she's found, then, if you prefer. First of all, disappearing this way isn't good for a young woman's reputation."

"But they've taken her! It's not her fault, she—"

"Please, dear. Yes, that's what we believe. But it may not be what everyone will believe. However, let's suppose they do. Let's suppose that she is found, and she is well, and she proceeds to solve the mystery of Mr. Bishop's death with her usual brilliance, or luck, or however she's managed such things in the past. No, let me finish."

She smoothed her dress. "We will, of course, be very grateful to her if that happens, and we will reward her suitably. What will you do?"

"I—I will—" Patrick stuck there. Thoughts of that awful meeting, Hilda and his mother being as cordial to each other as two blocks of ice, crowded into his mind, along with thoughts of Hilda laughing up at him, shouting at him angrily, taking his hand that day at the firehouse . . .

"I see that you have not thought it through. I suggest that you do so. Miss Johansson is a very attractive and intelligent young woman, who deserves to be treated with respect. I intend to do so, and I hope that I can persuade the rest of our family to do so as well. But respect, Patrick, is a far cry from love."

"Love." She'd said it. Patrick tried to deny it, but the words wouldn't come.

Mrs. Malloy watched him closely. "I see that I was right. You have let your emotions run away with your good judgment. Now, Patrick, let me say this once, for your own good, and then I'll have done with it.

"You cannot entertain thoughts of marriage to Miss Johansson. Don't say anything; I can see by your face that you have considered the matter. You will do yourself and her great harm if you persist."

"I thought you liked her! You hired her to find Uncle Dan, and she found him, and now you—"

"I do like her, and moreover, I respect her. She has come to this country and shown great courage and industry, as well as considerable intelligence. She has obtained a good position and kept it, and has been thrifty with her earnings. My opinion of her has nothing to do with the issue at hand. Have you considered the fact that if she marries anyone except another servant, she will lose her position? A live-in servant cannot be married to someone who works outside the household."

Patrick winced. That was an aspect of the problem he had tried to ignore. He had no wish to give up his job, no wish to spend a lifetime at someone else's bidding.

"Furthermore, she would be an outcast if she married outside her faith. She would be required to become a Catholic, and although we would rejoice at her conversion to the true faith, her family would not. Nor would your mother, your brothers and sisters, welcome her into the family. To them she would always be a Protestant, conversion or no. These things are important, Patrick! The two of you are not even allowed to enter one another's churches! You have never met her family, have you?"

"Not until today, when I talked to Sven." Patrick said no more, but his aunt nodded grimly.

"And she has met yours, or part of yours, only once, yes? And that, I understand, was not a happy occasion either."

Aunt Molly always knew everything that went on in the family. Patrick looked at his feet.

"I repeat, these things are important. You are worried about your friend, and quite properly. It is through her involvement with you that she was brought into this matter, for we would not have known about her otherwise. And I deeply regret asking her to take the risks she has taken. I am, of course, grateful that she found Mr. Malloy in time. I will try always to be a good friend to her, if she is found. But you, Patrick, you must leave off seeing her. You have become too fond of her. Like you, I hope and trust there will be a happy outcome to the present anxiety. But after this is over, you must not see her again."

Patrick stood, his hands in his pockets. He cleared his throat.

He loved Aunt Molly as he loved no one except his mother. She was as kind as she was indomitable. She had guided him, encouraged him, seen to it that Clancy didn't bully him too badly, refused to interfere in their battles (which Patrick had almost always won). She was, in a very real sense, the matriarch of his entire family. Everyone had adored her and done her bidding for as long as he could remember. Now was the time for him to promise to do as she asked.

He cleared his throat again. "I'm sorry, Aunt Molly. All I can think about just now is finding her. After that—well, I'll worry about other things after that. I've stayed too long. I'm sorry. I'll be off."

He kissed her cheek and was gone.

She stayed in her chair, her hands reaching in her pocket for her rosary.

"I tried," she whispered. "It's up to you now, Lord. Who knows . . ." She touched the crucifix to her lips, crossed herself, and began to pray silently.


Hilda had been fumbling blindly for a long time, or so it seemed to her. Now she reached her hand out another few inches and felt—nothing.

A doorway? Her heart pounding, she felt around a bit more.

No, only a corner. The passage, or tunnel, or whatever it was, turned to the right.

Should she follow it? Should she turn back and try the other direction, past her starting place?

The decision was too much. Weak with hunger, devastated by disappointment, she sank to the brick floor and wept once more.

"So you see, it just won't work out right now."

"But you have the money—you said it would be enough— you said they would come soon—we have waited for so long—" Sven, Gudrun, and Freya all spoke at once.

The man from the bank held up his hand. Lord, these dumb Swedes! "Things have *changed*, I'm telling you. The coal strike has begun to have its effect on industry. It'll get worse before it gets better. There just isn't the need for laborers that there was at the beginning of the year."

Sunday afternoon. The rain continued. The temperature had dropped. Autumn was upon them.

The Johansson family had been to church and had prayed earnestly for Hilda's safety. Now they sat in the cramped living room of their house, listening anxiously to the confusing things the man had to say. They weren't happy about any of it, not about what they were hearing, not about discussing business on a Sunday.

"I do not understand," said Sven, frowning. "How does that affect us and our family? We have work, all of us, and we have a good place to live. We can promise a home to our mother, our sisters, our brother. You said you could promise them work, that they could work off the rest of their passage."

The man rolled his eyes to the ceiling. "One more time! The government won't let any immigrants in unless they're guaranteed not to be a burden to real Americans."

"We know that, *ja*. But they would not be a burden, our family. They can all work hard, even little Erick."

"Maybe so. But they can't work if there aren't any jobs, can they? And the way things are with coal, it could be months before Mr. Vanderhoof can find them work. Your little brother—he's not old enough to work in the mines, is he?"

"He is eleven years old," said Gudrun. "Farmwork he can do. Factory work he can learn. But we would never allow him to work in a mine."

"Might not have a lot of choice when he gets a bit older, but eleven's a little young."

"There are no coal mines here, Mr. Andrews," said Sven, his large, square hands resting firmly on his knees. "Erick will not work in the mines."

"Who said anything about here? We said we'd bring your family to America. We never said South Bend, not for certain. They might have to work their way west, same as everybody else, and the boy'll work where he's told. But there's no point in talking about it right now, anyway. We just can't do anything until these strikers come to their senses."

Suddenly Sven stood, pushing back his chair with a harsh scrape. He towered over Mr. Andrews; his face was dark with anger.

"Sir, we will talk about this another time. Our family is in trouble just now. Our sister is lost. Now you say our mother, our brother, our sisters must wait yet more months to come to America. This is too much bad news for us. You will go now."

"Sure, anything you say." The smaller man stood and backed away. "It's your family, not mine. Do as you like."

"It is also our money, Mr. Andrews."

"Sure, sure!" He waved genially as he left the house, but with a nervous look back at Sven, looming in the doorway.

Gudrun and Freya looked at each other.

The two sisters didn't always get along. Freya resented Gudrun's domination; Gudrun found Freya's frivolity maddening. But they understood each other very well, and now the wordless communication that passed between them was one of complete accord.

Gudrun rose and smoothed her Sunday skirt. "Come, Freya.

We are upset. A walk will do us good."

Sven looked from one to the other. "It is cold. And rainy. Today you wish to walk?"

"We will change our clothes, but yes, we wish to walk. I will make some coffee for you."

When Gudrun spoke in that tone, even Sven obeyed. He shrugged and left the women to their own mysterious ways.

The two of them changed clothes in record time. Gudrun put a pot of coffee on the big black range and fetched two umbrellas from the stand.

"Do not," she instructed Sven, "allow the pot to boil dry. We cannot afford a new one, and it may be some time before we return. Come, Freya."

Hilda tried to struggle to her feet, but the effort was beyond her. Her head swam with the slightest movement and star bursts glittered out of the absolute darkness that enveloped her. Her stomach hurt more than she could ever remember.

But she could remember little. She no longer knew why she was imprisoned. Sometimes she forgot who she was.

Only her will remained intact. For some reason that she had now forgotten, it was important to follow this string she held, follow it back to its beginning. So follow it she would. Crawling slowly, so slowly, winding the muddy lace on her wrist as she went, she reached, after a period of time, the water jug.

Ah, yes. That was why she had to return. To drink. She could not lift the heavy jug, but it was filled brimful and overflowing. She let her head hang over it and lapped like a small, forlorn dog.

Though her prison was damp and chilly, it was stuffy. The cold water refreshed her momentarily, cleared her mind enough that she remembered there was something else she had to do—yes, of course. She had to go in the other direction. Follow the wall—somewhere.

Something about a door.

Yes. A door. A way out.

She took another drink and then crawled in what she hoped was the direction of the wall.

She hadn't gone far before she was brought up against an obstruction. Exploring it blindly with her fingers, she felt a different texture. This surface wasn't brick, it was wood.

A wall? Would she have to turn around, try one direction or the other back at the corner?

It wasn't until her questing fingers felt cold metal and traced its shape that she realized she had found what she was looking for.

The metal, her muddled mind was nearly sure, was a hinge. This was a door.

Trembling, she stood and moved her hands across the surface, feeling for a knob, or a latch, or . . .

Her fingers closed on a knob, a plain metal doorknob. She couldn't remember quite why she should feel so pleased, but she tried to turn the knob. Her muddy hands slipped on the smooth metal, so she caught up the hem of her skirt and used it.

The knob still wouldn't turn.

Gradually the fact penetrated Hilda's dimmed consciousness.

The door was locked.

She sank to the floor in a faint.

# 20

I once was lost, but now am found / Was blind, but now I see.

—John Newton, "Amazing Grace," 1779

NORAH had not felt like going out that Sunday afternoon. On a usual Sunday she would sleep late, dash to the latest possible Mass, and spend the rest of the day with her family or her current beau.

But nothing about this day was normal. She'd awakened early after a restless night and gone, for once, to an early Mass. She'd hoped the soothing routine would provide some comfort, but Hilda's face kept coming between her and her attempts at prayer.

None of her family or close friends were at church so early, so she was able to hasten out with little conversation. Stopping at her mother's house, she claimed a headache and said she wouldn't be there for Sunday dinner. Her mother had looked at her sharply. Norah didn't get headaches. But she'd escaped and returned to Tippecanoe Place, where she'd raided the pantry for a cold meal—she'd had no breakfast, and the cook took Sundays off, too—and then brooded.

Hilda had been missing for a day and a half now. She had left St. Patrick's rectory sometime before midnight Friday night, and never reached home.

The distance was only a little over two blocks, straight down Taylor Street from the Studebakers' back drive.

Norah had walked those two blocks twice today, once on the way to Mass and once on the way home. Both times she'd studied the sidewalk, the lawns, the street, as if she could somehow conjure up a vision of what had happened to Hilda.

But there was nothing. If there had ever been footprints, cigar ash, telltale scraps of paper or cloth (Norah had read some of the Sherlock Holmes stories), there was nothing now. Rain for a solid twenty-four hours had obliterated any traces there might have been. Neither close observation nor Norah's sheer force of will could make these mute surroundings speak.

So she retired to the servants' room of Tippecanoe Place, put some more coal on the fire, and then sat and ruminated for what seemed like hours.

The great house was very quiet. Everyone except the butler was out, and he had decided for once to take a proper nap upstairs in his room instead of falling asleep over a book in his favorite overstuffed chair downstairs.

Where was Hilda?

She had left the rectory for home and never arrived there. She could have been taken anywhere.

Norah tried to picture the scene. It's very dark. There are no streetlights closer than Washington Street, and the lights, gas or electric, in nearby houses have all been turned out. The moon is obscured by the clouds that will soon bring rain.

The hour is late, so the neighborhood is quiet. Everyone has settled down to sleep. The locusts and crickets keep up a steady rhythm, but there are no human noises save Hilda's quiet footfalls as she turns toward home. Oh, there is a murmur of voices, perhaps, as Mr. and Mrs. Malloy leave the rectory a few minutes after Hilda. Then the sound of their carriage wheels, their horses' hooves, on the brick pavement.

Is there the sound of another carriage, the one that's come to take Hilda away?

Does someone notice these sounds, unlikely at this time of night and unwelcome when a person's trying to sleep? The night is stiflingly warm, so the windows are open.

Mrs. Malloy might remember hearing another carriage. Or she might not. She was very concerned about her husband. It was something for Patrick to ask, at least, though just what use the information might be, Norah didn't know.

Norah herself could go and ask the neighbors. Yes, and get herself snubbed for her pains! These were well-to-do people, for the most part. They'd likely not welcome a nosy maid on their doorsteps on a lazy, rainy Sunday afternoon. Hilda could sometimes get away with that sort of thing, but she possessed a dogged persistence that Norah did not.

Moreover, the police had probably already asked those questions. They might not be frantically concerned about a missing servant, and an immigrant at that, but to even the meanest intelligence it was obvious that Hilda's disappearance was intimately connected with Mr. Bishop's death and Mr. Malloy's abduction, and the police were certainly concerned over those matters. Yes, they'd be looking for Hilda, if only to try to implicate her in the crimes.

Norah shifted restlessly in her chair. Her head was beginning to ache in earnest; it pounded with a dull rhythm that she could almost hear.

There ought to be a way to find Hilda. She, Norah, knew her better than anyone except perhaps Patrick. Certainly better than her family, who spent far less time with her than did Norah.

Some of Norah's family, the ones who'd been born in Ireland, had "the sight," or so they'd always said. Norah was a good daughter of the Church and scorned superstition, but she'd heard the tales of the little people, of the old women who had to be kept happy or your cow would stop giving milk, your hens would stop laying. She crossed herself hurriedly. She didn't believe in such things. Of course not. This was the twentieth century; if there had ever been leprechauns and witches, there weren't any now. On the other hand, she herself had experienced occasional flashes, going to a place for the first time and feeling sure she'd been there before, meeting a person and knowing what they were going to say . . . hmmm. Could it be that she had the gift?

As hard as she could over the pounding of her head, she concentrated on sending a message to Hilda. *Where are you? Tell me where you are. We must find you, Hilda. Where are you?*

Then she tried to empty her mind and listen. No answer formed in her consciousness. There was only the pounding, and silence.

When the silence was broken by a tap at the back door, it startled Norah so much she nearly fell out of her chair. With no one else to answer it, she went herself.

Two women stood at the door, their umbrellas dripping, the hems of their skirts sodden. Norah had never seen them before, but she recognized them instantly. The family resemblance was strong, and they both wore their blond hair in distinctive coronet braids.

"You're Hilda's sisters," she said in a voice that didn't quite hide her astonishment.

"And you, I think, are Miss Murphy," said the elder of the two. "May we come in?"

"Oh. Oh, yes. Sorry, I forgot me manners! It's just that I didn't expect—"

"We have come to talk to you about Hilda. I am Gudrun Johansson; this is my sister Freya."

"Norah Murphy." Norah bobbed a half curtsy. "Come to the sittin' room. There's a fire there; you must be cold."

Gudrun followed Norah, her bearing straight and severe. Freya, trailing behind, looked about her with unabashed curiosity. So this was how the ultrarich lived. The backstairs area, even, was far more luxurious than the house where she lived, or, for that matter, than the much grander house where she worked.

The two Johanssons settled themselves in front of the fire, and an awkward little silence ensued.

Norah's head pounded. She had never expected to meet these two sisters of Hilda's, and she didn't know what to say now that she had. They were not disposed to like her, she knew, and she had no reason to be particularly fond of them, either. But they were, after all, Hilda's family, and Hilda was her best friend. She cleared her throat.

"I suppose you've come about Hilda goin' missin'," she began. "Meself, I've been tryin' all mornin' to think where Hilda might be." She omitted mention of her experiment with telepathy; the very memory of it made her hot all over. Such silliness! "I'm thinkin' somebody might've heard the carriage that took her away, if it was a carriage, but it's likely the police've asked about that." She made a frustrated little gesture with her hands and arms. "It's only two blocks! How could they've gotten away with her in such a short distance!"

Gudrun frowned. "We, too, wonder about that. Miss Murphy, we are a family in distress. We need to find our sister, who is often able to solve problems that others cannot. We have another problem now, one that we will not trouble you with, but Hilda is needed. We thought you might be able to help us."

Even in Norah's agitation, she recognized that last sentence as remarkable—Hilda's family asking her, an Irishwoman, for help. Wisely, she made no comment, but allowed Gudrun to continue.

"Our brother Sven has said that we are not to try to find her, but we have decided that we must. She would do the same for us if— Miss Murphy, has something gone wrong with your furnace? I believe Hilda has said the house has a furnace?"

"Yes, but it's not been fired up yet this fall. What d'you mean, wrong?"

"That noise—I wondered about the radiators. The house where I work, it has a furnace, and sometimes air in the radiators will pound—"

"The pounding! You mean you hear it, too? I thought it was in me head!"

"It is dull, distant, but I hear it. I hear very well, better than most. If it is not the furnace, perhaps someone is working in the cellar—"

Norah stood, her face a little paler than usual. "There's no one else in the house except Mr. Williams, and he's asleep in his room. If there's someone in one of the cellars, it's someone who has no business there."

"Ooh!" Freya grabbed her sister's arm. "Should we get the police? Or maybe the butler?"

"Mr. Williams'd not thank us for wakin' him, and as for the police—the telephone's in Colonel George's office, and he keeps that door locked. I'll go careful, first, and see if we've need of help."

"We will come with you," said Gudrun in her most no-nonsense manner, and Norah didn't argue. The sounds were louder now that she was in the hallway, and she didn't relish the idea of confronting it—whatever it was—alone.

Seizing a candlestick and a box of matches from the mantel, she led the way to one of the many cellar doors.

It took three tries. Twice they listened carefully at the open doors and could hear the pounding noises only faintly, if at all. The third time—

"He's down there!" Norah whispered.

"He?"

"Whoever it is. I'm goin' down!" She lit her candle and descended the stairs, the candlestick in one hand and the railing gripped with the other, a grip that whitened her knuckles. Gudrun and Freya followed close behind.

"What is down here?" Freya breathed, her voice shaking ever so slightly.

"I don't know. Never been down here. Nothin' much, I don't think."

She came 'round the last turn of the stair and held her candle high, Gudrun and Freya so close they trod on her skirt.

"Why—there's nothing!"

There was, indeed, nothing. The room was small and low-ceilinged and contained nothing except dust and a few cobwebs. Someone evidently cleaned down here from time to time, but not often, and Norah could see why. The room was not used for storage, was not, apparently, used for any purpose whatever.

The pounding noise, however, was much louder, and came from—

"A door! Look, over there, there's a door!"

"But—we are underground, are we not?"

"Yes." Norah's voice had risen to a more normal level, with the absence of obvious threat, but it still shook a little. There was a good deal here that Norah didn't understand, and she was still frightened. "Yes, I don't understand what a door's doin' there, I—"

She broke off as the pounding stopped and from behind the door came a voice. Faint, but recognizably human.

"Help! Help me! Oh, *Herre Gud*, someone help!"

# 21

[Sleep is] meat for the hungry, drink for the thirsty . . .
—Miguel de Cervantes, *Don Quixote de la Mancha,*
1605–15

THE rescue had taken a little time. Norah, Gudrun, and Freya had all tried to crowd 'round the keyhole of the heavy wooden door at the same time, shouting to Hilda, weeping, each giving instructions which the others ignored.

It was Gudrun who, in the end, sorted things out. She thrust the others aside and knelt to the keyhole.

"Hilda, there is no key here," she said in slow, careful Swedish, as one might speak to a child. "We will find one, or we will chop the door down if we must. I will stay here and talk to you while Freya and Norah go for help."

She left Freya to translate that for Norah. The two sped up the stairs, leaving Gudrun in the dark uttering soothing, comforting words to Hilda, who was sobbing, able to give way now that help was at hand.

Norah had to wake Mr. Williams to ask for the key. He was irritable, but once he understood what was happening, he behaved surprisingly well.

"Hmph! In the old tunnel, is she? However did she get there?"

"I don't know, sir," said Norah tartly, "but the sooner we get her out—"

"Yes, yes, don't nag, girl. I'm coming."

The key, neatly labeled, was in the proper drawer in the butler's pantry. Mr. Williams applied a drop of oil to the key ("That lock's not been used in some years"), picked up an oil lamp, also kept in the pantry should the gas supply fail, and led the way down the steps. Then it was but the work of a moment to unlock the door and release a bleeding and nearly senseless Hilda.

That had been some hours ago. Mr. Williams had helped take Hilda up to her room, even allowing the use of the elevator, unheard of for servants. Then her sisters and Norah had removed her filthy, ruined clothes, bathed her, dressed and bandaged her scarred and cut hands and knees, and put her to bed with a cup of sweet, milky tea. "Food later," Gudrun had decreed. "Broth, perhaps."

While Hilda slept, Norah made a flying trip to Patrick's house with the good news. He, of course, had come back with her and had, under strict chaperonage, been allowed a brief glimpse of Hilda as she lay sleeping, her long blond hair unbraided and lying across her pillow like scattered sunlight. It was just as well, then, that both Norah and Gudrun were present.

Norah had then sent him home with the promise that he could return as soon as Hilda was up and dressed. He left with distinctly mixed feelings, unwilling to leave Hilda but happy to escape Gudrun's palpable disapproval.

Now Hilda was awake and sitting up in bed, eagerly partaking of the rich chicken broth Mrs. Sullivan had provided upon her return to the house. There were even a few noodles in it. Hilda had never eaten anything that tasted so good, though there was far too little of it.

"You can have more later," Norah said, handing the bowl and spoon to Freya, who stood by the bed. "Maybe by then you'll be strong enough to feed yourself."

Hilda made a face. "To be too weak even to hold a spoon! Never have I been weak. I am a strong person, I can do hard work, I—"

"Yes," said Gudrun dryly. She had been so greatly relieved to have Hilda back, and so shaken by her ghastly appearance, that she had been hard put to maintain her air of stolid calm. Now she struggled to reassert her sisterly authority. "We know how wonderful you are, and it is clear that your tongue has taken no harm. What we would like to know is what happened to you."

"Miss Johansson!" Norah was furious. "It's too soon for that! She must get her strength back before—"

"It is all right, Norah," said Hilda. She was tired of being looked after and treated like an invalid. Time to speak up for herself. "I am tired, and soon I will sleep, but now I would like to talk. There is little to tell, though."

She hitched herself up a little higher in her bed; Norah adjusted the pillows. "First, what day is it? How long was I in—that place?" She resisted the urge to shudder, but her voice reflected horror.

"It's Sunday. You went missin' on Friday. And to think you were right here in the house, or almost, the whole time, and we never—"

But Hilda wasn't interested in Norah's speculations. "Yes, and it was Friday when I found Mr. Malloy. Do you know about that? Has the word spread?"

Norah rolled her eyes. "And has Patrick been doin' anythin' else but talkin' to his uncle Dan, tryin' to find out where you might be?"

"That is good," said Hilda with satisfaction, ignoring Gudrun's glare. "Does Mr. Malloy remember anything more about who might have kidnapped him?"

"Not that I've heard. But what about you? Never mind about Dan Malloy, what happened to *you*?"

Hilda sighed. "I do not know. I was afraid Mr. Malloy might not know very much, for I think they did almost the same thing to me and I know nothing of who they were."

She told of starting to walk home and being enveloped in a

blanket, and then knowing nothing more until she awoke in the darkness. "I think they gave me laudanum, or maybe hit me on the head—" She raised a hand to her head and felt it carefully all over. "There is no lump, so it must have been the drug, to make me sleepy and stupid. Not *so* stupid, though. They drugged the water they left for me, just as they did for Mr. Malloy. But I did not drink it."

She readjusted herself. "But what was that place where they put me? It was big, I think. I could not see, it was dark, but I think it was an oddly shaped room for a cellar."

"Not a cellar, a tunnel. I asked Mr. Williams meself."

"A tunnel!"

Norah nodded. "I'd never heard of it before, but Mr. Williams says that Mr. Clem, when he built the house, thought it would be a good idea to have a tunnel to the factory, so that he could get there even if the weather was very bad. Mr. Williams says it's never been used, but he kept the door in working order and the key in the drawer, just in case."

Hilda made a face. "I wish Mr. Clem had never had the idea. It is a horrible place!"

"If they hadn't put you there, it'd have been someplace else. This way we found you, girl. Count your blessin's."

"But how did they get me there? Maybe from the other end—but that is far away."

"I think," said Norah with a sigh, "they just walked in with you, stole the key to the tunnel, and took you down the stairs. The back door was unlocked that night."

"Oh." Hilda tried to think what that meant, but it was too complicated. She yawned. "I will think more later. Now I sleep."

She closed her eyes. Norah and her sisters, with many questions still unasked, left her to her much needed rest.

Hilda woke in the middle of the night, woke at first to panic. Dark, it was dark, she was a prisoner . . . but no, it wasn't really dark. A little light filtered in from the streetlight down on the corner. And she was not a prisoner. She was in her own bed—

"Hilda! Are you all right?"

The voice came from the door. Norah.

"*Ja,* I am all right."

"You screamed. Can I come in?"

Hilda got up and opened the door, and then climbed hastily back into bed. The night was chilly.

"Ooh, you scared me! I heard you scream, and I thought they'd come to get you again!"

"No, I—I do not know why I screamed. I did not even know I had. I had a nightmare, I think. The men were carrying me in the blanket, and I could not breathe, I—"

She shuddered, and Norah, sitting on the edge of the bed, smoothed the bedclothes. "Likely you had the covers pulled up over your face. It's all right. No one could get in, really. The doors are all locked up tight and bolted. Mr. Williams checked three times." Norah yawned. "So if you're all right, I'll get back to me bed. You might lock your door if you're afraid at all."

She started to stand, but Hilda put a hand on her arm. "Norah. How did they know they could get into the house? How did they know about the tunnel? Even I did not know, and I have lived here for five years."

"I wondered, meself. They must've known you were workin' to find Mr. Malloy, an' who you were an' where you worked an' all. They might've reckoned the door'd be left unlocked for you. But the tunnel . . . I'm not thinkin' of any reason they'd take you there."

Hilda lay silent for a moment. Then she sat up. "Norah, I am hungry."

"Hungry! It's two in the mornin', girl!"

"I know. But I had nothing to eat for nearly two days, and then only a little broth, and I am hungry. Hear my stomach; it growls."

Norah sighed and stood. "I suppose I could go down and heat up the broth for you."

"I will come, too."

"Are you sure? Your sisters said you were to stay in bed."

"Gudrun said. She likes to tell people what to do. I do not feel weak anymore and I wish to get up."

"Oh, well . . . we'll have to be *awful* quiet, though."

They put on their wrappers and slippers and tiptoed down the back stairs, stifling giggles. Somehow the kitchen raid had turned into an adventure.

Preparing the broth didn't take long. Mrs. Sullivan had left it on a back burner of the big coal range, keeping warm. The noodles were spread out to dry in the pantry; Hilda helped herself to a large handful and dropped them in the broth.

"You're supposed to cook them before you put them in the soup," observed Norah, moving the pot to a hotter burner.

"I know, but this way they will cook while the soup gets hot. It is quicker, and I am *so* hungry. I will have some bread and butter while they cook."

"I don't know if you'd better. You're not supposed to eat much solid food after you've been fastin'. I heard Dan Malloy got sick as a dog when he tried to eat a good breakfast."

"Mr. Malloy is old, and he had been drugged. I am young and strong and I am not ill, only hungry." She cut a thick slice of bread from a fresh loaf, got the butter from the icebox, and spread it generously on the bread. Norah shrugged and followed suit.

"Norah, I been—I have been—thinking," said Hilda when she had eaten half the slice. "Those men, the ones who took me. They had to be friends of Mr. Clem or Colonel George."

Norah's mouth was full. She raised her eyebrows.

"Yes. Because they knew about the tunnel, knew where to find the key. And I think the men are old friends, too." She took another big bite and went on when she had swallowed. "I think that when the house was new, and the tunnel was new, Mr. Clem probably told people about it, showed it to them. He would have been proud of it then. But as the years went by and the tunnel was not used, he would have forgotten about it."

Norah nodded agreement. "Or else he'd have been embarrassed because it had turned out to be a bad idea."

"Yes, that, too. Mr. Clem did not have very many bad ideas. So he would not have told people in recent years. And I do not think that Colonel George would, either."

The soup was boiling. Norah put in a spoon, tested a noodle, and ladled some out into a bowl for Hilda, who had no trouble at all feeding herself.

She said not another word until she had finished her meal. Then she yawned. "I feel very much better," she announced. "Thank you, Norah."

"It's all very well," Norah grumbled as she cleared away the dishes and began to wash them. The kitchen must show no signs of their indulgences. "*You* don't have to be up in two or three hours to go to work." But it was a good-natured complaint, and she put an arm around Hilda as they headed for the stairs.

When they reached their bedrooms, though, Norah stopped and looked at Hilda. "If they're friends of the Studebakers," she whispered, "what are you goin' to do?"

Hilda shook her head solemnly. "I do not know."

# 22

To work! To work! In Heaven's name! / The wolf is at the door!
> —Charlotte Perkins Gilman, "The Wolf at the Door,"
> 1893

ILDA did not get up with Norah at the usual hour of five-thirty, but by nine she was awake and ready to face the day. She had slept, off and on, for eighteen or twenty hours since she had been rescued, and she felt thoroughly rested. Her hands were still bruised and puffy from beating on the door, but they didn't hurt too much. Her headache was completely gone, and she was once more ravenous.

Some money was tucked carefully under the clock on her bedside table, two dollar bills and a ten. They had found it in her clothes and saved it! She had forgotten all about it, but a wave of relief washed over her. She owed the two dollars to Colonel George and the rest to Mrs. Malloy for the ruined clothes. She would have been hard put to pay the debts out of her wages.

If she still had wages. If she still had a job.

How would Mr. Williams feel about her abduction? Would he believe her story? Even if he did, would he contrive to find something scandalous about the whole matter, something to provide cause for dismissal?

She set her lips tightly and began to dress. Whatever was

coming, it was better to face it as soon as possible.

There were two clean uniforms in her wardrobe. Neither had been mended, she discovered on closer inspection, so they were the ones she had left in the laundry. Mrs. Czeszewski, the laundress, didn't work at Tippecanoe Place on Saturdays. That meant Norah must have laundered these, along with all the rest of her duties. She had also ironed Hilda's good summer dress; it hung in its accustomed place. Hilda brushed away a tear and felt guilty about the things she had said when she was angry.

The third uniform must still be at the Malloys' house. She would have to go and reclaim it, and confess to the destruction of the borrowed clothes.

First, however, came breakfast, and then she would have to talk to Mr. Williams. The thought was almost enough to take away her appetite.

She dressed in one of the uniforms, braided her hair and pinned it atop her head, carefully tucked the money into her pocket, and went downstairs.

Mrs. Sullivan had, of course, discovered that some soup and bread were missing, but she was unusually indulgent about it. She even made fresh porridge for Hilda and boiled an egg.

"And that's as much as you should have for now. No bacon or sausage or fried potatoes. They're too greasy for a touchy stomach."

Hilda's stomach didn't feel at all touchy, just empty, but she meekly complied, remembering what Norah had told her about Mr. Malloy.

As soon as she had finished and washed her dishes, she sought out Mr. Williams, finding him, as was usual at that hour, in his pantry cleaning the silver.

"Ah, Hilda," he said stiffly. "I trust you slept well?"

"Yes, sir." She didn't mention the kitchen foray and hoped Mrs. Sullivan had kept quiet about it, too.

"You are recovered from your—er—misadventures?"

"I think so, sir."

"Very well. Colonel George asked to see you as soon as you were feeling well enough. He is in his office."

She was free to leave. Once out of the butler's sight and hearing, she expelled a long breath. He had not discharged her, had not even scolded her. Perhaps—perhaps he had been told to leave that chore to Colonel George. Why else would the colonel want to see her?

She went upstairs to the office, tucked away in a back corner of the main floor, entered, and curtsied.

"You asked to see me, sir?"

"Yes. Come in and sit down, Hilda."

He indicated a chair. She sat upright on the very edge, her nerves tightened to snapping point.

"Well, it seems that you were right about Dan Malloy and everyone else was wrong. Well done, Hilda."

She flushed a little at the unexpected compliment. "Thank you, sir. I only used common sense. Oh, and, sir, Mrs. Malloy gave me money, so I can return yours." If she was to leave the Studebakers' employ, she would not leave as a thief. She fished in her pocket and pulled out the two dollars. "The money is dirty, sir, I am sorry. It was in my pocket when I was in the tunnel."

"No need to give it back, Hilda. No, no, I insist. After all, it was my tunnel they put you in. I have to take some of the blame. Did you—er—have you any idea who the men were?"

Was it her imagination, or did he have more than a casual interest in her answer?

"No, sir. There were two of them, I think, because I heard them talk to one another. But they spoke in whispers, and I could hear only sounds, not words. And I could see nothing, of course. They put a blanket over me at first, and later there was a cloth over my eyes."

Colonel George made a face, but she thought he looked a little relieved. "I see. Well, I hope you'll be in no more danger. You must be very careful."

"Yes, sir." And, as he said nothing more, "Is that all, sir?"

"Yes. No! Confound it, I nearly forgot. The Malloys would like to see you. They said they could come here any time today."

Hilda was horrified. "Oh, no, sir! I would not put them to

the trouble. I will go there. If I have leave, sir," she added, and waited anxiously for his reply.

"Yes, of course, go if you feel well enough, and then do as you like for the rest of the day. I should think you'll need at least a day off to recover from your—er—privations. Perhaps you could—er—resume your normal duties tomorrow?"

"Yes, sir. Thank you, sir. Shall I go to the Malloys now?"

"If you like. I'll telephone and tell them you're coming. Thank you, Hilda." He turned to pick up the telephone and she escaped.

Her knees shook so badly she had to sit down on one of the five steps that led up to the office. She still had a job! Her life could go back to normal. She was dizzy with relief.

What was more, she was free for the day. Almost guiltily, she left the house by the forbidden porte cochere door. She could enjoy her few hours of freedom from the constraints of servitude, now that she knew she was going back to the security of her accustomed role.

She turned, as she went down the front drive, and looked back at the great stone house. It looked like a castle, almost, with its towers, its carved stonework, its great oak doors. The finest mansion in town, and her home.

If she and Patrick . . . but she didn't want to think about that just now.

This time Riggs was expecting her. "Come in, please. Mrs. Malloy will see you in the parlor." His manner was carefully neutral. Not certain whether he was addressing Hilda the maid or Miss Johansson the employee of the Malloys and rescuer of his master, he took no chances.

Mrs. Malloy was quite certain whom she was addressing. She rose to greet Hilda. "My dear! Are you sure you ought to be out of bed? You've had a terrible time."

Hilda curtsied. "I am well now, madam, thank you. It was not so bad. I was not drugged for so long, so I was not so ill as Mr. Malloy. Is he feeling better now?"

"Fighting fit and full of vinegar. He wants to start campaigning again, but I've made him wait. It isn't decent, what with poor Mr. Bishop hardly cold in his grave."

"No."

A little silence fell.

"Mrs. Malloy—"

"Hilda—"

They spoke at the same moment.

"I am sorry, madam."

"No, go ahead, please."

Hilda took a deep breath. "Madam, I must give you your money back. I worked for you for only two days, and then I ruined your maid's uniform and your underclothing. I am sorry, but the tunnel was dirty, and muddy when the rain came and trickled through the roof, and I tore off the lace to make a safety rope, because I thought I was in a cave, maybe, and I know the things were expensive, this is maybe not enough, but—"

"Child, child, hush! Do you think I care about a ruined petticoat? You keep that money. You earned it, and more. Another day or two, and Mr. Malloy might . . ." Her voice faded for a moment, and then she smiled. "But sit down, child. I don't think you're quite as strong yet as you think you are. There, on that chair."

She sat down herself, her little stool at her feet. "Miss Johansson, I didn't ask you here for an accounting, but to thank you for what you did, and tell you how sorry I am you encountered danger and unpleasantness on our behalf."

"Thank you, but I did little. I wished to solve the problem, to learn who killed Mr. Bishop and kidnapped Mr. Malloy. And I did not, even though they took me, too!"

"You did what I asked you to do. You found my husband for me. For that you have my eternal gratitude, and I believe Mr. Malloy plans to reward you in a more practical way."

"Oh, no, madam, you have given me too much already! I can take nothing more."

Mrs. Malloy looked at her, opened her mouth, and then shut it again. "Very well. I have no wish to embarrass you. Oh, and Agnes has your uniform for you. It cleaned up quite nicely. I suppose you will be resuming your usual duties?"

"Yes, madam, tomorrow. Colonel George has been good enough to allow me the rest of the day off."

"I should think so, after what you've been through. Well, enjoy your day. You've earned it. Get a good rest."

"Thank you, madam. I thought I would go and see Pat—Mr. Cavanaugh."

She could not interpret the look that spread across Mrs. Malloy's face as she offered her hand in farewell.


Patrick was not at the firehouse. The fireman who answered the door didn't know where he was, only that he was not expected on duty until ten o'clock that night. Disappointed, Hilda turned her steps toward home. She didn't dare seek out Patrick at his house; his mother had made her feelings about Hilda quite clear.

She was very tired when she reached Tippecanoe Place, too tired to trudge up the front drive and enter by any forbidden door. Perhaps Mrs. Malloy was right and she was not quite as strong as she thought.

"Hilda!"

Her heart lurched in terror before she saw who it was. He ran to her from the bench by the carriage house where he had sat waiting.

"Patrick! You frightened me!"

"I'm sorry. I came to see if you're all right."

"Only a little tired."

"Then sit down and tell me everything. If you've time, I mean?"

Hilda nodded. "I'm not to go back to work until tomorrow. They want me to rest."

They sat on the bench. "All I know," said Patrick, "is that they found you in the cellar somewhere."

"Not in the cellar. In the tunnel." She told her brief story.

"If I knew who they were, I'd— Ye've really got no idea?"

"No."

"Hilda, I—when I didn't know where you were, I—"

He didn't have to continue. Hilda nodded. "I know."

He was almost afraid to go on. "Hilda, I don't want you to be—to be where I don't know where you are. I don't want that, ever. But—but our families—and your job . . ."

She nodded again, drearily. She knew exactly what he meant, and there was nothing more to be said about it. Nothing to be done, either.

They sat silent. Each had wanted desperately to see the other, but now . . .

Patrick cleared his throat. "I'll see you as usual on Wednesday?"

"Yes. Unless I am expected to work, to make up for the time I have taken off."

"But that wouldn't be fair! You've been workin', you've been a prisoner, they can't—"

"Life is not always fair, Patrick."

He had no answer to that. At last he stood. "Ye're lookin' a bit pale, me girl, and tired. You'd best go and get that rest they promised you. I'll come on Wednesday."

He took her hand. Their eyes met for a moment; then Hilda looked away.

"I will see you then, Patrick, even if I cannot come out with you."

She walked to the basement stairs and down them, Patrick watching until she disappeared from view.

# 23

If nothing occurs to interfere with the resumption of mining . . . the coal famine should be quickly relieved.
    —*The New York Times* (editorial), October 19, 1902

AND so life returned to something resembling normality.
Hilda, fully recovered from her abduction, worked as
hard as she always had, or harder, to make up for lost
time. She stayed far away from the door to one particular cellar
and avoided being alone in the dark. She always locked her bedroom door, and Norah occasionally woke to muted screams
from the next room, but otherwise day succeeded day as they always had.

Hilda and Patrick walked out together on Wednesday and
Sunday afternoons, but the old companionship was gone. Hilda
no longer told Patrick what to do in her dictatorial fashion; they
never quarreled. In fact, they talked little as they walked in the
park through piles of fallen leaves or ate ice cream at the Phila-
delphia, the grand new candy shop and ice cream parlor on
Michigan Street. When they did speak, it was of neutral topics:
Hilda's work, or Patrick's, the comings and goings of the Studebaker family, city events. They strenuously avoided speaking of
their own families or of political matters. The election campaign
proceeded in somewhat muted fashion, Malloy facing no real

opposition, but for Hilda and Patrick, it might as well not have existed at all.

One thing they could talk about was the coal strike, which was growing ever more serious. September gave way to October. With winter coming on soon, there was no settlement in sight. The families with no coal for their furnaces or fireplaces, the owners of small factories with no coal to heat their boilers, grew more and more frantic. In Rochester, New York, residents began chopping down telephone poles for fuel.

Hilda and Patrick talked about it one Sunday afternoon in early October as they sat on the grass in Howard Park and watched the river flow past. It was a perfect Indian summer day. Red and orange and gold leaves drifted down from the oak and maple trees to float on the surface of the water and drift into the dark green shadows under the arches of the Jefferson Boulevard bridge. The sky was a deep blue, without a cloud in sight.

"But winter's comin', sure as we're sittin' here, and what we're to do with no coal, I'm sure I don't know." Patrick pulled up a blade of grass and began to chew on it.

"It is bad," Hilda agreed. "I think it is a terrible thing when the president asks them to agree and they will not."

For the newspapers, the past two days, had reported an abortive meeting called by President Roosevelt in Washington. Mine operators, with George Baer as their spokesman, and union men, led by John Mitchell, had assembled, but the meeting had accomplished nothing. The operators were adamant that they would not talk to "a criminal," as Mitchell was characterized by Baer.

"Things are apt to get worse before they get better," said Patrick gloomily. "There'll be more violence, you wait and see."

"The explosion in Kentucky, that was the worst thing so far. Patrick, the miners need more money and better working conditions, but *nothing* is worth the deaths of so many people."

"It's a war, Hilda, a war between the rich and the poor, and people get killed in wars."

The violence burgeoned, as Patrick had predicted. The National Guard moved in; one soldier shot a miner at Shenandoah.

Trains were wrecked; a bridge was blown up.

The national news occupied so much newspaper space that local news was nearly crowded out, especially old news. Every now and then the *Times* or the *Tribune* would remind readers that the murderer of John Bishop and the abductors of Daniel Malloy still roamed free, but the items grew shorter and less frequent. They never mentioned Hilda's ordeal. Even the Democratic *Times* found the misadventures of a servant less than newsworthy, once they were past.

The Sunday dinners Hilda had with her family were gloomy affairs these days. Hilda had been angry when she was told of the delay in bringing the rest of the family to America, but she hadn't reacted with the fury Gudrun, at least, had expected. Gudrun worried about Hilda a good deal lately.

"You eat nothing," she said the next Sunday as they sat at table. The weather had changed. October, nearing its midpoint, was behaving more like autumn, producing rain and wind. Gudrun had cooked a substantial cool-weather meal. "For you I even made *köttbullar*, your favorite, and you do not eat."

Hilda looked at the savory meatballs in cream sauce that lay untouched on her plate in their bed of homemade noodles. Listlessly, she picked up her fork, cut one of the meatballs, and conveyed a small portion to her mouth. "They are very good, Gudrun, but I am not hungry."

"Never are you hungry! The herring, the good *fruktsoppa*, all your favorites I make, and you push the food around on your plate and hide it under the potatoes. Anyone could break you in two, you are so thin!"

But it takes two to make a quarrel, and Hilda only lowered her eyes and murmured an apology. Gudrun gave up. She knew just how much time Hilda was spending with Patrick these days, and was very much afraid she knew what the trouble was. There were certain subjects even Gudrun was unwilling to broach.

By the next Sunday, however, the situation had changed, for the country and for the Johanssons. Hilda did not meet Patrick immediately after Sunday dinner as usual. Instead, she sat with her family in their tiny parlor, united in hostility toward Mr. Andrews.

"I cannot understand," said Sven, his annoyance in no way hidden by his courtesy. "The strike is over. The workers are to go back to the mines. The factories will work night and day to produce the goods they could not when there was no coal. Why can you not now bring our family here?"

"It's not me, you know, it's Mr. Vanderhoof. He doesn't want to make promises he can't keep, and he doesn't know—nobody knows—when full production will start again. Besides, winter's coming on soon, and the journey's much longer and more difficult in winter, you know. He doesn't want to put anyone on a ship that's going to sink, or make everybody sick in a storm. He cares about you people."

Hilda stood up suddenly and moved to stand before the man, hands on hips and eyes as hard as chips of ice. "I do not believe you, Mr. Andrews. The president himself has settled this strike, he himself has promised that everyone will be back to work soon. We have saved for years, my brother and my sisters and I, we have worked very hard to have enough money to bring our family to be with us here in America. Now your Mr. Vanderhoof has our money, and we do not have our family. I wish to talk to him myself!"

Andrews smiled. "Now, now, Miss Johansson, don't get all upset. This is a complicated arrangement, you know, what with all the government regulations and all the travel arrangements and everything. Your money is safe, and your family'll be here soon. Just be patient."

"I am not patient!"

"Hilda," said Sven with a frown, "I will take care of this matter."

"No, Sven, you must let me say what I have to say. Too long we have been patient. I wish to talk to Mr. Vanderhoof myself. You will tell him, Mr. Andrews, that I come to see him on Wednesday afternoon, at his store."

"Oh, I'll *tell* him. I can't guarantee he'll be there, though. He's got a business to run, and he's a very busy man."

They argued about it after he was gone. For once Gudrun took Hilda's side. "Hilda is right, Sven. Someone must speak to

Mr. Vanderhoof. Maybe to Hilda he will talk, because she is a pretty woman. Some men are like that. You, Sven, you will lose your temper with him, but Hilda maybe can make him tell her the truth."

What she did not say was that she was so happy to see Hilda interested in something again, she'd encourage her to do almost anything. At any rate, Sven capitulated. Hilda might talk to the man. Once. She was to report back to the family, and if further steps were needed, he, Sven, would be the one to take them.

Hilda was still seething when she met Patrick later. The rain that had kept up, off and on, for a week had begun again. It was too wet and chilly for them to walk out, so they sat in front of the fire in the cozy servants' room at Tippecanoe Place, making cinnamon toast to eat with the fresh pot of coffee Hilda had made.

Her appetite had returned with her anger. She dispensed butter and cinnamon sugar with a lavish hand, and took a big bite.

"He has stolen our money, Patrick," she said as soon as she had swallowed. "He has had it for nearly two months, and he has done nothing, nothing! Oh, Patrick, I am so angry I could—could—" She waved her hands in the air; crumbs flew everywhere.

Patrick, too, was glad to see her angry. A quiet, docile Hilda was not the one he knew. But he was nearly as upset as she over her situation.

"It's possible," he said. "I've heard it said he gambles on the horses."

"What's that about horses?" John Bolton walked into the room, bringing a faint smell of the stables with him. He walked over to the fire. "Move over a bit, there's a good girl. I'm wet through. Star cast a shoe while we were out, and I had to find it and then gentle her back home. If someone you know's having something to do with horses, he's a fool."

"He doesn't have to do with them, he gambles on them," said Patrick shortly. He didn't like John.

"Who does?"

"Mr. Vanderhoof, we think," said Hilda, and explained. She

got along well enough with John, though there had been a time when she was wary of him.

"Hmm. Funny you should be talking about him. I saw him today."

"Saw him! Where?"

"I took Star and Nell out for a good run this afternoon. They've not had enough exercise lately, and the rain hadn't started yet. Anyway, we went out south of town, and when Star started going a bit lame, I stopped and checked her feet. There was another carriage there, stopped alongside the road, and I saw Vanderhoof, pacing off a stretch of swampy land."

"But why?"

"Don't know. Didn't pay attention; I was worried about that fool horse."

"How do you know him?" said Patrick suspiciously.

"He runs a harness business, doesn't he? Not that he's there much, anymore, thinks himself too good to man the shop now that's he's made his packet off of it. But I've seen him there now and then. And what's it to you?"

Hilda silenced them both with a frown. "Where was this land, John? South of town, you said?"

"About five miles beyond the end of Michigan Street. Just woods and swamp. Can't imagine what anyone would be doing out there."

"Hmmm. I wonder . . ." The description sounded very much like the land Mr. Malloy had bought for a farm. Of course, Hilda couldn't be sure . . . "John, could you drive me out there?"

"What, now? No. I'm wet and I'm tired, and I told you, Star's missing a shoe. What d'you want to go out there for? There's nothing to see."

Patrick frowned.

"I just—would like to see where Mr. Vanderhoof was. I have an idea."

"What idea?" Patrick sounded petulant.

Hilda ignored him. "Hitch Nell to the small buggy. Or Sterling, if you think Nell's tired."

"It's raining, in case you hadn't noticed, Your Highness."

"Then I will drive. I am not afraid to get wet. John, this is important."

"I'll drive," said Patrick through set teeth, thinking about John and Hilda sitting together on the cramped seat of the buggy.

"You'll not! Drive a Studebaker horse pulling a Studebaker buggy? Not while I'm alive, thank you very much."

Hilda stamped her foot. "Stop quarreling! It does not matter who drives, but, John, you must come to show us the place. And yes, it must be now, for I will have no more time off until Wednesday, and I tell you again, this could be important. Change your wet clothes, if you must, and put on your waterproofs."

John threw up his hands. "I pity any man who marries you, the kind of nag you are." He shot Patrick a look. "You. Come and hitch up the dad-blamed horse while I change, then, if you're so set on helping your precious girl."

# 24

This used to be among my prayers—a piece of land not so very large, which would contain a garden ... and beyond ... a bit of wood.

—Horace, *Satires*, 30 B.C.

PATRICK insisted on going with them. "For if this is so all-fired important, then knowin' you, it's likely to be dangerous, and I'll not let you go alone."

"I would not be alone, Patrick. There is John."

"Huh! Fat lot of use he'd be."

Hilda sighed and said no more. She had no fear of danger, not this time, but she wasn't sorry to have Patrick accompany them. She was worried, and about more than one problem. She sat silent, mentally urging Sterling, the beautiful gray gelding, to a faster pace over the rutted, muddy road.

John pulled on the reins as they approached a wooded area. "Along about here somewhere. Don't know for sure."

"Yes," said Hilda with satisfaction. "I thought it might be. John, do you know who owns this land?"

"Vanderhoof, I'd think, from the way he was looking it over."

"Was anyone with him?"

"Just a coachman."

"Do you not think it strange that Mr. Vanderhoof came out, on a rainy autumn day, to look at another man's woods? Patrick, this land belongs to your uncle Dan. This is the place Clancy showed me."

John and Patrick frowned. Then John shrugged. "No business of mine what kind of fool thing a man wants to do. Maybe Vanderhoof wants to buy it."

"Maybe," Hilda said, considering. "Maybe that is what he wants to do with our money! But I do not think Mr. Malloy would wish to sell."

"There's that," Patrick admitted.

"I mean to find out what Mr. Vanderhoof does—is doing. We can go home now, John."

"And high time, too. A wild-goose chase if ever there was one. And who's going to clean the mud off this buggy, not to mention the horse, that's what I'd like to know!"

He turned the buggy, clucked to Sterling, and set off at a jarring trot that kept Hilda and Patrick silent and clinging to the coachwork all the way home.

After Patrick had grudgingly helped John clean off the mud, he rejoined Hilda in the servants' room. He smelled of the stables and there was mud on his Sunday suit. He wore a scowl, and Hilda, for once, chose to placate him.

"Come, Patrick, come to the laundry and I will clean your suit and your boots. I am grateful that you came with me today."

He allowed her to brush and sponge for a few minutes. Then he laid a hand on hers, halting the brush.

"It's all right. Me mother'll finish."

"She would not be happy that you got your good clothes dirty. I will do it. Turn around." She went on with her work. "If you had to tell her that you were with me when it happened, she would be *very* unhappy."

"I've had a talk with me mother."

Hilda froze.

"What did you say?" she asked finally, in a voice so different from her own that Patrick turned to see her expression.

"I told her I'd walk out with whoever I wanted to, that this was America, where things were different."

Hilda swallowed. "And what did she say?"

Patrick shrugged. "Not much. She didn't like it, but what could she do? You're a kind of heroine to the family, you know, ever since you found Uncle Dan and got into such trouble about it yourself. Mother is— Oh, it's pride, Hilda! She'd like you fine if she'd let herself, but she can't forget you're Protestant and you're me—the lady I like best. She's so everlastin' afraid we might—might marry one day."

It was the first time the word had been spoken between them. Their eyes met and held for a long moment before Hilda's were lowered.

"We cannot . . ."

She stopped speaking. Patrick held his breath.

"We cannot talk about it now, Patrick. I am worried about other things."

He breathed again, clinging to that word *now*. "Worried about Vanderhoof?" With great effort he managed to make his voice sound ordinary.

"Yes, about why he was at your uncle Dan's land today, and about what he does—is doing—with my family's money."

"I don't think you need to worry he's buyin' land with it. Land doesn't come as cheap as all that. There's forty acres there, you know, and even if it is a bit swampy in spots, it'd go for a good two hundred dollars."

"Yes, and he has four hundred of our good dollars!"

She clapped a hand to her mouth. Mr. Andrews had always insisted that they keep the amount of money a secret—"If you won't keep it in a bank, at least don't spread it around that you have all that at home. Not everybody's honest, you know." And Sven had agreed that it was a sensible precaution. Now she had divulged the secret! Surely, though, it didn't matter so much now, when the money was gone anyway.

But Patrick was looking at her with astonishment. "Four hundred dollars? Have you gone mad, girl?"

Something in his tone frightened her. "What do you mean?"

"I mean that passage for the likes of us costs about twenty, twenty-five dollars. Didn't you know that? Your family's been charged four times too much!"

The blow, on top of everything else she had endured in the past few weeks, undid her. Tears began to roll down her cheeks. They became sobs that she was powerless to stop. Patrick, frightened, supported her, led her back to the servants' room, pushed her onto the sofa. Still she sobbed uncontrollably, while Patrick stood helpless, patting her hand.

"Saints alive, what've you *done* to her?" Norah stood in the doorway, shocked.

"I don't know, she just—fell to pieces."

"Ice. Get some from the icebox, crush it up fine, and wrap it in a damp towel. Quick!"

Norah tried to soothe Hilda until Patrick came back with the ice pack, then took it and clapped it to the back of Hilda's neck. Hilda yelped and tried to push it away, but Norah persisted until the sobs had turned to hiccups and Hilda, exhausted, was persuaded to lie down on the sofa.

Norah sat with a sigh of relief and tossed the sodden towel to Patrick. "Here, throw out what's left of the ice an' hang the towel over a rack to dry. Then come back an' tell me what in the world's goin' on."

When Patrick returned and tried to explain, he was at a loss. "I told her she'd been cheated on the price to bring her family here. She was already thinkin' they'd been robbed of the money, for Vanderhoof's taken it and there's no sign of her family comin'. But I don't know why she went so—so—"

"It is the last thing," came a choked voice from the sofa. "The thing—what do you say when one extra thing is more than you can bear?"

"The straw that broke the camel's back?" hazarded Norah.

"Yes. And it is not a straw. All our money!" The sobs threatened to begin again.

"Now, then, you'll not get anywhere with that." Norah spoke with the privilege of long friendship. "I'd think you'd have more spunk, girl! Stop that bawlin' an' let's figure out what you're to do about it. You want me to make some tea? Or coffee, you're always pinin' for coffee."

Hilda sat up, sniffled, and wiped a hand across her face.

"Not the kind of coffee you make. I will do it."

Patrick and Norah winked at each other. The real Hilda was back.

They sat over Hilda's good, strong coffee and tried to make sense of the tangle.

"First of all, you need to know who it is that's taken the extra money," said Patrick. "Is it Andrews or Vanderhoof?"

Hilda thought about that. "It is Mr. Andrews who has always come to see us, but he is only an agent for Mr. Vanderhoof, and a little afraid of him, I think. I do not think he would dare steal the money."

"How would he know? Vanderhoof, I mean. If Andrews told you a tale about how much it was goin' to cost, an' it was way more than it should be, he could have just taken the extra, given Vanderhoof the real price, and nobody's the wiser."

Hilda shook her head. "I do not think he would do that. There would be too much danger that someone would say something to Mr. Vanderhoof one day. Because I think it is not just us, our family, that he has treated this way. He has helped many immigrants to bring their families to America. Helped," she added, with a bitter note in her voice.

Patrick had heard anger from her, many times. He had heard laughter and tears, mischief and affection, indignation and approval and conceit and discouragement, but never before bitterness.

Hilda had grown wise to the world, and Patrick was saddened beyond measure. Something precious was gone forever.

"What're you goin' to do about it?" It never occurred to Norah that Hilda would do nothing.

"I do not know. I must think. I do not understand about the land."

"What land?" Norah asked, and the whole thing had to be explained to her.

"I don't see what that's got to do with anythin'," she said, finally. "If he's stolen your money, what do you care what he's doin' with it?"

"Because it is Mr. Malloy's land. I like your uncle Dan, Patrick. He and Mrs. Malloy have been good to me."

Unlike the rest of me family, thought Patrick, with his own bitterness, but he did not speak.

"And I am afraid," Hilda went on, "that maybe Mr. Vanderhoof tries—is trying—to steal Mr. Malloy's land. If he is a thief in one way, perhaps he is in other ways, too."

"Hmmm. Maybe he was the one who sold the land to Uncle Dan in the first place."

"But then why— Oh, it is foolish!" She put her coffee cup down on its saucer with a thump that would have cracked any but the heavy crockery used by the servants. "It is no good to guess. I must know. And I will begin with Clancy Malloy."

"Clancy?" said Patrick with a frown.

"Oh, do not look that way! I have told you again and again that I do not like Clancy and he does not like me. I do not wish to talk to him, but I must. Your uncle Dan is too busy with his campaign to talk to me, and Clancy was the one who actually bought the land for his father. He will know who sold it."

Patrick was almost satisfied, but he still didn't like the idea of Hilda and Clancy together. "I've got a better idea. Why don't I ask him? It's nearly sundown, you couldn't get over there and back in time, an' the next chance you'd have wouldn't be till Wednesday. I can go there now, chase him down if he's not home, and get the facts you want. If it's not too late by the time I find him, I can even leave a note for you this evenin'. First thing in the mornin', for sure."

Hilda, for once, agreed to the sensible suggestion and sent Patrick on his way. As she climbed the many stairs to her bedroom, she admitted to herself that she was grateful to Patrick. She had no wish to talk to Clancy. She had a headache from weeping, not one of her worst headaches, but bad enough. She was weary and disillusioned and wished only to be done with the matter, to have her family's money back, to have—she realized with sharp longing—to have her mother there for comfort. None of those things seemed likely to happen soon.

She napped briefly and woke with her head feeling better but her spirits unrefreshed. Supper, she thought. Maybe some of her weight of gloom was due to hunger.

She went downstairs and was greeted in the kitchen by the butler, who handed her a note.

"That young man of yours gave it to me," he said with a sniff. "He wanted to come in and talk to you, but of course I couldn't allow that, so he wrote the note. I hope, Hilda, that you have not misunderstood your position in this household. Merely because you were given a brief leave of absence does not mean—"

But Hilda had ceased to listen. Patrick's note read:

> *Dear Hilda,*
> *I must talk to you as soon as you can get away from that fool of a butler. I'll wait outside until I have to go on duty at ten. This is urgent!*

# 25

I can resist everything except temptation.
—Oscar Wilde, *Lady Windermere's Fan,* 1892

THE urgent news that Patrick had to convey was so startling that Hilda could not at first take it in.

"He doesn't *own* the land?"

"Hush! You'll bring Mr. Williams out here if you yell like that."

They were seated on the stone bench by the carriage house, huddled in their cloaks, little protection against the soft, steady rain.

"Tell me again. Start at the beginning. I did not understand."

"The way Clancy tells it, Uncle Dan'd been wantin' that land for a long time. Clancy never could see it, it bein' swampy an' all, but Uncle Dan was determined, if he could get it for the right price. Well, he finally got the owner, Mr. Matthews—don't know him—beaten down to what Uncle Dan thought was reasonable. But he—Matthews—said Uncle Dan'd have to buy right away, and me uncle was goin' out of town for a couple of weeks. So he got the money from the bank an' gave it to Clancy to close the deal."

"Yes, yes, that I understand, but then?"

"Well, what happened then was that Clancy turned thief, nothin' more nor less than that, though I'm sorry to say it of me own cousin. There was a horse he had his eye on, so he just took the money and bought the horse. Uncle Dan wasn't goin' to be back to town for a while, an' he didn't plan to clear the land right away, anyway. Clancy reckoned he'd make the money back, runnin' the horse an' bettin' on it. Then he could buy the land an' nobody'd ever know.

"Trouble was, o' course, the horse kept losin', an' so did the other horses Clancy bet on. He's deep in debt now, an' Uncle Dan still doesn't know about the land, an' Clancy, he's scared stiff."

"Why did Clancy tell you this? I would think he would be afraid to say anything to anybody."

"I told him if he didn't tell me the truth, I'd go and ask Vanderhoof. He didn't like that idea. An' I can still beat Clancy in a fair fight if I need to, an' he didn't like the idea of that, neither."

Hilda didn't much care, herself, for the idea of Patrick fighting with Clancy. No matter who won, both were bound to get hurt. And fistfights weren't a civilized way to settle anything. She kept those thoughts to herself and said only, "I still do not understand what Mr. Vanderhoof has to do with the land."

"I don't either, but I've got an idea. An' tomorrow mornin', soon as I get off duty, I'm goin' to check it out."

"What? What is your idea?"

"I think Vanderhoof bought that land from Matthews."


A note arrived for Hilda just before noon the next day. "I was right. I checked the deed. I think you need to talk to Vanderhoof, but I want to go with you. Come out at five and we'll talk."

Hilda and Patrick had had unauthorized meetings before at times when she was, strictly speaking, on duty. They had found a good place to do it, a niche where they could not be seen from any vantage point inside the house.

They had to keep it brief.

"When did your family pay over the money to Andrews?" Patrick asked without preamble.

"The middle of August."

"The deed to the land was transferred on the twenty-second."

"Oh." Hilda's voice was bleak. "Then it is true. I had hoped, maybe . . ."

"We still don't know for certain, but it's likely."

"How much did the land cost? He might still have enough left—"

Patrick shook his head at the note of renewed hope in her voice. "Ah, me girl, if he's a thief he'll have spent it all. Not on the land. It cost him nearly two hundred dollars, about what I thought. But there'd be plenty of other things to spend it on. He's a gambler, for a start. I told you, I've seen him at the tracks.

"No, your money's gone, Hilda, if things are the way we think they are. But if Vanderhoof's a thief, it's our business to see him in jail where he belongs."

"We are immigrants, Patrick." Her voice was spiritless again. "He is a big, important businessman, he had important friends, in politics even . . . we have no chance . . ."

"Now what's the sense of talkin' like that? I'm a citizen now, an' you will be soon, an' we both got our rights. Me uncle Dan'll help, too, see if he doesn't. But first we've got to know the truth. So we'll go see Vanderhoof on Wednesday afternoon."

Hilda smiled a little. "Yes, Patrick," she said with unaccustomed meekness.

She did a good bit of thinking between Monday and Wednesday, and when she met Patrick after lunch she was full of apprehension.

"Patrick. I am not a fearful woman, am I?"

"You! You're the bravest woman I've ever known, even countin' me mother."

"But I am afraid now, Patrick. What will Mr. Vanderhoof say if we accuse him of being a thief?"

"Ah, but we won't accuse him of nothin', not at first, anyway."

"We will not?"

"No. We'll go in, an' you'll say you're worried 'cause your family's not been brought here yet. An you'll say you've heard of a way they could maybe come a little cheaper than what he's chargin'. Pretty it up a little, say you know they won't be so comfortable, but you don't want for them to spend another hard winter in Sweden. An' can you please have your money back, except o' course for any he's had to spend for his trouble. You'll be real polite. An' then we'll see what he says."

"I will want to spit at him."

"An' me, too, but we won't, not to begin with. You catch more flies with honey than with vinegar, me mother says. An you're the best liar I've ever known."

He said it as a compliment, and Hilda took it as such. She took his hand, briefly, and smiled at him, a smile so like her old self that his knees turned to rubber and he nearly stumbled.

Things did not, however, work out quite the way they had planned. They walked quickly in the crisp autumn air to the harness shop, a large, impressive business on South Main Street, and Patrick asked for Mr. Vanderhoof. The man at the counter looked superior.

"Mr. Vanderhoof does not see anyone without an appointment."

"I have an appointment," said Hilda, remembering just in time to sound subservient. "I am Miss Johansson. I asked Mr. Andrews to tell Mr. Vanderhoof I wished to see him this afternoon."

"Ah, yes, he mentioned something to me. But you see, Mr. Vanderhoof is out of town."

"When will he be back?"

"I couldn't say. He is in Chicago on business. He's a very busy man, as I'm sure you know."

Well, that seemed to be that. Hilda and Patrick looked at each other; Patrick shrugged.

"I'll be comin' in every day or so," he told the clerk, "tryin' to make an appointment. Or I might send me uncle. Dan Malloy, you might have heard of him."

They turned away, but not before noting and appreciating the change in the young clerk's expression.

"Drat!" said Patrick when they had left the building.

"Yes. But we will try again— Patrick!"

She clutched his arm.

"What? What's wrong?"

"That delivery van, Patrick!"

"Yes, it's one of Vanderhoof's. But what—?"

"I saw it at the fair, Patrick. From the balloon. I could not read the lettering on the sides from up there, but I know it was this van, or one just like it. It was behind the grandstand."

"Well, we saw him at the fair, remember?"

"But he would not go there in a delivery van, Patrick, not a rich man like him who has a carriage."

"Oh. Well, I suppose he had a delivery to make. Maybe part of the harness for one of the racehorses gave way and they had to get a new—rein or whatever it was—in a hurry."

"I saw it not long after you went away with Clancy," Hilda continued, as if Patrick had not spoken. "And I noticed it because the horse, the horse drawing the van, I mean, was very upset. Why was it upset, Patrick?"

Patrick took her arm and drew her away, across the street. When they were too far from the shop to be overheard, he said, very close to her ear, "Are you sayin' what I think you're sayin'?"

"I am saying only that something happened in that wagon that made the horse very nervous. In Sweden once I saw a horse act that way, wild, out of control. It was at butchering time. The horse had smelled fresh blood."

"A horse'll act up over any little thing."

"I know that! I am not stupid!"

"Then stop shoutin' at the top of your lungs!" he said in a furious whisper.

"And you, you will stop telling me what to do and think!"

They glared at each other, but after a moment Patrick realized Hilda was no longer looking at him, but at something she was seeing in her mind.

"Patrick. You told me you thought Mr. Malloy was taken away in a closed wagon."

"Yes—oh! Hilda, you don't think—"

"Yes. It would be about the right time."

"All right, then. If we're not both mad—wait, let me just work this out. Let's see. Bishop is killed."

"In his carriage, perhaps."

"Yes. That would be just after Clancy came to get me. They leave Bishop there while they try to think what to do. Then they see me uncle nosin' 'round, an' they quick bundle him into the wagon. If he was strugglin', that'd make the horse uneasy, right enough."

"Patrick, I am sorry to say this, but why did they not kill him, too?"

"Because they'd seen a way to make him the scapegoat! You said it right from the first—that they'd taken him away to make it look like he'd done it an' run off! Somebody was thinkin' quick, Hilda. They threw a blanket over Uncle Dan, knocked him out, an' took his hat an' coat an' stick. Then they took Bishop under the grandstand—he was already dead, o' course—an' somebody—well—made it seem as if they was killin' him, with somebody watchin.' It was pure luck for them that Father Faherty came along when he did."

"It was dangerous for them, Patrick. If the wrong person had seen them—"

"Well, then, maybe they just planned to leave me uncle's things there. Maybe it was only when Father Faherty came that they decided on their playactin'. He was a witness after their own heart. Nearsighted, too old an' slow to do much, an' as honest as a saint, so everybody'd believe him."

Hilda closed her eyes against the evil image in her mind, and then opened them again. "And it was Mr. Vanderhoof's wagon. Patrick, he is a thief. He is a wicked man. But to do such a—such a savage thing, and to his own candidate. He is an important Republican, Mr. Vanderhoof. Why, Patrick? Why would he kill Mr. Bishop?"

Patrick shook his head.

Hilda groped for an explanation. "You have said you have seen Mr. Vanderhoof in places where there is gambling. Patrick, did you see him making bets at the fair?"

He rolled his eyes. "Hilda, it's over a month gone by, and I was lookin' for me uncle after I left you—an' findin' a dead body, an' all. How do you expect me to remember if I saw one man, with hundreds and hundreds of people all over the place?"

"But if we do not know why, we will never be sure. And until we are sure, and the man is caught, I will still be afraid to go to sleep for the nightmares—"

"Ye're havin' nightmares? Why did you not tell me?"

"I did not want you to worry. It is nothing. I am sorry I said it, but you—"

"And do you really think there's still somethin' to be feared?"

She took a deep breath, and when she spoke, it was quietly enough to please Patrick, if he'd still been worried about being overheard. "Not in the daylight, I do not fear. But when night falls, I remember that someone has killed, and he knows that Mr. Malloy and I might one day remember something. So yes, I am afraid."

"And you never told me that, neither."

"I was ashamed." Now her voice was so low he could scarcely hear her. "I do not wish to be fearful. I told you earlier I feared Mr. Vanderhoof, and now I fear him even more. It must have been his men who put me in that awful place, Patrick. They are Republicans, like the Studebakers. They would know the house, they would have heard about the tunnel, maybe—oh, I wish to be strong and smart, as I used to be, but—"

She made a despairing gesture with her hands and looked down, embarrassed.

Patrick looked at her old summer hat, the straw frayed in one place, the pink ribbon beginning to come unwound, and thought how much he would like to buy her a pretty new one. How much he would like to buy her a little house, furnish it to her liking, take care of her so she would never have to be afraid again . . . and how impossible it all was.

He cleared his throat. "Hilda, I don't like you bein' afraid. And that's maybe one thing I can help you with. I think, before we try to tell the police all this, we need to have a good talk with Clancy Malloy. There's things he's not tellin', an' it's time he did."

# 26

How sharper than a serpent's tooth it is / To have a thankless child!
　　　　　—William Shakespeare, *King Lear*, 1605

C LANCY was not at home, they were informed by Riggs the butler. Hilda looked at him, suspicious of the phrase, and opened her mouth, but Patrick got in first.

"And does that mean he's not here, or he's told you to say that? I can ask me aunt, you know."

Riggs bowed stiffly. "Mr. Clancy is out, Mr. Patrick. I believe he took out his horse. I do not know when he might return."

Hilda grimaced. It was a lovely autumn afternoon, the sky blue, the air cool and bracing—just the sort of day for a long ride. Hilda had never ridden anything but the plodding old workhorse on the farm back in Sweden, but on such rare days as this she had always stayed out for as long as she dared, for pure pleasure. Clancy, with a fine mount under him and no responsibilities at home, might well be out until dusk, by which time she had to be back at Tippecanoe Place.

"Do you know where he went, Mr. Riggs? It is important for us to speak with him."

"I'm sorry, Miss Hilda. I don't know. Out to the country,

probably. He likes to ride hard and fast, and a paved street is no place for that sort of thing. But just where, I couldn't say."

It was hopeless, then. She would have turned to leave, but Patrick spoke.

"Then tell me aunt we're here, if you please. She's here, is she?"

"Yes, Mr. Patrick. If you'll take a seat in the parlor, I'll tell her."

"But, Patrick," said Hilda when they were alone, "we do not need to talk to Mrs. Malloy."

"She might be able to tell us somethin', you never know. But what I want to do is wait for Clancy. He's got to come back sometime."

"I cannot wait until 'sometime.' I must be home by sunset; you know that."

"If Aunt Molly telephones to old Williams, you can stay."

Hilda's eyes grew big with the audacity of it. Then she smiled a little. "Mr. Williams will not be happy to receive such a call."

"And that's throwin' roses at it. But he might as well get used to the idea that things've changed, an' you're somethin' more than just a servant now."

Mrs. Malloy, entering silently as usual, saw the smile Patrick got in return for that, and sighed inwardly. There was trouble ahead for these two, sure as the blessed saints. Such children they were, thinking they could change the way the world spins.

She coughed gently to announce her presence. They stood hastily. She put her face up to Patrick's to be kissed and nodded graciously to Hilda, who curtsied.

"What a pleasant surprise, dear," she said sweetly. "And, Miss Johansson, I'm always glad to see you."

Hilda, supersensitive to nuances from Patrick's family, flushed a little. "I would have sent you a note, madam, to ask if I might come, but it is Mr. Clancy we wished to talk to."

"And as he isn't home, we thought we'd spend a little time with such a charmin' lady as yourself, Aunt Molly."

She smiled and shook her head. "Oh, sit down, the pair of you, and, Patrick, don't you go wasting your blarney on me, who's heard it from the time you could talk. What is it you need from Clancy this time?"

That, thought Hilda, was for Patrick to answer. She could hardly tell Clancy's mother that he was suspected of knowing a good deal more than he had said about the Bishop-Malloy affair. And though she was as proficient a liar as Patrick had said, she couldn't lie to his aunt Molly, a lady for whom she had the most profound respect.

And one who would detect a lie before it was well out of someone's mouth.

Patrick, fortunately, had enough good sense to realize that himself.

"Ye'll not like what we have to say," he began, all the beguilement gone from his manner.

Mrs. Malloy seemed to stiffen, to draw herself in, to harden. "If it's about what happened to poor Mr. Bishop, and to Mr. Malloy, I've not liked anything about it from the first. Tell me."

"We think Clancy knows some things he's not told."

"And why do you think that?" She wasn't going to help them, but she wasn't going to give way, either.

"We know that Clancy has lied about—about something else, and it has to do with Mr. Vanderhoof somehow. You know, the harness shop?"

"I know. What is it that my son has lied about?" Her voice was like ice.

"He—he never bought that land for Uncle Dan."

"The farm? Of course he did. Mr. Malloy gave him the money, and Clancy—"

"Clancy bought his horse with it, Aunt Molly. I'm sorry. He told me so himself."

She seemed scarcely to breathe, she sat so still.

Hilda saw her knuckles whiten on the arms of her chair. Her mouth worked. Finally she said, "And Mr. Vanderhoof? What has he to do with this?"

"All we know for certain is that Vanderhoof bought the land

Uncle Dan wanted. And Hilda saw one of the vans from the harness shop at the grandstand at the fair."

"And you wish to ask Clancy more about that day."

"Yes, madam," said Hilda quietly. "I am sorry to distress you, madam."

"Very well. You may wait here until he returns." Mrs. Malloy stood, slowly, painfully. She seemed to have grown much older in the few minutes they had sat talking. "You will excuse me. I will see that some refreshment is brought to you."

Hilda and Patrick stood politely until she had left the room.

"I couldn't ask her to call Mr. Williams," said Patrick. "Not after that."

"No. It does not matter. He will be angry, but I do not care. It is such a little thing, compared to . . . Patrick, it is not fair! She is a good woman, and she should not suffer so!"

"An' aren't you the one told me life isn't always fair?"

They waited. Riggs, silently reproving, brought a tray with tea and cookies. They drank the tea and crumbled the cookies. Somewhere a clock struck the quarters, one dragging slowly after another.

Riggs came to light the fire in the parlor and remove the tray. "Mrs. Malloy asks me to say that she is sorry she cannot rejoin you. She has a headache."

Patrick stood and faced him. "Ye don't have to put on the act with me, you know. You smacked me backside more than once when I was a lad givin' you grief, and I can see you'd like to do it now. I know well enough what's wrong with Aunt Molly, and I know you think it's my fault. Man, I only told her what the trouble was, I didn't cause it."

"No, Mr. Patrick," said Riggs, looking almost human for once. "I don't blame you. I've known well enough there was trouble coming from that quarter, if you'll excuse my saying so. I'm only sorry that Mrs. Malloy's having to bear the brunt of it."

"Where's me uncle, then?"

"He is going straight from the store to a campaign meeting. I thought it best not to disturb him, but if you think I should telephone—"

"No. Bad news'll keep. Make the call if Aunt Molly tells you to, but not otherwise."

"Yes, Mr. Patrick. Can I get you anything else, sir? Miss?"

"We're not hungry, thanks. But, Riggs, when Clancy comes home, tell me aunt, will you? I'll feel better if she's here when we talk to him. "

Riggs inclined his head and left with the tray.

"You think he will tell the truth if Mrs. Malloy is here?"

"More likely, wouldn't you say?"

Hilda sighed. "Yes, I suppose that is true, but it will be hard for her."

They were silent. The clock ticked. The shadows in the parlor lengthened. Riggs came in again, drew the draperies, turned on the electric lamps, stirred the fire, and departed.

"It is odd, Patrick. I been—have been—thinking. Here in this house you are a member of a family with a butler. You are waited on; you are 'Mr. Patrick, sir.' At Tippecanoe Place you are a friend of a servant and Mr. Williams tells you what to do."

Patrick nodded. "And at home I'm one of seven kids, all doin' me mother's biddin', and not much money to spare. At the firehouse I'm just like anyone else. This is America, me girl. There's classes here, like everywhere else, but here they've got all mixed up, and they've got nothin' to do with whether your grandfather had a title or whether he took his cap off to someone with a title. Here a man can work hard and earn money and make somethin' of himself.

"That's the only hope we've got, Hilda, you and me. Maybe we won't always be fireman and servant. Maybe—"

"We will still be Protestant and Catholic, Patrick. And our families will still not like each other."

"Aunt Molly likes you, and Uncle Dan. And your sisters came to Norah for help in finding you. Cracks are beginnin' to open, Hilda. If we can be patient—"

They both heard the front door open. There was a murmur: Riggs's voice.

"Yes, well, tell them they've had a wait for nothing. I've been riding and I intend to have a hot bath and change clothes, and then I'm going out for dinner."

Another murmur. "Mother! Why does she— Oh, all right! But I've still got to change."

"Clancy, you will come now, please."

It was Mrs. Malloy's voice, as unyielding as marble.

"But, Mother! I stink of horse!"

"You do. You've ridden that horse too hard, as usual. But there are worse smells. Come, Clancy."

Unwillingly, uneasily, Clancy entered the parlor, followed by Mrs. Malloy.

Now that the moment had come, Hilda was feeling very awkward. She knew what she wanted to ask Clancy, but the presence of his mother was inhibiting.

Perhaps Mrs. Malloy felt Hilda's apprehension, for she took matters into her own hands. "Patrick has told me something I would not have believed from anyone else, Clancy."

Clancy shot Patrick a look of loathing. Mrs. Malloy continued. "Perhaps you would care to explain to me why you stole your father's money to buy a horse."

"I—it wasn't like that, Mother. I borrowed the money, only until I could win enough—I thought Gladiator was a really good horse, just what I wanted, but he's turned out not quite fast enough, or he needs a better trainer—I would have paid the money back as soon as he started winning, I—"

"I see. You knew how much your father wanted that land, you knew that the purchase had to be made quickly, and you chose to spend the money elsewhere. The result is that the land has been lost to another purchaser, Mr. Vanderhoof."

Clancy went white; Hilda thought he was going to faint. "Vanderhoof bought that land? He never told me—"

"I think," said Patrick, "we need to know just what your dealings with Vanderhoof are. We already know the man's a crook. He's stolen Hilda's money, the money she and her brother and sisters saved to bring their family here from Sweden. It's the trick of a dirty scoundrel, and if you know any more about him, we need to hear it."

Mrs. Malloy, as implacable as a Greek mother in one of the ancient tragedies, continued. "You said, Clancy, that Mr. Vanderhoof didn't tell you he'd bought the land. He knew, then, something about it. He knew you had betrayed your father's trust. Perhaps he promised not to tell in return for—for what, Clancy?"

# 27

As to what are called the masses, and common men—there are no common men. All men are at last of a size.
—Ralph Waldo Emerson, *Representative Men,* 1850

THERE was a long silence. Clancy's glance darted from one to another of his listeners. He moistened his lips.

"I didn't know anything, not really!" he finally said. "I—I just saw him there, at the fair. Later, when there was trouble, he told me he didn't want to be involved, and if I'd keep my mouth shut, he'd keep his shut about the land. I don't know how he knew, I—"

"When did you see Mr. Vanderhoof at the fair?" Hilda's voice was almost as hard as Mrs. Malloy's.

"I don't know what right you think you've got to question me!"

"The right," said his mother, "of a person whom I have employed, and a person who has been harmed. Answer her question, Clancy."

"I don't remember when I saw him!"

"Ye never could tell a good lie, Clancy Malloy, even when you were a lad." Patrick's tone was matter-of-fact. "I'd thrash the truth out of you then. Do I, beggin' your pardon, Aunt Molly, do I have to do it now?"

Clancy sagged in his chair. "Oh, all right, all right. You're making a fuss over nothing. I saw him get into Mr. Bishop's carriage, and later I recognized his voice when the two of them were quarreling."

"And you heard what they were saying." Hilda made it a statement.

Clancy nodded sullenly. "I don't know if it was true, though, what Bishop said."

"If it had not been true, I doubt that Mr. Vanderhoof would have wanted you to suppress it," said his mother. "Tell us, Clancy, and stop making excuses."

He slouched even lower. "Bishop told Vanderhoof he'd heard rumors it was Vanderhoof's men, scabs he'd hired, who touched off that mine explosion in Kentucky. He wanted to know if the scabs—if it was just an accident, or—"

No one could speak.

Mrs. Malloy looked at her son as if she had never seen him before.

Patrick looked at him, too, and saw the spoiled, sulky cousin he'd never much liked, the son of two people he loved, the son who was breaking his mother's heart as they sat there in the beautifully furnished parlor.

Clancy looked at no one.

Hilda's look was inward. She saw the men dying in the mine, saw her youngest brother among them, if he had been brought to America and put to work there as Mr. Andrews had hinted. Tears ran down her face. "That's why," she whispered to herself. "That's why he killed."

Mrs. Malloy finally found her voice. "And you did what, then?"

"I thought I'd do better to get away from there, but Father saw me. He'd been too far away to hear what they said, but he could hear that there was a quarrel. He thought we should intervene, but I—I wanted reinforcements, so I went for Patrick. When we got back, Father wasn't to be found, but we did find Bishop. We separated, Patrick and I, and that's when Vanderhoof saw me and said—what he said to me."

"And you knew that Mr. Bishop was dead. You knew, later, that your father was missing, and then that Miss Johansson had been kidnapped. And you said nothing."

"I was thinking about it! And then Father came back home . . . and anyway, I didn't *know* Vanderhoof had anything to do with it! Not for certain. You can't go around accusing a man without proof. And suppose he did do it? You wanted me to expose a murderer, a man who'd know I was the one who went to the police? What do you think would have happened to me? He's a powerful man, Vanderhoof. If it ever gets out, what I've told you, we'll none of us be safe."

"*If* it gets out?" Patrick stood, his face white with anger. "Ye can't mean to tell me you think we'll keep this to ourselves! The man killed Bishop, he came damn near to killin' Uncle Dan an' Hilda, he maybe killed dozens o' men down in Kentucky, an' you want us to keep *quiet*?"

"Sit down, Patrick. And you will not swear in my parlor."

"Sorry, Aunt Molly, but—"

"This has gone far enough. Be silent and let me think."

They bowed to the strongest will in the room, though Hilda had to bite her tongue, and Patrick's breast heaved with suppressed emotion.

At last Mrs. Malloy spoke. "Patrick, will you ring for Riggs, please?"

To the butler, when he came into the room, she said, "A serious matter has arisen, Riggs. Will you telephone to Mr. Malloy, please, and tell him I require his presence at home as soon as it is convenient? And he might invite Mayor Fogarty to come with him."

"Excuse me, madam—"

"Yes, Miss Johansson?"

"If it is no trouble, could Mr. Riggs also telephone to Mr. Williams? I am out long past my time, and he will be—annoyed."

"Certainly. Riggs, tell him I detained Miss Johansson, and I apologize."

The butler left, and Mrs. Malloy summoned one last morsel

of strength. "Now, Patrick, you had best see Miss Johansson home. I think this is, for now, a family matter. We will deal with it as Mr. Malloy sees fit. You will both understand, I know, that it will be better, and safer, for you to say nothing to anyone at present. But please be assured that I will do my utmost to see justice done."

They spoke little on the way home. Hilda, at one point, said, "It must be true, Patrick. About the explosion, and the miners. He would not have killed Mr. Bishop if it had not been true."

Patrick simply nodded his head and they continued in silence. Hilda fell into bed the moment she reached her room.

For the next four days she heard nothing. The newspapers made public no startling revelations. Patrick did not come to call. She could not speak of the matter to Norah, but her mind could consider nothing else, so they went about their work in strained silence, Norah thinking something had gone badly wrong between Hilda and Patrick.

On Sunday morning, as she left Tippecanoe Place to go to church, Patrick was waiting on the drive. He fell into step with her.

"Patrick! What has happened? Has no one done anything? What—"

"I don't know anythin' more'n you do, except Aunt Molly wants you—an' your family, all of 'em—to come over to the house after church."

Hilda quailed. "They will not like it, Patrick, Sven especially, and Gudrun. Always we go to their house for dinner after church. Gudrun will have it cooked and ready—"

"Aunt Molly said, if that was the way of it, to come after dinner, but that you'd all be welcome to take dinner with us."

"Your family will be there, too?"

"Not all the cousins an' such—just me mum an' me brothers an' sisters."

"I think," said Hilda, a vivid picture in her mind of a silent and antagonistic group picking at their food, "it would be better to come after the meal. If I can make them come at all."

"Aunt Molly said she has a nice surprise for you all."

"I do not know how there can be anything nice about this terrible thing," said Hilda tartly. "Do you know nothing else?"

"Nothin'."

"Then I see you after dinner."

"With your family."

She waited until church was over and the Sunday meal well under way before broaching the subject. "There is something I must tell you," she said, putting down her fork.

"Yes, little one?" said Sven.

Good. He was in a kindly mood. "We have been invited, all of us, to the home of Mr. and Mrs. Malloy this afternoon after dinner. Sven, I know you do not like the Irish, but they have been kind to me, at least Mrs. Malloy has. And I was to tell you that she has a surprise for us, something we will like."

Sven frowned, but before he could open his mouth, Gudrun said, "They are very important people, the Malloys. It is an honor to be asked to their house. We will go."

"Sister!"

"Sven," said Gudrun in a dangerous tone, "I have now met some of the Irish, and they are not bad people. Norah Murphy is a very good friend to our Hilda, and a nice enough woman. We are told in church that all men are our brothers, and I am the eldest daughter in this house. I am able to make some of the decisions. We, Freya and Hilda and I, we will go to the Malloys'. You may do as you wish."

In the end, Sven would not allow his womenfolk to venture into such dangerous territory without his presence, so, glowering all the way, he accompanied them to the Malloy house.

They were shown in with great courtesy by Riggs. Even Sven was subdued by their reception, and bore his introduction to the Malloys in a dignified manner.

The two parlors had been thrown into one for the occasion. The visitors arrayed themselves on chairs and sofas. The Cavanaughs, gathered together in one corner, did their best to ignore the Johanssons, but Patrick defied them and slipped away to join Hilda.

Clancy, Hilda noted, was not there.

Mrs. Malloy stood in the middle of the room. "I am very pleased, Miss Johansson, to welcome your family to my home. Mr. Johansson, it is especially a pleasure to meet such a fine craftsman as I know you to be."

Clever Aunt Molly, thought Patrick admiringly. Flatter the most unwilling guest.

"I have asked you all here today for several reasons. First, to all of you who know our son, Clancy, I wish to tell you that he has been offered a fine job in New York, and has already left to take it up."

The Cavanaughs broke into delighted exclamations. Hilda and Patrick exchanged a look that said, as plainly as words, So that's what they decided to do with him.

"Second, some of you may also know Mr. Vanderhoof, but you may not know that various interests have suddenly required his presence abroad for an indefinite time. This means he will no longer be able to carry on his assistance in bringing immigrant families to South Bend, which is an unfortunate circumstance for the Johanssons." She bowed to them, catching Hilda's eye with an imperious *Keep still.*

"So, in view of the very great help Miss Hilda Johansson has given this family, Mr. Malloy has something he would like to give to you, Mr. Johansson."

Sven, astonished, looked at Mr. Malloy, who stood and took his wife's place.

"Mr. Johansson?"

Sven stood and stepped forward.

"I have here the schedule for your family's arrival in New York. Their ship leaves Sweden at the end of this week. Now, Miss Hilda, I can see you're thinking they can't be ready by then, but I've sent them a cablegram explaining everything, and they'll be there."

Sven took the paper from Mr. Malloy and gravely shook his hand with a word of thanks. Gudrun, Hilda, and Freya said not a word, for tears robbed them of speech.

"And the last thing we've got to say is that Patrick, here, deserves our thanks for all he's done during our recent troubles.

But I've asked him, and he says there's nothing he wants for himself, so I take leave, sister of mine, to give you what he'd like you to have."

Patrick's mother looked startled. "Brenda," Mr. Malloy went on, "you'll have to wait till spring when the weather's better, but I believe you've always wanted to go back to Ireland for a visit?"

Now it was the women of the Cavanaugh clan who dissolved into tears.

Mrs. Malloy took command again. "And now I hope you'll all enjoy some cookies and punch and get to know one another." She walked over and deliberately held out her hands to Patrick and Hilda, who stood at her bidding. "If it were not for these two young people, you two fine families might never have met." And boldly, Patrick on one arm and Hilda on the other, she began to move around the room speaking to her guests.


Hilda and Patrick were the last to leave the Malloys' house, so they walked back to Tippecanoe Place alone together. "They still do not like me," said Hilda.

"No, but Aunt Molly does. Funny, she gave me a speech once about how impossible it was, us being together, and now she acts like this."

"Perhaps she thought it was her duty to warn you," said Hilda, wiser in the ways of women. "But I think she does not mind, really."

"Maybe. Your sisters, they talked to me, but Sven wouldn't."

"It is partly that he does not like to have to be grateful, and now he must be grateful for what your uncle Dan has done for us. It makes him cross."

They walked in comfortable silence for a little.

"And I will tell you," said Hilda, "what it is that makes *me* cross, and worse than cross, angry! I do not mind so much that Clancy is not to be punished. He was very wicked, but he maybe did not do anything that was against the law."

"Sayin' nothin' when you know about a crime is against the law," said Patrick. "So is stealin' your father's money. But I'm not so sure he isn't bein' punished. He'll hate bein' a little frog in a big pond, and he'll hate workin' for a livin'. It might just be the makin' of him."

"But Mr. Vanderhoof! He is a murderer! He cannot be allowed just to go away. It is not fair at all!"

"Remember we've both said the world isn't fair? He's a big man, Hilda. Big men can do things the little people can't. An' he probably never killed or kidnapped anybody himself, with his own hands. We may never know who actually did the evil deeds for him. Oh, I know, I know." He held up his hand against her protest. "Orderin' somebody to do it is just as bad, but it's different to the law, 'specially if he didn't really order it. You know, just let his men know that's what he wanted, without sayin' it."

"And what about the money he stole from us, and probably from other people as well? Does he not deserve punishment for that?"

"He does. An' maybe someday we'll live in a world where men like him get what they deserve. But not yet, Hilda. Not yet."

They walked on through the fading autumn afternoon, two of the little people of the world, seizing what happiness they could for now, the happiness of simply being together.

# Afterword

O N Tuesday, November 4, 1902, Daniel Malloy was elected to one of the at-large positions on the St. Joseph County Council. He ran unopposed.

On Monday, November 24, 1902, Mrs. Johansson and her children Elsa, Birgit, and Erick arrived at the Chicago and Southern station in South Bend. Mr. Malloy's generosity had provided them with a second-class journey, rather than steerage, so they were in good health and spirits. The Thanksgiving celebration in the Johansson household the following Thursday was heartfelt.

Thanksgiving at the Malloy house was somewhat less exuberant, with Clancy unable to come home. But Mr. Malloy had the satisfaction of knowing he had his farm again, having worked out an arrangement with Mr. Vanderhoof's lawyers to buy it back. Mr. Malloy also sold Clancy's horse, Gladiator, to pay Clancy's debts.

Mrs. Vanderhoof and the children left South Bend to join her husband. No one was quite sure exactly where they went.